Totally Bound Publishing books by Desiree Holt

Single Books
Crude Oil
Beg Me
Down and Dirty
Interlude
Intermission
Four Play
Game On
Swingtime
Party of Three
All Jacked Up
Top or Bottom
Rodeo Heat
Night Heat
Cupid's Shaft
Trouble in Cowboy Boots

Strike Force
Unconditional Surrender
Lock and Load
Advance to the Rear
Take No Quarter

The Sentinels
The Edge of Morning
Night Moves
Dark Stranger
Animal Instinct
Mated
Silent Hunters

Corporate Heat
Where Danger Hides
Double Deception
Masquerade

I0680953

Cat's Eyes
Pretty Kitty
On the Prowl

Erector Set
Erected
Hammered
Nailed

Galaxy
Retrograde
Critical Density
Supernova
Absolute Zero

Anthologies
Night of the Senses: Carnal Caresses
Christmas Goes Camo: Melting the Ice
Treble: Trouble at the Treble T
Subspace: Head Games
Bound to the Billionaire: Made for Him
Three's a Charm: Double Entry

Collections
Heatwave: Summer Spice
Feral: Black Cat Fever
Clandestine Classics: Northanger Abbey
A Little Bit Cupid: Hot Pants and Valentines

Galaxy

ABSOLUTE ZERO

DESIREE HOLT

Absolute Zero
ISBN # 978-1-83943-769-4
©Copyright Desiree Holt 2022
Cover Art by Claire Siemaszkiewicz ©Copyright January 2022
Interior text design by Claire Siemaszkiewicz
Totally Bound Publishing

This is a work of fiction. All characters, places and events are from the author's imagination and should not be confused with fact. Any resemblance to persons, living or dead, events or places is purely coincidental.

All rights reserved. No part of this publication may be reproduced in any material form, whether by printing, photocopying, scanning or otherwise without the written permission of the publisher, Totally Bound Publishing.

Applications should be addressed in the first instance, in writing, to Totally Bound Publishing. Unauthorised or restricted acts in relation to this publication may result in civil proceedings and/or criminal prosecution.

The author and illustrator have asserted their respective rights under the Copyright Designs and Patents Acts 1988 (as amended) to be identified as the author of this book and illustrator of the artwork.

Published in 2022 by Totally Bound Publishing, United Kingdom.

No part of this book may be reproduced, scanned, or distributed in any printed or electronic form without permission. Please do not participate in or encourage piracy of copyrighted materials in violation of the authors' rights. Purchase only authorised copies.

Totally Bound Publishing is an imprint of Totally Entwined Group Limited.

If you purchased this book without a cover you should be aware that this book is stolen property. It was reported as "unsold and destroyed" to the publisher and neither the author nor the publisher has received any payment for this "stripped book".

ABSOLUTE ZERO

Dedication

To my fabulous editor Rebecca Fairfax who hand-carries me through every book and makes sure it's whipped into shape. Oh, and look for her in the book!

Dear Readers,

Writing a book is a labor of love for me. My characters take over my life and I work to make them come alive for all of you. But I could not do it without the help of key people in my life. My team. First and foremost, my wonderful beta reader, Margie Hager, who has a super critical eye and finds all my mistakes. Then there is my incredible son, Steven Horwitz, who despite running a successful business of his own, manages the financial side of mine and is also a marketing guru. And let me introduce you to Maria Connor, author assistant extraordinaire and very talented author. When my life was turned upside down, I was honored that she stepped in to co-write this book with me and give it her special flare. She is a top-notch talented author and I am honored to work with her. Please check out more books by her and look for more collaborative efforts from the two of us.

Special thanks to former SEAL and *New York Times* bestselling author Jack Carr for all his help and information.

And finally, there is you, my readers, without whom there would be no Desiree Holt. You enrich my life and inspire me.

Chapter One

If someone had explained to Sierra Hunt what absolute zero was, she would have told them that it was exactly where she was. At a total standstill. And her pounding head wasn't helping the situation. She pried her eyes open and looked around. Where was she, anyway? Her hotel room? No, not hers, but one like it. Then whose? She scrunched her forehead trying to remember exactly where she was and how she'd gotten here. Was this a repeat of Jeremy's situation?

Shit.

Jeremy. Her brother. Then it all came rushing back at her.

The trip. The last chance. Then the disappointment and depression. The depressing phone call to her brother. The man in the lobby.

They had spent a fortune on attorney fees trying to arrange an appeal, but all for nothing. Every attempt after the first one had been denied and now every option that they'd had was exhausted. Every attorney she had consulted — if quick brushoffs could be called consulting — explained they had no additional grounds. The three other attorneys she'd tried previously had all told her they saw nothing to indicate there were grounds for yet another appeal. And the governor's office would not take her call.

Jeremy was already showing the physical effects of being in prison, and she'd begun to fear for his mental health as well.

Cheryl Andrews, Jeremy's wonderful girlfriend, somehow continued to believe in him but then she'd became ill with a bad case of the flu and had died in days. Jeremy still had not recovered from the loss.

Sierra had flown here to New Orleans to meet with a high-profile attorney who she'd been told was a champion of difficult cases like this. He was her last chance, the man she was told who could find a loophole. He'd refused to make an appointment, but she figured if she just showed up, he'd at least have to give her fifteen minutes. She'd waited all day in his office, only to have him tell her she should accept the fact her brother was guilty and prepare herself for the fact he would die in prison. She left his office depressed and discouraged. She had one option left, but she couldn't exercise it until the morning, damn it.

On top of that, for the past few weeks she'd had the uncomfortable feeling someone was watching her. Following her. She'd been doing weird things to see if that was true, but if it was, whoever was on her tail was very good at it.

Exhausted, she'd been paying no attention to anything as she made her way through the hotel lobby. Hot tea, she told herself. That was what she needed to soothe her nerves. The drinks wagon was still open in the lobby, and the scent of the various brews tantalized her senses. She chose peach, a flavor that always helped her relax.

Then, as she turned away to head toward the elevators, she bumped smack into a solid wall of masculinity, spilling her hot tea all over the shirt of the man standing in front of her.

"Oh, my god! I am so sorry."

She looked up...and up. The first thing she noticed was he could model for a photo of warriors. He was tall, lean, muscular, with a shadow of a beard lining his jaw. His eyes were a piercing blue, and the whole image was accented by a stripe of white hair that ran backward from his forehead. For a moment she was frozen in place, mesmerized. Then reality jabbed her. She grabbed napkins from the drinks wagon and tried to blot his shirt dry, but he stayed her hand.

"I'll handle it. Don't worry." But he was pulling the damp material away from his chest and removing the hot liquid from his skin.

His voice was rich and deep and sent shivers along her spine. A sharply defined jawline and angular cheekbones were highlighted by electric blue eyes and thick lashes. His lips, curved into a hint of a smile, looked as if they were usually set in a grim line. She wondered what had created that change.

"No, no, I am so sorry. I—"

Flustered, she made things worse because she was still holding the now half-empty cup of tea and more splashed out of it. When she turned to toss the cup into the trash, her hand bumped the metal edge of the counter. She dropped her purse which then fell open, scattering her things on the floor.

If she could have melted into space, she would have done it. Instead, she crouched down, doing her best to gather items and stuff them back into her purse. And of course, the stranger insisted on helping her.

She grabbed her key card from her purse, and in the process scattered some of the contents again. *God*. If only the floor would just open up and swallow her.

"You going to your room? Come on, I'll make sure you get there."

Go with a strange man up to her room? Was she crazy? Absolutely not!

"No, thanks, I—"

"You're bleeding." The stranger took her hand and lifted it. "You must have hit it pretty hard on the counter."

She glanced down, shocked to see blood welling from a long cut and running down over her fingers. *Holy god. What next?*

The stranger grabbed more napkins and pressed them against the cut.

"You can't let something like that go. It needs attention. If you'd rather, I can take you to a walk-in clinic—?"

"No. Please." That was all she needed. "I just want to get to my room."

"Do you have bandages? Antiseptic? If not, you could be courting an infection. I can fix it, at least temporarily."

She was so rattled she didn't even have the brains to refuse. Instead, she let him lead her across the lobby to the elevators. Inside the car, he punched the button for the tenth floor.

"I'm on nine," she protested.

"But the first aid's on the tenth, in my room."

He was taking her to *his* room? What if he…?

"Don't worry." He grinned at her. "I'm not planning to attack you. That is, unless you want me to. Ah, here we are."

Still in a daze, she followed him down the hall and into his hotel room. She had to admit he was very efficient in cleaning and bandaging her cut.

"Are you a doctor?"

He shook his head. "Former SEAL. We learn how to field dress wounds. Okay, there you are." He frowned. "You're still trembling. What can I get for you?"

"Can you just hold me for a minute? I've had the day from hell and this hasn't helped."

For a moment he looked as if he were about to refuse. But then, just as she was about to get up, he put his arm around her and pulled her against him.

"We should at least introduce ourselves. I'm…"

She held up her hand. "No names, okay? I… It's better this way." She tried a smile. "More mysterious."

"Okay. Just call me Eagle, then." His mouth curved into a hint of a very sexy grin. "That was my call sign in the SEALs."

She figured the streak in his hair had something to do with that.

When she didn't respond, he shrugged. "Okay. No problem."

And still he held her.

His touch was gentle for a man his size, and that was what probably broke the dam of her emotions. One minute she was sitting there, the next she was crying all over his shirt, tears she'd been holding back since this whole nightmare started.

Everything after that was a blur. She was blubbering on his shoulder, then hugging him.

"I'm going to kiss you," he said slowly. "If you don't want it, just say so. That's okay. Really. I'm not in the habit of forcing myself on women."

But there was no force involved, except maybe for her clutching him so desperately and kissing him so hungrily, as if that could erase this whole nightmare. It seemed her body's needs had awakened after dozing for months. *Awakened by a man who could best be described as sex on a stick.*

And this morning, her body hummed pleasantly with intense satisfaction, even as it flushed with embarrassment.

Oh, my god! Oh, my god!

This is not me. I don't do things like this. Ever.

But apparently she did.

My god, I've never even met the man before. I must have been out of my mind.

She'd chalk it up to severe emotional stress combined with exhaustion and depression. Lifting the sheet and blanket covering her, she peeked at her body. *Oh, god!* Just as she suspected. She was completely naked. *Crap!* What in hell had she done?

She closed her eyes…and it all came slamming back into her.

Oh, dear sweet lord.

At last the tears stopped flowing. She knew she should leave the room, but it felt so good just sitting there, hugged to his body. One minute he was stroking her back gently, the next they were kissing. As their kisses grew hotter, so did her body. Then it was as if someone had flipped a switch.

She was so lost in it that she didn't even stop to wonder why she was doing this with a complete stranger. Instead, kisses that shut down her brain were exchanged. Kisses that were hot and demanding and involved a whole lot of tongue. Clothes somehow disappeared. Hands coasted over naked skin, touching and squeezing and stroking. While he cupped her breasts in his palms, brushing the nipples with his thumbs, she reached between their two bodies to wrap her fingers around his rigid, thick cock.

His body was so hard, his muscles so well-defined that she could trace the outline with her fingers. The hair on his chest was soft over the chiseled planes beneath it and all made more enticing by the heat that rose from him.

They tumbled onto the bed, barely taking time to strip back the covers. She lay beneath him, his fingers braceleting her wrists, holding her in place so she was literally immobilized beneath him. Rather than frightening, it made her nipples peak and the walls of her pussy tingle in anticipation.

Heat blazed in his eyes as he raked them over her naked body while his hands touched her everywhere. At each stroke of his fingers, another fire ignited until she was squirming with need. She tried to reach between them to find his jutting cock again, but he brushed her hand away.

"Too close," he rasped.

He swirled his tongue around her nipples, grazing them with his teeth before trailing his tongue down her body to her shockingly heated sex. She hadn't been with anyone in so long she'd almost forgotten what it was like, but apparently her body woke up in a hurry.

Nudging her thighs apart, he settled himself between them and bent his head to lap greedily at the wet folds of her sex. Each stroke of his tongue ignited more flames, awoke more nerves. Her inner walls fluttered, seeking something to fill her greedy channel, seeking his cock that was so hot as it brushed against her skin. She had never been this aroused before, this hot, her body this needy.

"I can't wait," he panted. "I have to be inside you right now. Next time will be slower, I promise."

He grabbed one of the condoms he'd dumped on the nightstand and rolled it on with hands that shook slightly. Then bending her legs back so she was wide open to him, he drove into her, filling every inch of her. She was grateful she was so wet that she could take him easily.

He stared intently into her eyes, hunger blazing in his, then set up a rhythm that was unrelenting and fast. But she was ready. Oh, more than ready, a shock after going for so long without. He pounded into her, his movement almost frenzied.

"Look at me," he growled, desperation in his voice.

She lifted her gaze to lock with his, mesmerized by the heat smoldering in those deep blue eyes.

"I can't hold off much longer."

"Don't...hold back," she gasped, the orgasm already rolling up from deep inside her.

"Let go," he told her.

And she did.

They exploded together, an upsurge of volcanic proportions, her inner walls quaking with spasms as they gripped his shaft, milking him again and again.

Then they were done.

He collapsed forward on his elbows, doing his best to catch his breath while studying her face as if memorizing every inch of it.

Sierra had no idea how long they lay there like that, too weak, she was sure, to even move. Finally, he eased himself from her body, pinching the condom closed and moved into the bathroom to dispose of it. Then he crawled into bed next to her, pulling her body against his and…

Sierra's eyes flew open again, and the rest of the night came flooding back. They'd had sex so many different ways she was surprised they'd gotten any sleep. The connection was so spectacular it shocked the hell out of her. And with everything they'd done, why wasn't she more tired this morning?

Morning! It was morning?

Holy hell, she had to get out of here. She had urgent business to take care of.

Stay, her body screamed. *This guy is a keeper.*

Keeper? How could she even think about that with desperation and disaster like twin devils beating on her head. And god only knew what he thought of her, blubbering all over him then falling into bed with him the way she had, with no holds barred. None. Just completely unrestrained sex.

Good lord. What the hell had she been thinking?

Jeremy. How had she let herself forget about Jeremy and his looming deadline and fall into bed with a total stranger?

A *hot* stranger.

Well, maybe it was all the unrelenting stress she'd been dealing with. Maybe it was because she didn't know him and had no intentions of anything beyond this one night, but still, no excuse. She probably should have worried that he was a killer or something, but then she thought, no, a killer wouldn't make sixteen kinds of erotic love to her.

Okay. Okay, okay, okay. Enough of that. She had to get out of here. The clock was running out on her brother, and she had only one option left to her. She'd saved it for last because she'd hoped like hell one of the attorneys would come through for her. She blessed the anonymous person who had called late one night and left a message for her to reach out to Senator Alicia Kane.

Of course, if Senator Kane had used these people, they must charge both arms and legs. Sierra had money but not that much, especially after attorney after attorney had drained it with legal fees that had accomplished nothing.

She'd borrow it if she had to, because if that didn't work, she was out of options.

Looking frantically around the room, she saw her clothes draped over the back of a chair with her purse on the table next to it. Obviously, he'd folded them, because she remembered ripping them off last night and tossing them aside so fast they'd looked like refugees from a windstorm. Heat crept up her entire body as she remembered her reaction to him and the things they'd done.

Where was he, the stranger who she'd fucked her brains out with?

No, not really a stranger, not after the things they'd done together. And she knew his name, right? At least his first name. Eagle. Well, he looked like one with the white streak down his hair. A duffel bag sat beside the chair where her clothes lay, and a laptop sat on the desk. But where was he?

Then from behind the closed bathroom door, she heard the sound of the shower running.

Good. Maybe she could get out of here before she had to face him. What on god's green earth was she doing spending a whole night fucking some hot stranger while Jeremy's future was so disastrous? She had definitely lost her mind as well as any residual common sense.

Wriggling out of bed, she dragged the sheet so she was at least partially covered while she grabbed her clothes from the chair. She forced herself to check her purse before she did anything else. There was no reason to think he'd robbed her. He certainly hadn't looked like he needed money, but then, what the hell did she know? She'd spent the night having imaginative sex with a man who didn't even know her name.

She wanted to stick her head in the toilet and flush it.

Okay, money and keys still there.

Dropping the purse, she began pulling on her clothes, not paying much attention to how well she did it, just yanking them on as fast as she could. She'd worry about showering and taking care of her hair later. Right now, all she wanted was out of here.

Chapter Two

Sierra had just stepped into her second shoe when the door to the bathroom opened, and her 'date' walked out, wearing nothing but glowing skin and a towel knotted at the waist.

Kill me now, please.

"Leaving?" He cocked an eyebrow. "I was planning on offering you breakfast."

"What? Oh, um. No. I have to..." She hurried toward the door. "I have to leave."

"Wait. I want to buy you breakfast." He grinned. "I'd offer to shake hands but..." He gestured at the towel at his waist. "I want to make sure this stays in place."

She shook her head and moved toward the door again.

"I can't. Sorry."

She had to take care of business today. Jeremy's fate was a black cloud enveloping her, and she had no time for anything else. Last night had been a huge mistake.

"Hey, wait." Eagle started toward her.

She yanked the door open. "Gotta go."

"But I didn't even get your name! I want to make up for being such an asshole."

She didn't know what to say to that so she just dashed out of the room and hurried down the corridor, losing one of her shoes in her haste. She picked it up and ran, one foot unshod, to the elevator. She glanced at the room numbers and gave thanks she was on a different floor.

She jabbed the elevator button a dozen times, silently urging it to get here fast.

"Hey!"

Don't look. Don't look.

So of course she looked. He was standing just outside the open door to his room, wearing nothing but the towel and watching her. Thank the lord the elevator arrived just then. She leaped into it, bumping into three people who looked at her as if she had just escaped an asylum. After last night's stupidity, maybe she needed one.

The doors slid shut, and she punched the button for her floor. The moment the doors opened, she jumped out and hurried down to her room. Inside, she collapsed on the bed, throwing her arm over her eyes.

What in god's name had she done?

She certainly enjoyed sex as much as the next person — at least she had until Jeremy had been arrested and her whole life had focused on his situation. But she had never been one for sex with strangers, and certainly not a stranger she'd met in a hotel lobby. What had she been thinking?

I wasn't, and that's the problem. I just wanted a little time to blot out the disaster ruling my life.

She finally managed to push herself off the bed, strip off her clothes and step into a steaming-hot shower. She managed to keep her hand out of the water so the bandage didn't get wet. And she'd have to do something about that today. The smart thing would be to scrub her body so there was no memory of the sexy stranger with the streak in his hair. But it seemed these days she wasn't smart because all she could think of as she lathered herself was what it would feel like if it were his hands doing this.

God!

Just the memory of his electric touch, his ability to know just how and where to stroke her, set her hormones racing again. The pulse between her legs began to throb, and her nipples ached.

Stop it!

She had to wipe this whole episode from her mind. She had important things to take care of today and thinking about Mr. Sex God wasn't one of them. She turned the shower to icy cold and stood under it until every hormone in her body ran for cover. Then she dried off and wrapped herself in the hotel robe hanging on the back of the door.

Thankful for the coffee setup in the room, she fixed herself a cup then dug into her purse for the slip of paper with the name and phone number on it. She sat at the desk, gathered her shit together and dialed the number.

"Senator Kane's office."

"Uh, yes, my name is Sierra Hunt. I was given this number by a mutual friend. He said he would call the senator ahead of time to clear the way for me."

"Oh, yes, Miss Hunt. Apparently, he called the senator at home last night. She said to put you right through."

"Thank you."

Okay, one hurdle conquered.

"Hold one minute, please."

Another voice came on the phone.

"Good morning, Miss Hunt. This is Senator Kane. I understand you have a problem that I might help with?"

"Yes." Sierra swallowed. She explained about Jeremy. "I was told to ask you about something called Galaxy and for their unlisted cell phone number. That they'd really helped you with your sister."

Silence hung thick for a moment. Was the woman just going to hang up?

"I won't ask you who referred you because that person values anonymity much like Galaxy does. The fact that he called me says a lot for you."

Was the woman going to do this? Give her the information?

"Thank you." She held her breath.

"I'm going to give you the name and number of the man who helped my sister. Tell him I gave you his contact information."

Sierra wrote it down, her hand shaking slightly. If this didn't work, she had no place left to turn. "Thank you very much."

When she hung up, she programmed the number into her cell right away. But what was so mysterious about something called Galaxy that they didn't even have an office or a listed phone number?

Oh, well, here I go.

"Yes?" The male voice barked the greeting.

Well, this didn't sound very friendly.

"Is this John 'Rocket' Hardin?"

"Who wants to know?"

"My name is Sierra Hunt. Senator Alicia Kane told me I could call this number and book a flight to nowhere. Listen, Mr. Hardin"—she held back the

torrent of words that wanted to rush from her mouth —
"I am beyond desperate, and Senator Kane said Galaxy
could help me. Can you? Please?"

"I won't know until you tell me what this emergency
is."

She swallowed, hard, and tried to tell him in the
fewest words possible. He didn't sound like a man with
a lot of time on his hands.

"My brother is about to be jailed for life for a murder
he did not commit. I know you must have heard that
story a million times, but I swear to you, it's true. And
I'm out of options. Senator Kane said —"

"Hold on."

Two long minutes of silence followed while Sierra
clutched her cell phone. Then the same voice came back
on the phone.

"Senator Kane referred you?" the man asked again.

"She did."

"And she knows your story?"

"She wouldn't refer me without my telling her,"
Sierra told him.

Another moment of silence, and she did her best to
keep a lid on her impatience. Then he was back.

"Write this down. Someone will meet you at this
address at five o'clock. It's where we keep the plane."

She entered it in her cell. It was in Tampa, of all
places, where she and her brother lived and where the
crime he was accused of had taken place. "A *plane*?"

"Yes. Is that a problem?"

*No. No, nothing would be a problem if he would just agree
to help me.*

"Of course not. But can you tell me who will be
there? Will it be you?"

"I'm tied up a little so one of my partners will handle this. I hope that's okay. The plane will be waiting for you at five o'clock. Don't be late."

A plane. This was the weirdest appointment she'd ever had, and she still didn't know who she was meeting, but if they could help Jeremy, she didn't care. Relief washed over her that they'd even agreed to have someone make contact with her. She'd have to hustle her ass and get on a flight right now.

She looked at her watch. Okay. Time to get dressed and get moving.

* * * *

Vic 'Eagle' Bodine pressed the button to close the garage door and headed for his bedroom to unload his duffel. He stood for a moment at the windows overlooking the Hillsborough River. He and Viper had chosen to buy houses on Davis Islands across from downtown Tampa because they wanted the water. It had played a big part in so much of his life. They lived close enough to share transportation but far enough apart to maintain their privacy. And the view over the water was better than a tranquilizer, as far as he was concerned.

He had volunteered to stay behind at the location of Galaxy's last assignment after successfully closing it. It had been his turn to do the wrap-up with the client and that was fine, but he was glad to be home. Rather than bother 'Saint' Francis, their pilot, to come fetch him, he'd booked an early commercial flight back to Tampa. He was looking forward to a day doing nothing.

Or maybe just having erotic dreams about the woman he'd spent the night with. He couldn't get the images out of his mind. How was it possible to make such an intense connection with a complete stranger in just a few short hours? Her soft body beneath him, her diamond-hard nipples pressing into his chest. His cock swollen and demanding as it filled her cunt. Her swollen clit that he'd teased with little nips and tugs with his teeth. His fingers braceleting her wrists, holding them in place.

He had a brief image of her restrained with those same wrists tied to the headboard, immobilizing her while he feasted on her body. Every dirty thought he'd ever had flashed in his brain, swelling his dick and causing it to press uncomfortably against his fly.

At once he made the supreme effort to corral his thoughts. He hadn't even known her for twenty-four hours, for fuck's sake. But oh, god, how he wanted to spank that nicely rounded ass, see how long she could hold back when he tormented her clit with a vibrator, plunge himself into the dark heat of her ass.

Until the phone call this morning. That had been a pitcher of cold water on his thoughts and certainly sent his dick to naptime.

"I'm passing this along to you," Rocket said. "We just finished that case in Houston, and Mallory and I are still trying to get back to normal after Santa Clarita. Plus we're arranging to get her moved here. This woman's set for a five-o'clock flight to nowhere on the Gulfstream. She has directions to the hangar. Meet her. See what her story is. If it's worth taking on, then give us a call."

"What's her story? Did you get a hint of it?"

"Her brother is about to be sentenced to life in prison in two weeks for a murder she swears he did not commit. His current lawyer has given up, as well as all the others she's contacted since he was arrested. The prosecutor won't talk to her, and she can't get in to see the governor and plead his case herself. Eagle, she sounds desperate."

"I've heard a lot of people say they're innocent," Eagle pointed out.

"Yeah, me too," Rocket agreed. "But I'm telling you, there's something in the sound of her voice that makes me believe her. Senator Kane must have, and so did I. She's the real deal. Her name is Sierra Hunt. She lives right here in Tampa. She called my number, and I'm passing her along to you. It's your turn at bat, anyway."

"Okay. I'll let you know how it goes."

"Good enough. Just make sure if we take this, whatever it is, we're done before the end of the month. Peyton and Blaze will kill you if they have to postpone the wedding."

"No sweat." Eagle laughed. "That would be certain death."

"Good luck."

He spent some time clearing up stuff that had accumulated for the past couple of days and doing his best to wipe the memory of the very sexy, very desirable woman from his brain. The one he'd spent an unexpected hot night with. The one he'd probably never see again, sad to say. At four o'clock he changed out of his jeans to what he called his client outfit— slacks and a soft-collared shirt. He and his partners all agreed suits and ties were for executions and weddings. He avoided the one and dreaded the other.

Since he was driving against the flow of traffic to get to the outskirts of Tampa where they hangered the plane, he made good time getting there. The first thing they'd done when they'd formed Galaxy was to buy this very large piece of land at the edge of the city. There was actually a whole community of homes with hangars and two runways, but they wanted isolation for what they did. They couldn't afford for it to be anyone's business except their own.

So Tom Hernandez had done all the work and pulled all the strings to get them the same FAA approval and same arrangements with the Tampa International tower as the unique community and they were in business.

An immense hangar had been constructed and they had built a small house on the property for any time that their pilot needed to pull an overnight on the premises.

The entire property was electronically fenced, bordered with thick trees that prevented anyone driving by on the highway from seeing what was there and was wired for every possible kind of security. Cameras were hidden around both the house and the hangar, and Tom had found them a top-notch, top-secret security firm to manage it. All meetings and conferences with clients were held on the plane so there was no chance of eavesdropping. And the only way to destroy the place was to bomb it, and the likelihood of that happening was zilch.

He pulled up to the iron gate and waved his coded card at the reader set into one of the stone pillars, then drove up to the paved area near the hangar and parked his car.

The plane was already out on the tarmac. He spotted the car belonging to Saint parked in the turnoff area beside a silver rental sedan. He slid into line next to the sedan and headed toward the plane, looking around.

Where the hell was the client?

Saint came to the cabin entrance, saw him scanning the area and jerked his head toward the interior of the plane.

"She's inside. She got here about twenty minutes ago. I didn't see any sense in letting her just sit out there in her car, so I brought her in, told her you were on your way and gave her a cup of coffee."

"Well, aren't you the great host."

Saint glared at him. "Be nice. She's a messy wreck."

Eagle sighed. Weren't they all?

He locked his car and trudged up the stairway into the plane.

"She's in the seating area in the middle of the cabin." Saint inclined his head. "She's got her coffee, but she's so nervous I'm worried she might spill it."

"Okay, thanks. I've got it from here."

The woman was turned away from him when Eagle approached. Her thick blonde hair was pulled back in a tight ponytail, and she was so obviously on edge that she practically vibrated.

"Hello," he began. "Welcome to Galaxy. I'm —"

She turned to look at him, and he stopped, his jaw practically hitting the floor. *This* was Sierra Hunt, the new client? The woman with whom he'd had the best sex of his life? *Holy fucking shit! Twice over!*

Sierra stared back at him, so obviously shaken and nervous she dropped her cup, spilling coffee on the floor and shattering the ceramic.

Eagle found his voice first as he stared at his hot date from the night before, trying to unfreeze his brain at the same time he was telling his cock to stay at rest. *Holy fucking shit again. What are the odds, anyway?*

Then they both spoke at the same time.

"You're Vic Bodine?"

"*You're* Sierra Hunt?"

What the fuck?

27

Chapter Three

Eagle hoped his mouth wasn't hanging open because he was sure his jaw had dropped at least a foot. Not even in his wildest dreams had he imagined his client would turn out to be the woman he'd fucked seven ways from Sunday. The hottest woman he'd ever met, and he'd met a damn lot of them. The only one he'd ever fucked without knowing her name.

Again images from the night before slammed into his brain, along with thoughts of all the dirty things he'd like to do to her. How was it possible to make that kind of connection with a total stranger in just a few short hours? Only his ingrained SEAL discipline allowed him to maintain control over his demanding cock.

Her hair looked just as much like silky gold as it had the night he met her. Even though it was now neatly pulled back in a tail that his hands itched to stroke. He remembered the feel of the soft skin of her cheeks over her high cheekbones. The heat in her jade-green eyes framed by long, thick lashes. The way she'd looked at him at the height of her orgasm. Before he could even breathe, his cock hardened and threatened to break the zipper on his slacks. *And wouldn't that just be a fucking hit.*

Damn!

No woman had ever affected him like this and that was saying a damn lot. Images of their night together flashed through his brain like a video in fast forward.

Now what did he do?

Act like the professional I am.

"Nice to see you again. Sorry it's under these circumstances." He held out his hand, hoping when she touched it, he could control himself.

Fuck! What was he, sixteen?

Sierra bounced out of her seat, looking for a moment like she was planning to run off the plane. She stared at him as if she'd seen a ghost.

"I swear, uh, I swear I didn't know it was you when I called," she blurted out. "I don't want you to think I'd be using what happened between us to get you to do something. I would never presume like that." She blew out a breath. "Look. Maybe I should just leave. If you want to cancel, I'll understand. I can try to find someone else."

Cancel? That hadn't even occurred to him. In fact, he was positive she'd had no idea who he was when they spent that incredible night together. He might have been stupid blind with sexual desire, but his radar would still have picked up something like that.

No, she was as shocked as he was.

He cleared his throat.

"Sierra, I have no intention of canceling. Nor do I regret that night for one single minute. If we need to put it aside—just for the moment—to deal with this, we can do that. But first just let me clean up this little mess here."

"I can do it. I'm so sorry about this. I—"

He shook his head. "No worries. There. All done. Now, how about sitting down again, settling yourself in, and letting me get you some more coffee."

"Yes, please. If you think you can trust me with it again."

"Happens to all of us. Cream? Sugar?"

She shook her head, so he took care of the housekeeping chore then filled two mugs, black, and handed one to her. Then he took the opposite seat.

"If you went to the trouble of searching us out," he told her, "I'm pretty damn sure you have a desperate situation. That's why people come to us."

She nodded and took a sip of her drink. "Desperate doesn't begin to describe it. Last night was, um…" She looked down at her hands.

He chuckled. "Stress relief?"

He couldn't believe she actually blushed.

"It's okay. Been there, done that." He lowered his voice. "And by the way, it was fantastic. No, spectacular."

"Um, thank you." She wet her lower lip with the tip of her tongue, making his cock beg for mercy. "But," she went on, "I understand if you have a personal conflict here because of it. I really do."

He wanted to laugh. If personal conflicts arose because of attractions, none of the partners would have been with the women they now shared their lives with. Blaze was engaged to Peyton, and that was probably the only situation in the partnership that had started out without a relationship of some kind. She'd come to them as a client but, before anyone could blink, she was living with him. Viper had rescued Hannah from people who wanted to pin a murder on her and had her locked up. They'd been hot and heavy between the sheets before twenty-four hours had passed. And Rocket and Mallory, well, they'd had hot sex in a cave while hiding from the Taliban and things hadn't cooled down during their five years apart.

Maybe it was becoming their trademark. In any case, he could handle this professionally. He was a SEAL, for fuck's sake. He could separate the personal from the professional in his life. Just like in the military, he had a mission and he could stick to it.

Sierra had a serious problem and had come to him for help. He was going to give it to her, even while his cock kept trying to send him messages. And he wasn't going to let go of the connection they'd made. He'd just have to make sure it didn't fuck up his head, which he knew he could handle.

He gave her what he hoped was a reassuring smile.

"Let's get this out of the way first. That night happened by accident, but I wouldn't take back a single minute of it. And I'd like to think it was Fate bringing us together again today. You obviously have a desperate situation that I believe Galaxy can help you with. I—"

"But you don't even know what it is yet," she interrupted.

He shook his head. "Doesn't matter. People only contact us because we're a last resort. I like to think I can read people and what I get from you is an honest person at the end of her rope. You came to us for help, and we're going to see that you get it. It's what we do."

She studied him for a long moment before she spoke again.

"Thank you. I mean it." She was so tense every muscle in her body was rigid. "I don't—" She stopped, swallowed and took a deep breath. "I was told you definitely are the best last resort and right now that's what I really, really need."

She was still pale and her hands trembled just the tiniest bit as she gripped her mug. but determination lined her face. He'd seen the look of desperation in Sierra's eyes, and Galaxy had been created to help people like that.

"It's what we're here for," he assured her and rose from his seat. "Let me tell Saint to get ready for takeoff. As soon as we're at cruising altitude, I'll get you a refill on the coffee and you can tell me what's put that anxious look in your eyes."

"Thank you."

"So it's a go?" Saint asked when Eagle stuck his head into the cockpit.

"Roger that."

"Okay. Have a seat, and we'll get going."

Sierra looked up at him when he walked back into the cabin.

"Thank you for doing this. I mean, at least for being willing to listen to me."

Eagle took the seat opposite her. He buckled himself in, then reached forward and took her hands in his. They were ice cold, and he closed his fingers around them, trying to infuse some warmth into them.

"Sierra, I don't know how complicated this is, but I promise you, whatever it is, Galaxy can handle it."

"I hope so, because you really are my last resort."

The roar of the engines swelled, the plane began to move and before long they were rolling down the runway. Eagle held Sierra's hands all through takeoff and until they reached cruising altitude. When they leveled off, she seemed to relax a little. Eagle released the latch on his seatbelt and pushed out of his seat.

"Let me get those coffee refills," he told her, glad that all his SEAL training allowed him to put last night in the corner for the moment.

When they were both settled with fresh drinks, he gave her what he hoped was a reassuring smile.

"Okay. Whenever you're ready. And tell it however you want to."

He waited, his position relaxed while she sipped the coffee and visibly gathered her thoughts.

"My brother Jeremy is a really good guy," she began. "And I'm not saying that just because he's my brother. He is definitely one of the best. Leads a really normal life. He's an architect here in Tampa with a highly respected firm. About to make associate, as a matter of fact. And had a great girlfriend who adored him."

"Sounds like he has everything going for him."

"He does. He's got it all, which is why this whole thing makes no sense at all."

"What thing?" he prompted.

"This thing that sounds like a bad movie that's been done too many times. I'm not even sure you'll believe me. You might think I'm making this up." She took another sip of her coffee, studying her mug.

"I promise I won't think that. You have my word. People who get referred to us don't make up their stories."

"People keep telling me it's an open-and-shut case and why don't I just get on with my life?" Anguish edged her voice. "But I know my brother, and he didn't do this."

"Why don't you let me judge for myself. Okay?" He hoped his voice sounded reassuring enough.

"Okay. So. About six months ago Jeremy met a client for dinner at the Verdana Hotel downtown in Tampa.

Business meeting dinner. From what I can tell it lasted about two hours."

He quirked an eyebrow. "From what you can tell?"

"When you hear the rest of the story, you'll know why I'm not so sure. Anyway. He got a text message from a client who also wanted to meet. When Jeremy told him he had dinner plans, the client texted back that he'd like to meet for a drink after that. Jeremy was waiting for him in the bar, nursing a drink, chatting with the woman on the bar stool next to him about nothing. She told him she was waiting for someone, too. She got a call shortly after that, said goodbye, and he took out his phone to text his client and see where he was. He says that's all he remembers."

Eagle was getting a nasty feeling as he listened. This already sounded like the beginning of a disaster.

"What happened when he woke up? Where was he? Had he made it home?"

She shook her head. "He was in a room in the hotel, naked, with a screaming headache. He heard pounding on the door, but before he could manage to get up, it opened and three men walked in. By the time he was able to get his eyes open and ask a question, he realized there was a dead woman lying next to him."

"Sounds like a bad movie." Eagle echoed her. "Especially if it was the woman he was talking to in the bar."

"Which, of course, it was." She took another swallow of coffee. "He swears he was drugged, because his brain wasn't functioning, and he couldn't make sense of anything. He was set up, Mister, um…"

"Eagle will do."

She managed a poor caricature of a smile. "Okay. Eagle."

Her hands were trembling again, so he took the mug from her, set it in its holder and wrapped his own hands around hers.

"Go on," he urged in a voice as gentle as he could make it. The telling of the story was always an emotional trip for clients.

"He was arrested, booked and held without bail." She drew in a breath and let it out slowly. "I had to fight to see him, but I knew something was wrong. I hired the best defense attorney this city has to offer, and he assured me he did the best he could. If so, he wasn't worth his fee, because, Eagle? It felt like Jeremy's conviction was a foregone conclusion. The way the prosecuting attorney presented the case, you'd think he was a monster. The bartender testified he thought they knew each other, which is a lie. Someone else, a woman who said she was a friend of the murdered woman, testified her friend had been seeing Jeremy secretly so he could keep it from his girlfriend."

"They must have had some evidence to proceed, then to deny all the requests for an appeal."

She nodded. "A glass in the room with his fingerprints. They also matched prints on the woman's neck. The bartender swearing he heard Jeremy proposition this woman. Another glass with her lipstick on it, and the remains of a drink, which — how fortunate for them — had traces of a date rape drug in it. A guest at the hotel who came forward and said she saw him practically dragging the woman down the hall. She thought the woman was just drunk. But it was all faked. It had to be."

"I assume the police interviewed her?" Blaze asked.

"If you can call it that." She grimaced. "If they didn't do any better than the prosecutor who questioned her on the stand, then I'd just call it a farce."

Eagle's bad feeling about this whole thing solidified.

"You were at the trial, right?" Eagle asked.

"You bet your ass I was."

He had to bite his lip to keep from smiling. She was getting angry now, which was a lot better than nervous and frightened.

"Based on the fact that your brother is still in prison, I assume it did not go well."

"Nothing went well." She drained her mug and held it out to Eagle. "Could I possibly bother you for more?"

"Sure thing."

Apparently, she'd used the brief time while he got her refill to pull herself back together because when she reached for the mug, he could see the tremors were gone.

"Okay." He nodded. "Let's go back to the trial."

She took him through it all. The few witnesses who had seen Jeremy with the woman. The hotel manager who'd unlocked the door to the room and he and two men from hotel security had found him with the body. Some woman who'd testified she was the murder victim's friend. That the victim had told her she was involved with someone, but she'd learned he wasn't unattached. But she had been meeting him at the hotel to have it out with him.

"Did the roommate know the man's name?"

Sierra shook her head. "Nobody knew anything. That's what's so scary. The prosecutor built a case that had Jeremy arranging to meet this woman after his dinner. To straighten things out, they said. In other words, to get rid of her. And he had a solid case, or at least everyone else seemed to think so."

"But not you."

She shook her head. "No. Not me. I know Jeremy, and they don't."

As she continued her story, Eagle agreed that something was definitely off kilter here.

"The appeals process gave us nothing. One was automatically filed after the jury verdict and punishment phase. I studied everything about reasons to appeal after that first one. His attorney told me none of the requirements had been met. He wouldn't even try. He said the evidence was too strong and there just were no grounds."

"I thought you could apply for an appeal if you could prove the original defense was flawed."

"That's true. I looked it up. But the other lawyers I contacted said the same thing, including the last one I went to New Orleans to see. He barely looked at the case file before telling me there were no grounds for one." She ran her hand over her hair. "Eagle, I have so much stuff on my computer that I've managed to get hold of, and no one will take a look at it. And I have no idea why."

"Okay. Let me refill our coffee again."

He rinsed the mugs and poured hot liquid into them then placed them on a small tray. He also snagged some fresh muffins. Saint always stocked the pastry cupboard when they had a possible client and, right now, he was sure Sierra needed all the sugar energy she could get. He set everything up on the serving trays that were part of the seats, then leaned back.

"Now. Take me through it one more time and don't leave anything out. Not even the tiniest detail."

It took more than an hour, with Eagle asking questions about certain points, sometimes even repeating them. Finally he sat back in the chair, satisfied he'd gotten as much as he could for the moment. And that she was the real deal. From his years as a SEAL, he'd learned to distinguish bullshit from the real stuff, and Sierra Hunt was genuine. She wasn't conning him for some undetermined reason, and both her fear for her brother and her story rang true.

Okay, then. Moving forward.

"You know, I didn't even ask you if you live here too or somewhere else."

"I do. He lives downtown because he likes the busy environment, and a lot of his friends live there, too. I live in South Tampa in a totally rehabbed Craftsman bungalow that I love. My office is in Midtown."

"Are you an architect like your brother?"

She shook her head. "I'm a computer and information systems manager for an engineering design firm."

"Wow." He blinked. "I'm impressed."

She scowled. "Because you don't think it's a job for a woman?"

He laughed. "Hell, no. If my partners thought I believed that, they'd disown me. One of them is engaged to a well-known romance author, another to a woman who researches trouble spots in the world and writes about them and the third is hooked up with a drone engineer."

Sierra's eyes widened. "Holy crap! Well. I take back my words."

"So about your job. Did you get time off without a problem?"

"Actually, I did. My boss has met Jeremy, and he thinks he got a raw deal, too. He's willing to work my projects around whatever I have to do."

"Sounds like a great guy."

"He is. I don't know what I'd do if he didn't give me the flexibility I needed for this. Oh, and one more thing."

"What's that?"

"I've had the feeling for weeks now that someone is following me, but nothing is obvious, and I don't know how to check."

"Following you?"

"Yes. As if to keep tabs on what I'm doing. Why would anyone do that if I wasn't rocking the boat?"

"Good question."

And one he'd discuss with his partners when they met to talk about their new client. And that would be ASAP.

In Galaxy, it had become standard practice for the partners when they took on a new client to meet at one of their homes to plot strategy and decide who would do what. That would be the first order of business. Was he taking this case? Hell, yeah! And not just because Sierra rang all his chimes, either. Her story made his bullshit meter fly off the charts, and not in her direction.

He glanced out of the small window. "It's sunset already. Let me tell Saint to head home."

Hope flashed in her eyes. "Does this mean you'll take this on? That you'll help me?"

"Hell, yes. I just don't like the smell of this."

In fact, the smell was so bad he wanted to hold his nose. She reached for her purse in the seat next to her. "I can write you a retainer check right now if you want. I don't know what you charge but I make a really good living and I have some cash reserves. I—"

He held up a hand. "Let's leave our fee out of it for the moment."

"But—"

He gave her what he hoped was an encouraging smile. "We won't bankrupt you, I promise. We're in a unique position to pick and choose our clients not based on what they can pay."

She frowned at him. "Listen, I don't want you to—"

"It's okay, Sierra. I promise it will all be good. Is that your laptop in the case next to you?"

"It is." She nodded, then gave a tiny grin. "I never leave home without it."

"Okay, I think what we should do is head to my place and order in some dinner. I'll have my partners meet us there. We always dial each other in at the beginning of a case. And they should meet you. That work for you?"

"Uh, good. Thank you."

They flew in silence for the next few moments, Eagle studying the woman across from him and hoping to fuck his hard-earned discipline could help him keep his dick in his pants. He didn't ever remember having this problem before. No woman had threatened his self-control the way Sierra Hunt did. Or made him more committed to resolving her situation. And that was saying something, because Galaxy had a total commitment to each and every client they took on.

He was glad when Saint's voice came over the intercom and derailed his thoughts.

"Fifteen minutes to touchdown."

Eagle took out his cell. "I'm texting the guys to meet me at my place. We all have the codes to each other's homes so they can let themselves in if they get there before us. We'll get some dinner in then we'll go through that list of all the people you've talked to," he told her. "And pick apart the case against Jeremy one item at a time. It's going to be okay, Sierra. We're going to make sure."

He realized he had a personal reason for doing this but hell! So had his partners with certain cases that had come to them. and that had turned out well for them. Maybe he'd be as lucky as they were.

As they headed home, he sent a message to his partners.

New client. Sierra Hunt. Recommended by Senator Kane. Check her out.

By the time they landed, the sun had dropped even lower at the horizon and his brain was already going full tilt with things that needed to be done. And his partners had texted him back, each message the same.

She checks out. We're on.

Chapter Four

Sierra's head was spinning, and she wondered if she had stepped into some kind of weird dream by mistake. How bizarre was it, she thought, that the man she'd had the best sex of her life with turned out to be part of the organization who she had been told could help her with her problem? Her hormones and her emotions were doing a wild dance in her body, and she knew she'd better get both of them under control.

But now he was taking her to his house? Did he do that with all his clients? Did all the partners do it? From what she'd learned from Senator Kane, they held all their meetings on the plane, just as they'd done today.

"I have to ask you." She wet her lips. "Am I getting special privileges because of, you know, last night?"

He smiled at her. "I just think it's better in this case if my partners hear all of this right from you. Listen. We connected last night, and I know you feel it, too. But business always comes first, so let me give you my address."

She stood there and watched while Eagle texted the address of his townhouse to her phone.

"Okay. Go ahead and plug the address into your GPS," he instructed. "But I think it's best if you just follow me. The address is in case for some reason we get separated, and you get lost."

"I'm good," she told him. "I live in this city, remember?"

"Just not ever leaving anything to chance," he told her, "and it will make me feel better. Let's get going. Follow me, and I'll keep watch to see if you have any kind of a tail."

"Okay."

She trusted him. That was the oddest part. She'd learned most men could not be trusted, certainly with the disaster of Jeremy's situation. There didn't seem to be an area of her personal life where, up to now, she'd been able to have faith in any man she met.

Maybe I just choose poorly, personally and professionally.

But there was something about Eagle that she connected with right away, and how weird was that?

Confident that she'd found someone who could help her and who would not betray her in any way, or lead her into harm, she followed him down the driveway and out onto the street. The land where the plane was hangered was on the edge of the city, so she stayed on his tail until they were into the more populated area. She had a pretty good idea where they were going, but it didn't hurt to be sure.

She followed him onto the street which ran a little downhill toward a cross street and a traffic light. Sierra tapped her brakes to stop, but the car didn't even slow down. Worried that she'd rear-end Eagle, she yanked the wheel to the right into a turn lane to avoid hitting

Eagle's rear bumper, but the car kept moving at the same speed. Pumping the brake seemed to have no effect at all.

As traffic continued to move forward, she realized there were cars pulling into the right turn lane ahead of her. She was beginning to panic, still pumping the brakes, her hands sweaty on the steering wheel. Then she spotted a narrow alleyway between two buildings and yanked the wheel enough to turn into it. Giving thanks there were no cars parked there, she drove into the side of one building, jerking the wheel to the right as she did it so she hit the wall broadside.

She was slammed forward and back again as the car hit the wall, but at least it stopped. The airbag exploded, pressing her against the seat and spraying powder everywhere. Her hands shook as she managed to reach the ignition to turn it off. She heard a sound that she was sure was her heart beating extra hard, but it turned out to be Eagle banging on her window.

"Open the window," he was shouting. "Can you reach the controls? Can you open the window?"

Her head was hurting, and she was shaking like a leaf, but she pushed enough of the airbag aside to press the lever for the window. As soon as it rolled down, Eagle reached inside, unlocked her door and opened it. Using a knife he took from a sheath beneath his pantleg, he slashed the airbag, unfastened her seat belt and wrenched her out of the car.

Sierra saw that he had pulled into the alley and stopped behind her, blocking anyone else from entering. She collapsed against him, shaking, realizing how close she'd come to death.

"It's okay." His voice was low and soothing. "It's okay, Sierra. I've got you."

His strong arms around her and the warmth of his chest against her body were the only things that took the edge off her nerves. She forced herself to take slow breaths until her pulse leveled out, then she took a step back.

"My car wouldn't stop," she told him.

"I know." His face was calm, but his voice had a steely edge to it. "Are you okay if I take a few minutes to check around here? And I want to call the guys."

"Yes. Yes, sure. Do whatever you need to."

"Just give me a sec," he told her.

But she twisted her hands together to keep them from shaking, as his fingers flew over the keyboard on his cell phone.

"I think we should have a doctor check you over, but—" he told her when he was finished.

"I'm fine," she insisted. "Really. I need to get my car looked at."

"But I think we'll wait until we get you to my place." He went on speaking as if she hadn't interrupted him. "We'll call the doctor then. I want to get you out of here as soon as possible. I'll take care of your car. No worries. But we have some other things to deal with first." He looked over his shoulder. "Like the crowd behind us that seems very interested in what happened."

She peeked over his shoulder and saw a group of people on the sidewalk and spilling into the alley, staring at them with obvious curiosity.

"Do you need help?" someone shouted out.

"Thanks, but we've got it," Eagle told them. "I just need to make arrangements for my wife's car to be towed and get her home."

His wife? Sierra stared up at him. He just winked at her.

"Play along with me," he murmured in her ear. "It makes things a lot simpler."

"Okay," she whispered. She figured anyone who saw the way she was clinging to him wouldn't have any doubts.

"Sir? Do you need any help here?"

A police car had pulled up, and the cop had walked over to where they were standing.

"Oh, thanks, but we're good." Eagle nodded his head toward her car. "I think my wife's car had a mechanical problem. I'm just glad she wasn't hurt."

The cop studied her. "Have you been drinking, ma'am?"

"What? No. No, no, no. Not at all."

"And I've really got this under control," Eagle assured him. He took out his cell. "In fact, I'm calling for a tow right now."

The cop frowned. "You sure? There was no other car involved?"

"No car, no drinking," Eagle assured him. "But thanks for stopping. We appreciate it but we've got it under control."

Sierra let out a breath when the cop finally moved off, after taking down both their license numbers and the license plate of the car. She stepped away from Eagle, and they both watched the cop walk away. It occurred to her that Eagle kept her face as well as his turned away from the people watching.

"You think whoever did this is out there?" she asked, keeping her voice low and quiet.

"I think there's a good chance he has *someone* watching. I want to make it as impossible as I can for anyone to take pictures of our faces."

"But—" Then her eyes widened. "Whoever it is already knows what I look like. Obviously. So it's your picture you're avoiding."

"One of the things my partners and I learned early on is anonymity is the key to success. We've gone to great lengths to make sure ownership of the business, the plane, our vehicles, even our homes are listed under a shell corporation. Surprise is a great weapon. We've had some pretty powerful people involved in cases we've taken so, yeah, anonymity is one of the keys to our success." His mouth curved in a hint of a smile. "We don't like people to be able to prepare for us."

"That cop is still sitting there in his car," she told him.

"I'm sure he's running the plates to make sure they aren't stolen," he murmured in her ear. "Let's get out of the alley so I can make some phone calls in private."

He had parked his car across the entrance to the alley and now he sat her in the front passenger seat, facing away from the street.

"Just give me one second to check out your car."

She ignored the small crowd that had gathered. When they saw the cop driving away and figured there wasn't much excitement, they began to disperse. She watched Eagle walk around her car then get down on his hands and knees and look underneath it. As he rose, another car pulled up behind his at the entrance to the alley and two men, equally as tall and tough-looking as Eagle, got out and walked toward them.

They had the same lean, hard bodies Eagle did. One had dark brown hair that hung just below his collar and had a neatly trimmed scruff on his chin. The other had ebony-black hair just below his collar with a thicker beard growth lining his jaw. Sunglasses blocked their eyes and partially obscured their faces. They both looked as if they could defeat an army without any help. Before breakfast.

They exchanged guy greetings with Eagle who then led them over to the car where Sierra was sitting and introduced them.

"Meet Scott Hamilton and Matt Roman," he told her. "Blaze and Viper. Guys, meet Sierra Hunt. She's our newest client."

They shook hands with her, their grips strong and reassuring. They hadn't even done anything yet, but she already felt better.

"Thank you for, uh, taking my case," she told them.

"Eagle says you need our help," Blaze told her, "so that's good enough for us." He looked at his partner. "What do we need here?"

"I want her car towed to our usual garage. I think someone dicked around with it, and we need to make sure. Take pictures of whatever was done then get it fixed."

"And figure out who did it," Viper added.

Eagle nodded. "That goes without saying. Okay, I'm taking her back to my house. Can you two please take care of the car and keep people away from it until the tow truck gets here? Then come to my place. What about Rocket?"

"He's running a little behind today. He and Mallory are still getting organized, what with her move here and all."

"Okay." Eagle raked his fingers through his hair. "Hope she's not planning another trip to a place where she might get killed."

"Actually," Blaze told him, "she's promised no more life-or-death trips at all."

"Thank god for that. Okay, check in with him and see if he can get to my place after he's done with whatever they're in the middle of."

"He already said he would, so go ahead and get Sierra out of here. We'll do what has to be done."

Listening to them, Sierra began to hope that, for the first time since this whole nightmare started, she'd found people who could help her.

Eagle touched her elbow. "Let's get going. I want you safely in my house, then we can order in some food."

"You think I'm in danger." When he just looked at her, she sighed. "Of course you do. It just shocks me that anyone would want to hurt me."

"I think someone doesn't want your brother to go free and I think they'll do anything to keep that from happening. I have a feeling the problem with your car wasn't just mechanical."

She stared at him. "Well, whoever is blocking this has done a lot of things, but I never thought they'd try to kill me."

"Desperate people do desperate things. Come on. Let's go."

Viper quietly dispersed what was left of the crowd, and Blaze was talking on the phone, most likely to a garage. Eagle helped her into the car, fastened her seat belt and closed the door. She leaned back in her seat and closed her eyes. Things just kept getting worse. She knew she was missing something, but she couldn't see what. No matter how much research she did or who she tried to talk to, she could not figure out why anyone would frame her brother for this murder.

And she refused to believe he was guilty. She knew him better than that. No questions asked. She felt as if she were in a nightmare from which she could not wake up. And it kept running through her mind as they drove through the city.

"Sierra?"

Eagle's deep voice broke into her thoughts, and she sat up, looking around and realizing they were in a garage. They had crossed the bridge to Davis Islands, a beautiful paradise right at the edge of downtown Tampa, filled with gorgeous homes, quirky restaurants and incredible views of Hillsborough Bay.

She blinked and turned to the man in the driver's seat.

"Sorry." She scrubbed her hands over her face. "I must have checked out for a few minutes there. It took us a long time to go a very short distance."

"Just making sure no one was on our tail."

A little sliver of fear sliced through her. "You thought they'd follow us."

He shrugged. "It seemed logical, and I don't take any chances." He gave one of her hands a gentle squeeze, his touch unexpectedly comforting. "Come on. Let's go inside."

He led her through a door from the garage into a laundry room. Why did it always surprise her that men did laundry? She had no idea what she expected when she learned they were going to his house. Maybe an austere, masculine environment. White walls. Brown rugs. Nothing on the walls but a massive television set. Minimal furniture.

But she stepped out of the laundry room into a kitchen that made her eyes widen. The counters had expensive granite tops and the cupboards were a soft blue. There were things scattered on the counter, but it didn't look messy, just…busy.

The living room floor was polished hardwood with a large soft gray area rug, and furniture that was chosen for comfort as well as style. But it was the view from the wall of sliding glass doors that really took her breath away. A large patio stretched from the glass and centered in it was a good-sized swimming pool with a hot tub at one end. Massive sunshade solar screening protected it all from insects and birds. Plus, residents could see out, but others could not see in. She recognized it because Jeremy had shown her a house he'd designed that had the same type of screening all around a massive covered back patio similar to this.

The sun was just now dipping below the horizon and its reflection off the pool and the waters of the bay made a stunning view. She thought it surely one of the most beautiful landscapes she'd ever seen, and she'd lived in Tampa a long time.

"This is incredible." Sierra stood in the doorway, then turned slowly around, taking everything in.

Eagle chuckled softly. "Did you think I lived in a warehouse?"

"Actually I had no idea, but I have to say I'm really impressed." Standing there, she felt an unexpected serenity wash over her.

"After so long in the SEALs and with the kind of work Galaxy takes on, I needed a place where I could rest my brain as well as my body."

"You certainly accomplished that."

"When Viper bought a house here, I caught the bug. Lucky for me a home came on the market shortly after that because there's hardly ever anything for sale. Okay. There's a bathroom just down that little hallway there in case you need it. I'm going to order dinner. Being guys, when we work, we stick to the basics, which usually means pizza. If you'd prefer something else —"

"I love pizza," she assured him. "Any of the standard kinds works for me, if that's okay."

"Perfect. I'll go make the call."

Either Eagle had exquisite taste or a top-notch decorator. The small bathroom, like the rest of the place, was exquisitely decorated in shades of gray and soft blue. He even had matching guest towels and soap and lotion dispensers. Now her curiosity was really piqued.

She'd taken her purse in the bathroom with her to freshen up so now, buffed and polished as much as possible, she hunted him down in the kitchen.

"Very nice place," she told him.

"Thanks, but I can't take much of the credit. Two of the Galaxy fiancées were a very big help."

"Well, they did a great job."

She blew out a breath, suddenly unsure of how to act.

As if he read her mind, he reached out for her and pulled her toward him.

"We've got a few minutes before the others get here, and I want to make sure you understand something."

Apprehension coursed through her.

"Why do I get the feeling I'm not going to like what you have to say?"

His warm smile sent little flutters skipping through her.

"Why don't you hear what that is before jumping to conclusions." He stroked her arms in a soft, gentle motion. "The night we met, I felt as if I'd been thunderstruck. I won't lie about the fact that I've probably had more than my share of women, or that I enjoy being with women. A lot. But I do try to treat them all with respect."

"O-kay." What was he getting at? And what did this have to do with anything?

"Meeting you was like being hit with a ton of bricks. I don't ever remember a woman having that effect on me. And, pure truth, the sex was beyond incredible. When you just walked out yesterday morning, I felt as if I'd been smacked with a block of ice."

He slid his hands up to cup her face. "Cards on the table? That was more than incidental sex, as far as I was concerned. A lot more. At least it was to me, and I'm hoping it was to you."

She studied his face, trying to read what was behind his expression. Then she drew a breath and let it out slowly.

"I'm almost afraid to say yes."

He still cradled her face in his warm palms.

"Don't be. Afraid that is. I've learned from all my years in the military that sometimes things happen just because they're supposed to. We don't have to rush anything. We have plenty of time. And it's not going to affect the case at all, even if you say no. We can take it really slow, but let's not turn our backs on it either."

He brushed his mouth over hers, the contact sizzling. Then, just as he slid his tongue along the seam of her lips, his cell phone rang. He lifted his mouth, swallowed a sigh and hit Accept.

"Yeah, Blaze. What's going on? Uh-huh. Uh-huh. Yeah. Well, fucking damn." Every muscle in his face tightened. "Okay. You both get over here. Rocket texted he'd be here in another hour. We need to do some planning. Yeah. Okay."

He disconnected and shoved the phone in his pocket, anger flashing in his eyes.

"What is it?" she asked. "What's wrong? What did Blaze have to say?"

Eagle took a deep breath and forced a calmness he obviously hadn't been feeling. He took both her hands in his and wrapped his fingers around them.

"There's a problem with your car," he began.

"Well, I figured that, since you didn't seem too happy with the call. What's the problem?"

"The guys had it towed to the garage we always use and one of our mechanics went over it. It seems someone cut your brake line."

Shock stabbed at her. "What?"

"Not all the way through, just enough to create a slow leak. They called Saint and asked him to check the spot at the hangar where you were parked. There's enough droplets there to indicate a slow leak."

All of a sudden, she felt weak and began to tremble. Someone in this whole complex case was actually trying to kill her. *Oh, god!*

"Here." Eagle guided her to one of the bar stools at the counter. "Have a seat."

Her laugh was edged with a touch of hysteria as she eased herself up onto the stool.

"I can't believe someone really wants to get rid of me. Why? Because I'm a pest?"

Eagle shook his head. "I'd say because you're pushing someone's buttons. Someone has a secret they don't want uncovered. Which gives a whole lot of validity to your theory that your brother is being framed."

She rubbed her hands over her face. "I feel as if I'm living in a nightmare."

"I know. But we're going to help you get out of it. Meanwhile let me get you something to drink to settle you down as much as possible. What would you like? Water? Coffee? Tea?"

"Do you have any wine, by any chance?"

He smiled. "I have a Riesling I'm especially fond of. Will that do it?"

"Yes, please."

She twisted her hands together to keep them from trembling while he filled a wineglass and placed it on the counter in front of her. Lifting it with both hands, she took a healthy swallow, then another one.

"I don't usually drink wine that way." She managed a smile. "But I needed it this time."

"No problem. But let's get your mind on something constructive. How about moving into the dining room where the table's big enough for all of us and our laptops or tablets? Grab your wine and I'll bring your laptop."

They had just seated themselves at the table when the doorbell rang. Eagle answered and Blaze and Viper followed him into the dining room.

"Sorry we didn't have better news about your car," Blaze told her.

"What's the deal with it?" Eagle asked.

"Rich showed us exactly where the damage is. Someone who knew precisely what they were doing made just enough of a slit in the brake line for the fluid to leak slowly. Wherever it finally broke, there'd be some kind of incident that would either kill the driver or injure them badly."

"But an injury would not necessarily get Sierra off their backs," Eagle pointed out, "assuming that's what they wanted."

"You're right," Viper agreed. "But if she was injured, it would get her out of the field of action and certainly put her in a more vulnerable position for some other kind of attack."

Sierra was glad she was sitting down because she suddenly felt weak all over. Eagle reached for her hand under the table and gave it a reassuring squeeze. She wondered if last night hadn't happened, how he'd be handling this, then decided it didn't matter. By whatever stroke of fate, she'd landed in the best situation possible, and she wasn't going to ask any questions.

"Anyway," he went on, "there's no way to tell how long it's been leaking. Saint found the puddle at the hangar, but there's probably more where her car was parked at her house. One of us needs to get out there and take a look."

Blaze nodded. "I agree. So then the question is, who is Sierra a danger to? Who wants her brother locked away for good without her interference, wants it so badly they seem to have gone to a lot of trouble to make it happen?"

"Hopefully there's something in all her files, documents and what all else Sierra's got that will give us a clue of some kind."

"Anyway," Blaze said, "Rich is going over the rest of the car inch by inch to see if there's any other damage and taking pictures of everything as he does."

Eagle frowned. "No fingerprints, I'm guessing."

"Not one," Viper told him. "I'm sure whoever did this wore gloves. Still, Rich is going to replace the entire braking system, and he'll keep all the pieces of the existing one to go over thoroughly."

"Wait." Sierra held up her hand. "That sounds expensive."

"We'll take care of it," Eagle assured her. "That was definitely a disaster on its way to happening. And proof that someone is tracking you."

The doorbell rang again. Viper opened the door to a pizza guy and carried in their dinner. Rocket arrived on the heels of the delivery, and in moments they were all seated around the dining room table with slices of pizza and open laptops.

Sierra took a bite, swallowed and washed it down with a sip of wine. Then she drew in a breath and let it out slowly. She figured this was as good a time as any to get the money thing out in the open.

"Before we go any further," she began, "I would really like to discuss your fee. Eagle didn't want to talk with me about it, and Senator Kane said your charges were flexible, whatever that means. I make a good living and I'm not without resources, but you should know right off that a lot of that has gone to paying legal fees to attorneys who wasted my money and my time. I—"

Blaze held up a hand.

"I'm surprised Eagle didn't explain it to you, but, yes, our fees our flexible. They range from six figures to zero, depending."

Sierra frowned. "On what?

"The case. The client. I guess Senator Kane might not have mentioned this, but we started Galaxy when we won the super lottery of more than a billion dollars."

"What?" Sierra stared at them. *What the hell? A billion dollars?*

"We used part of it as startup funds and we invested a lot of it, plus we have many clients who are flush and can afford the highest fees we charge."

"Depends on the situation," Viper added. "We like having that flexibility. So you see, there won't be a problem with you paying a fee."

She turned to look at Eagle. "I still don't understand. How much are you charging me?"

"We don't take kindly to people trying to kill our clients," he told her. "In fact, it makes us very angry, so you get charged the Alpha fee."

"Alpha? What are you talking about? How much?"

"Zero." He grinned. "I think you can afford that."

Sierra was stunned. They weren't charging her anything? "Wait. There has to be a catch here. What am I missing?"

Blaze leaned toward her. "Nothing. Sierra, we like being in a position to do this. You can argue with Eagle about it, but as far as we're concerned, it's time to get to work."

"But what if…?"

Blaze shook his head. "No what-ifs, Sierra — we're all former SEALs. We know how to plan and execute even the most impossible missions and even with little to no time to do it. SEALs know how to do this. We don't fail. We'll get to the bottom of this, I promise you. Right now we're all going to go through the documents

Eagle says you have and see what we can find that's the least bit out of place."

"Just take another sip of wine," Eagle said in a soft voice, "and let's get to work."

Chapter Five

For the next several hours, getting down to work was exactly what they did.

"We usually hold meetings like this on the plane," Eagle told Sierra. "The only thoroughly soundproof and isolated place we had, until recently."

Sierra lifted an eyebrow. "And now?"

"We all decided the best thing to do was soundproof all our houses, so we found a company that specializes in it and had them do all of ours. That way we could have meetings like this one tonight without worrying someone was out on the street with a parabolic reflector catching our sound. In our line of work, that's critical."

"Wow." She exhaled slowly. "I feel as if I'm in a movie."

Eagle winked at her. "So do we. Okay, let's get to work"

He had her send all the documents on her laptop to everyone so they could each look at them. As they read through them, they peppered her with questions.

"I've told you all I can," she said at last. "I only know what's in those court documents, in the interviews — which is damn little — and what Jeremy told me. You think I haven't gone over these a million times?"

Eagle took one of her hands in his, ignoring the side glances his partners gave them.

"We know you have. But sometimes there can be a little something stuck in a corner that doesn't seem important, then it is. So any little thing you can think of. Anything that Jeremy might have said. Have even mentioned in passing. Some little inconsequential thing. Because if, as you say, he's completely innocent —"

"He is." She slammed a hand on the table. "Not you, too. Please. I am so tired of people questioning his guilt. You look at all those files and you'll see the evidence against him is very flimsy. But it was just as if nobody heard a thing I said. As if their minds were already made up, and nothing I said made any difference."

She rubbed her forehead.

"I can believe how frustrating it was," Eagle told her. "What did his girlfriend say during all this time? She must have been distressed, too."

"She was floored. She said the whole thing was impossible. Swore up and down that he wasn't seeing anyone else."

She remembered how passionate Cheryl had been about that and how devastated she was by the whole thing.

"She got sick before the end of the trial," Sierra told him. "I think it was because she was so worn down physically and emotionally by the investigation, and the trial and the battle for an appeal. Like me, she was killing herself talking to anyone she could find and telling them that this was all a horrible mistake."

"Is she working on this with you?" Rocket asked.

Sierra had to swallow the lump in her throat. "We lost her to the flu about three months ago. Jeremy still hasn't recovered." When the men all exchanged glances, she frowned. "What?"

Eagle cleared his throat. "We're very sorry for your loss."

She got the feeling there was more to it, but Blaze jumped back into the discussion.

"Listen, guys. You see everything that's here. I've gone over it a zillion times and scoured my brain, but nothing pops up. Jeremy lived a very normal life. Had a great career, a nice condo on the water, a terrific girlfriend. Everyone loved him. His boss, his friends. Even the guy whose car hit him. He —"

"Wait," Rocket interrupted. "What? He was in an accident? When? Was anyone hurt? When did it happen?"

"Hold it, guys." Eagle held up a hand. "She's already had a bad enough day. Take a breath."

Rocket gave her a crooked smile. "Sorry, Sierra. Automatic reflex on anything that veers from the norm. Tell me about this accident."

Sierra took another swallow of her wine then set the glass down. She figured she'd better watch it before she fell on her face at the table, but she needed something to settle her jangling nerves.

"It was at night. Jeremy had just taken Cheryl home, and he was headed to his own place. He said he had turned a corner when a car pulled out of a driveway. I'm guessing the heavy rain was making it hard to see and as the other car pulled out, it banged into his right fender."

"Where did it happen?" Viper asked.

"Jeremy said it was right near The Library. That private club on Bayshore Boulevard. When Jeremy got out to see the damage, the other driver jumped out of his vehicle and was nervous as hell. He handed Jeremy a wad of cash to cover it, jumped back into his car and managed to take off."

"And Jeremy didn't get the license plate or anything?"

"It was pouring rain," she repeated. "He was dog tired, and the cash more than covered the damage to his car. I think he was just glad it wasn't worse. Why?"

"I'm not sure, but it's odd that the other driver didn't want to exchange information," Rocket mused.

"I thought so, too," she agreed. "But that would have meant calling the police to file an accident report. Jeremy said the guy told him his boss was in the car and didn't want to take the time to deal with a police report and all the insurance paperwork. The money he gave my brother covered the repairs and then some."

Again the men exchanged looks.

"What?" she asked.

"My brain doesn't like things that don't fit neatly. Your brother didn't think it was unusual that this other driver seemed anxious to get away from the whole thing? Didn't want him to get the police and the insurance company involved?"

Sierra shrugged. "Jeremy designed buildings for some very wealthy people in this town. He was always telling me about their odd habits and personalities. And how they always figured they could buy their way out of everything. That's why he didn't think this was so odd. Besides, it was pouring with rain, and he was just as happy not to have to stand in it."

"How long after that before he was arrested at the hotel?"

Sierra frowned, going over the time frame in her mind. "About three weeks? But what does one have to do with the other?"

Again the men exchanged glances.

"I'll look into it," Eagle said. "Let's not create a situation if none exists."

Blaze shook his head. "I think one of us should do that. Not you. I know you're itching to dig into this, but you need to stay glued to Sierra's side. Whoever these guys are, they were bold enough to get close enough to her car to damage it...at her house."

A sick feeling washed through her.

"What you're saying...?" She shook her head. "What you're telling me is that no place is safe. Right?"

"Correct," he told her. "Even though I hate to say it. Which is why Eagle is going to stay glued to you like a second skin until this is resolved."

Glued to me?

Unbidden, erotic images began to dance in her brain, and in the midst of all this stress she had to squeeze her thighs together to contain the vibrations running through her.

Blaze cleared his throat. "Sierra, give me your address. I'm going to run out to your house and check out your driveway and your garage. I'll need the garage door opener, too."

"I don't have a garage," she told him. "My house is a Craftsman bungalow and there's an attached breezeway for parking."

"Well, damn," he swore. "Easy enough for someone to sneak in after dark. If he knew what he was doing, cutting a brake line was a snap. I need to see if I can find any signs of brake fluid leakage."

"I thought maybe Eagle could look when he takes me home tonight." Again they exchanged looks. She was going to have to learn to decipher them. "What?"

"Sierra." Eagle took one of her hands in his again, something she realized she'd come to enjoy. "You won't be going home tonight. Or, as a matter of fact, any night until we get this cleared up. It's not safe for you there."

Not go home?

"Not even if you hire someone to guard me?"

"They obviously know where you live. If they were bold enough to damage your car in an open breezeway, a guard at your house is not going to stop them. You can't go home until we get this wrapped up."

"Are you kidding?" She stared at him. "B-but I need things. Clothes. Personal things. I mean—"

"Got it covered," Blaze told her and punched a number on his cell. "Peyton? Yeah, listen, honey. Viper picked me up earlier, and I was going to have him take me home, but I've got a little errand to run. One, by the way, I think well suited to you. Uh-huh. Yeah, kind of like with Hannah. Okay, see you in a few." He disconnected and looked at Sierra. "My fiancée's on the way. I think we've got your problem solved the best we can under the circumstances."

"Good idea," Eagle agreed. "And while we're waiting for her, let's divvy up who is doing what tomorrow."

Sierra was amazed at the efficiency with which they drew up what they called their 'mission,' assigning responsibilities and organizing their plan. Peyton West arrived in the middle of it and put Sierra at ease immediately. Of medium height, she was casually dressed in a T-shirt and jeans. Thick, glossy chestnut hair was pulled back tight into a ponytail, and sympathy for Sierra's situation warmed her dark green eyes.

"Come on, let's get some privacy. Blaze and I are going to stop by your house on the way home. If you give me a list of what you want, I'll pack it all up for you and bring it in the morning."

Peyton led her into the kitchen where she made hot tea for both of them, then sat at the counter with Sierra, doing her best to assure her she was in good hands.

"I know this is rough," she told Sierra. "We've all been through it. A killer was after my sister. Corporate killers were after Hannah, Viper's fiancée. And Rocket had to rescue his fiancée, Mallory Kane, from a drug cartel."

Sierra just shook her head.

"It sounds like it's dangerous to hang out with these guys."

"Not at all," Peyton assured her. "The danger is in being away from them. I promise you, whatever this is, they'll get to the bottom of it, and keep you safe while they do it."

Her voice was so warm, her eyes so reassuring, that unexpectedly Sierra's eyes filled with tears. She swiped at them with her hand.

"Sorry. I'm not usually a weeping willow. I think all the stress, and looking at the reality of it from the guys' point of view has just…just…"

Peyton reached over and squeezed her hand. "Understandable. Been there, done that, got the war story to prove it. I will say this. You couldn't be in better hands. If anyone can get to the bottom of this and help your brother, these are the guys. Now" — she took out her cell — "why don't you give me that list of things you'd like me to pick up for you. I know it's weird having a stranger paw through your stuff, but I promise I'll be as sensitive as possible."

Since she didn't seem to have much choice in the matter, Sierra took the cell and began typing in the items she could think of. Since she had no idea how long she'd be here, she wanted to make sure she was well supplied. And she could always do laundry. She swallowed a smile as she remembered the immaculate laundry room they'd entered this place through.

"I can't tell you how much I appreciate this, Peyton. I mean, you don't even know me, yet you — "

Peyton held up a hand.

"We've all been there in some form or other. I was the first addition to the group, so their habits are old hat to me now. Let me fix more tea, and I can try to answer your questions. Make you more comfortable in the situation."

"We're going to call it a night," Eagle told them when they came back into the dining room. "Sierra, I don't mean this is a bad way, but you look like you could use a good night's sleep."

She almost laughed.

"I didn't think such a thing was on my schedule again."

"We're going to make sure it is. Okay, guys. Everyone's got their mission assignment. Let's check in mid-morning to see where we are." He reached for her hand, a signal to the others that this was more than a regular mission. "I'll be working on my computer from here. Like we said, there's something fishy about that accident. I'm going to see if I can find out why."

After they were gone, Eagle cleaned up the remains of the pizza. Sierra could see him quietly keeping an eye on her.

"I'm okay," she insisted. "Really."

"Sierra, I could see how the more you got into the retelling of things, the more stressed out you got. And with good reason." He gave her arm a little squeeze. "This whole thing smells funny. It's the kind of thing that usually happens if there's big money involved, and all my senses tell me that's what's behind all of this."

"I've been thinking the same thing," she agreed. "But how? Where? Why would someone set Jeremy up to take the fall for killing someone? And who would that be?"

"Obviously we don't know yet, but everything you showed us? There's glaring holes in there that no one wanted to see. We had a similar situation when someone tried to kill Peyton's sister and brother-in-law to protect the son of a rich lawyer. A partner, by the way, in the law firm where her brother-in-law worked. Which is one reason we're all convinced there's a lot of shit shoved behind a curtain in this case. And there's got to be a lot of power behind it, like there was in Peyton's case, for everyone to ignore all the things they should have checked out."

Sierra's body tightened again with tension.

"Come on." He took her hand and led her down a wide hallway and waved at all the open doors. "Let's get you settled for the night. FYI, I have three bedrooms here, and you can choose any of the others if you'd like." He pointed to an open set of double doors and the big master bedroom beyond them, and cleared his throat. "But I'm hoping you'll decide to share this one with me."

She appreciated the fact he was leaving the decision up to her and not automatically expecting her to share his bed just because they'd already had sex. It took her less than a minute to decide. It was good he'd given her the option, but right now she wanted to cuddle up to his strong, sexy body more than she wanted to sleep alone in a big bed. Whatever happened, well, maybe some good hot sex was just what she needed right now.

He took both of her hands in his and pulled her slightly closer.

"Listen. I have no idea what forces were at work in the universe that made last night happen, but they did. And I for one am very glad they did. I know we haven't even known each other twenty-four hours, but we made a connection that few people are fortunate enough to experience. Don't pull back because of this."

"But—" She chewed her bottom lip.

"My partners and I are going to get this done for you. If anyone can, it's us. And I want to keep you with me so I can protect you, but also because...I can't believe I'm saying this...I don't want to be away from you. I want to make sure that we really started something fantastic. Okay?"

How could she refuse? Wonderful sex and a man who wanted to help and protect her.

"Okay, then I, um, think I'll share this one, if it's okay with you. I mean, since you offered." *Crap.* She sounded like an addle-brained idiot.

He winked. "It would be my pleasure."

"But first," she told him, "I'd love a shower, if that's okay. Oh, and I guess I also need something to sleep in."

"One shower coming right up. Then we'll take care of the other."

He led her through the double doorway into the master suite then to the big bathroom. It was all decorated in the same muted blues and grays as everywhere else. The shower was enormous, with a big rain showerhead and a built-in bench.

"There's liquid soap in the dispenser." He pointed to the small, recessed shelf. "It might be a little masculine for your taste, though. Sorry."

She almost giggled. "I can handle it. No worries. You weren't exactly expecting guests."

"The towel racks are heated. I'll hang a fresh one right here. Holler if you need anything." He turned on the shower before walking out of the bathroom.

Sierra kicked off her shoes and stripped off her clothes, leaving them in a pile on the floor. Maybe Eagle had an old shirt or something she could wear until Peyton arrived with her things. She stepped into the shower and turned it up as hot as she could stand it. She let the heated streams caress her body in an attempt to wash away the tension that was her constant companion.

She had no idea how long she stood there, eyes closed, trying to let her muscles relax. She was a little disappointed that he had just walked away like that. She had hoped, when he'd asked her to sleep with him... She had just reached for the body wash when she heard the shower door open and close.

"I think I can handle that for you," a deep voice said.

The soft body wash splashed on her shoulders, and his strong hands began massaging it into her taut muscles. Despite her brain telling her she was jumping too soon too fast, she let herself enjoy the touch of firm fingers kneading the tension gripping her body.

"You don't know how hard it's been for me to keep my hands off you today," he continued. The deep voice was as erotic as it was comforting.

"Mmm." She closed her eyes, reveling in his touch. "That feels so good."

"Okay, enough of that," Eagle told her, his deep, rough voice more soothing than soft music. "Time to unwind this sexy body."

Closing her eyes, she deliberately wiped every thought from her mind except for the here and now in this shower. Eagle's fingers dug deep into her locked muscles, his thumbs pressing and kneading until very, very slowly the tension began to slide away.

She thought of nothing except his touch and the slickness of the body wash and the soft stream of water sluicing over her. She just stood there, forcing everything else out of her mind, because god knew she needed it. At some point, when she vaguely realized Eagle had lathered her body and rinsed it twice, she understood that his fingers had changed from therapeutic to instruments of arousal.

And she thought how glad she was that she'd decided to share his bedroom with him.

She had been leaning against the shower wall, facing him while he glided his hands over the front of her body, but now he turned her to face the wall. Placing her hands against the tile, he nudged her legs apart and began again to work his magic with his fingers. He stroked the curve of her spine, of her hips then down each of her legs. His touch was light, teasing, and the muscles of her pussy suddenly came to life and vibrated. That was the only word for it.

Eagle slid his hand along the inside of one leg, from ankle to thigh, gently stroking the skin then barely brushing the lips of her pussy as he worked his way down the other leg.

Touch me there!

She wanted to scream the words, but they stuck in her throat. Instead, she just clawed the tiles in front of her as his wicked fingers teased and touched. And stroked. But not *there*.

"Am I going too fast for you?" His voice vibrated with sexual hunger.

"No. Don't stop. Don't stop."

"Okay." He nipped her neck. "Just checking."

Back to her shoulders, stroking and rubbing, and sliding his palms down her back until he reached the curves of her ass. He molded his palms to them, making slow, circular motions before easing two coated fingers into the crevice of her ass. When a soft moan drifted from her lips, a low chuckle rumbled up from Eagle's throat.

"You have the sweetest ass in the world," he told her, his lips against her ear. He closed his teeth over the lobe and tugged on it. "Sweet and sexy. You have no idea the things I want to do to it."

A shiver raced over the surface of her skin and as if it were connected by a chain to her hungry pussy, all her inner muscles clenched. When he pressed the tip of one finger against her opening, she moaned even louder and pushed back against him.

"One of these days," he murmured in that low sexy voice, "you're gonna feel my cock back here. I'm going to fuck that sweet ass of yours until you beg for mercy. Make you come like a maniac then do it all over again."

"Yessss."

Now, she wanted to say, startling herself because she was mostly a follower of conventional sex. But this man made her want to throw off all restraint and open herself up to every erotic situation possible.

When he took his hand away, she wanted to cry at the loss of contact, but he gave her no time to dwell on it. Instead, he turned her to face him and went to work on her front. He used the showerhead to rinse off all the body wash, then cupped each of her breasts in his palms.

"Such sweet tits," he murmured. "So round and plump. They fit right into my hands. And those nipples are just begging for my mouth."

He cradled the flesh around one taut nipple and closed his mouth over it, scraping it with his teeth before sucking on it. Another little moan drifted from her mouth and she gripped his shoulders, digging her fingers into the flesh. He worked the one bud until she was ready to scream from the pleasure before moving his mouth to the other one. He pinched the pebbled skin and bit down on it gently, making her pussy clench with need.

More, she wanted to tell him. *Please. More.*

As if he'd heard her silent words, he knelt before her, nudged her thighs apart and peeled open the lips to her very hungry cunt. At the first stroke of his tongue over her clit, she nearly ignited, electricity shooting through her entire body. She grabbed his upper arms to steady herself, feeling the hard muscle beneath her touch.

Taking the sensitive bundle of flesh between his teeth, he gave it a series of tiny bites, each one sending more intense sensations rioting through her. The more he ate at her, the hungrier her body became. She wanted him inside her so badly. Wanted to squeeze him with her inner muscles and milk him for all she was worth.

But he was in control and he was taking his time. Lifting one leg and resting it on his shoulder, he held her in place with his hands on her ass and proceeded to nibble away at her cunt until she was screaming with need. The pulse in her inner walls fluttered insistently, and it was all she could do not to beg him to fuck her right then and there.

When at last he slid two fingers into her, she pushed hard against him and came at once. The muscles of her pussy pulsed and throbbed, milking his fingers. He pulled her clit into his mouth and sucked hard on it until the last tiny spasm subsided. Easing his fingers from her body, he propped her against the shower wall and took her mouth in a kiss that was both gentle and hungry.

At last, her breathing slowed. Eagle eased his mouth and fingers from her body and rose to his feet. When he kissed her, even with the shower spraying over them she could taste herself on his tongue. She gripped his shoulders and clung to him, satisfied yet hungrier than ever for him.

Then she realized something was missing, besides the feel of his cock inside her.

"You didn't..." She studied his face. "You didn't come."

"Not yet." He brushed his mouth over hers. "Glad you noticed."

She watched as he took a step back, opened the glass door, reached out to the edge of the vanity counter and grabbed a condom. He unwrapped it and rolled it onto his very swollen dick with efficient movements, then nudged her legs apart with his knee. When his gaze locked with hers, she saw heat blazing in his eyes and a hunger so intense it sent chills down her spine.

Moving a hand between her thighs, he slid two fingers back between the swollen lips of her cunt and eased them inside her.

"Still wet." His deep voice was thick with lust. "I like that, darlin'. I always want you wet and ready for me."

With one strong, muscular arm around her waist, he lifted her enough to use his other hand to ease his cock into her waiting heat. She clenched her inner muscles around his thickness and wound her legs around his waist. She dug her heels in the small of his back, tightening her body to his so his dick filled her completely.

"Fuck!" he growled and banded his arms around her. "Fair warning. I'm not gonna last very long."

"Just do it," she urged. "Fuck me. Hard."

She had no idea where this intense sexual desire was coming from, except that Eagle Bodine made her hotter and needier than any man she'd ever been with.

Pressing his open mouth to hers, he gripped her hard and moved his hips, slamming his dick in and out of her with an intensity that almost bordered on desperation.

"Touch yourself," he whispered. "I'll hold you up."

She managed to inch one of her hands between them, found her clit and began to stroke it, just the way she did when she was alone. She'd never guessed how much it would turn her on to do it with someone watching. As she moved her hand, her knuckles brushed the area at the base of his cock, and he moved in and out of her with ferocious speed, the feel of it making her more aroused.

"I'm so close," he whispered. "I can feel your pussy squeezing me. Take a breath and ride with me."

She pulled her hand loose so she could use both to hold on to him as he pounded into her. His cock was so big and thick it stretched her to her fullest. As close to the edge as they clearly both were, it took only seconds before they exploded in an intense orgasm. Sierra closed her eyes and hung on for dear life as his dick pulsed inside her and her inner walls clutched at him again and again.

At last, when the final shudder had subsided, when their heartbeats had slowed to somewhat normal, when he'd poured every drop of himself into her, he eased from the grip of her body and lowered her feet to the floor. Before he did anything else, he slid open the shower door and dropped the condom into the waste basket beside it. Then, with the shower still pouring down on them, he lathered her body again then slowly washed the suds away.

He cradled her face in his palms for a moment.

"You know, I feel like we're doing this backwards. The other night…"

"Was great," she assured him in a languid voice.

"Now I feel like I can't get enough of you. The things I want to do to you. With you…"

"Will happen. Listen." She let out a slow breath and tried to gather her scattered thoughts. "That was a big first for me. I don't go around jumping into bed with strange men. But I don't regret a single moment of it."

"Good, because neither do I."

She felt as limp as a dishrag when he lifted her from the shower, stood her on the mat and dried her with a warm towel. Then he grabbed one of his T-shirts which he'd left on the vanity counter and eased it over her head, lifted her again and sat her on the counter.

"Don't move," he said.

Sierra gave a weak little laugh. "As if I could."

She watched in a cloud of pleasant lassitude while he finished drying himself and yanked on a pair of boxer briefs. Just as he hung up the towel he'd been using, his cell phone, beside her on the counter, played a tune.

"It's Blaze," he told her. "Yeah. Everything good? Oh? Interesting. Uh-huh. Uh-huh. Yeah. Do that. Good deal. Okay, we'll see you guys in the morning."

Sierra watched him, but his face never changed expression. *Damn*, she thought, *he's good at that.*

"Everything good?" she asked.

"Peyton has a full suitcase for you, and your house is locked up tight as a drum." He hesitated as if trying to phrase his words.

"What? Please don't try to hide things from me. I hate that."

"Blaze found an oil puddle in your breezeway, evidence that your line had been cut just enough to produce a slow leak. Just like the evidence we found at the hangar, only there was more there, because you'd driven your car out, which sent oil flushing through the engine. They probably got in while you were in New Orleans." He paused. "They kept most of the lights off in the house, and he kept watch while Peyton packed your things. He said a car passed your house twice while they were there, so he called our friend Danny Tardello."

"Who's he, and what does he do?"

"He installed all our security systems. We're having one installed at your house but not until morning. If the house is all lit up tonight, whoever was following us and you will be all over this. Tomorrow there'll be a cable service truck in your driveway, but the guys will be putting in the security system."

"So am I going back there to stay?"

"Hell, no." Eagle practically snapped the words out. "Not until this is all over. And maybe not even then." He winked, then his face sobered again. "But whoever this is won't know that. Sierra, all your digging has scared someone, and they can't afford to let it go. That makes you a target."

She started to shiver as the reality of the situation washed over her again.

Eagle wrapped his arms around her and pulled her close to his body.

"I promise you no one will get to you."

He stroked her hair, a gesture that sent a different kind of warmth through her body.

"Thank you," she murmured.

"For what?"

"For taking me on as a client. For insisting I stay here with you. For, well, everything."

He was silent for a moment, long enough that she began to worry about what he'd say next.

"I've been a loner a long time," he said at last. "I watched each of my partners meet the right woman for them, but me? I was just hanging loose and sampling all the goodies. Until I met you." He tilted her face up so he could look into her eyes. "Until this sexy blonde spilled her tea all over me in the hotel lobby."

"Yeah." She forced a laugh. "For once being clumsy paid off."

He grinned. "It was a lucky clumsy. And in one night, I knew my days of being single were gone. I'm just damn glad someone was watching over us and made that happen. And let me tell you, that's a weird thing for me to say. But it's what I believe, Sierra. And I think you do, too."

"Yes." She nodded and managed a little smile. She still wasn't sure it wouldn't all be snatched away from her, the way her luck had been going lately. But she trusted Eagle.

"Well, darlin', it's been quite a day and that orgasm was so intense it just about did me in." He cupped her chin and pressed his mouth lightly to hers, then traced the outline with the tip of his tongue. "In fact, that was…incredible."

"For me, too," she told him in a soft voice.

"Just so you know," he told her, "I could have gone longer tonight if I hadn't been on a sex marathon with you last night. Which, by the way, was incredible. No, more than that, it was amazing."

She touched his cheek, brushing her fingertips over the light scruff.

"For me too. Like I said before, this isn't a habit for me—"

He pressed his fingers to her mouth.

"You don't think I can tell? Something's happening here, Sierra, and I promise you I'm not gonna do anything to destroy it. And we're going to fix this thing with your brother."

He picked her up and carried her to the bedroom, stripping back the covers and laying her down on some of the softest linens she'd ever touched. She wasn't so out of it that she missed the fact the sheets were like a soft cloud of cotton and the comforter was puffy and warm. She supposed he had the Galaxy women to thank for those, too.

What a contradiction this man was — one hundred percent macho, unbreakably tough, a warrior, an incredible lover, a man with an exciting sexual appetite and gentle and caring on top of that. And her body was still totally drained from some of the best sex in her life, ever.

Just as she drifted off to sleep, she gave one last thought to how fortunate she was that circumstance had brought Eagle Bodine into her life. If anyone could attack her problems, he and Galaxy were the ones.

Chapter Six

"As long as she's alive she's a danger to me. To us."

Darius Holland ground his teeth as he spat out the words.

"We never expected her to go this far," Neil Maguire, sitting in one of the armchairs, reminded him. "But, Darius, she's been turned down by every lawyer she's approached, as we'd arranged. She's out of options."

"We can't count on that," Darius protested. "Somehow she's brought strangers into this, and I don't like the feeling I'm getting."

The two men were dissecting the latest and most disturbing piece of information they'd received late today. Smart enough to know they should not be discussing this in any place outside of their homes, they chose to meet at Darius' because he had a soundproof den.

They had been friends since college and business partners since they'd graduated. That had given them a lot of years together to build up an enormously successful business enterprise. They'd discovered early on that the way up the ladder of success was not to give an inch in any deal and to always press their advantage. It might have given them the reputation of being ruthless and some other not-so-nice adjectives, but it had made them rich beyond their wildest imaginations.

A lot of secrets have been revealed in this room, Darius thought. When he died, his children should just burn the house down and the secrets with it. At least he'd taken care to make sure his ex-wife would have nothing. What a bitch she'd turned out to be. He'd been very honest with her from the beginning, and until the children were born, she'd seemed amenable to all his suggestions, at least to a point. But then overnight, she had seemed to turn into another person. It had been worth every dime of the divorce settlement to be rid of her.

He took a healthy swallow of the whiskey in his glass and eased himself into a seat on the couch, then turned to look at Neil.

"I can't believe this whole fucking thing isn't behind us yet." He wanted to throw his drink across the room. "That goddamned woman. I'll say it again. We should have found a way to get rid of her before this."

"Oh, right," Neil snorted. "You think that spotlight wouldn't have shone brighter?"

"We know how to make that happen," Darius told him. "A prescription for sleeping pills. A note that she couldn't live any longer with the hopelessness of her brother's situation. Any number of ways. Getting to her should be easy since she doesn't have any kind of security options."

"And you think some hotshot wouldn't have decided to take a closer look at whatever we chose? No, an accident is the best solution. Except it seems we can't even make that happen the way it should."

"She does seem like the bad penny that just keeps turning up," Darius pointed out. "What I'm interested in is where someone like Sierra Hunt would come into contact with people who are this mysterious and practically invisible. She's hardly someone that would move in shadowy circles so who the hell would she contact to put her in touch with these people, anyway?"

"Maybe we should start investigating her background more," Neil suggested. "We might find the answer there. Someone we weren't aware she knew or had a connection to. And why the hell didn't we do it before?"

"Because we didn't think there was a need. Remember? For two smart men, we're being very stupid. It's been five hours since this all started today." Darius bit the words off. "Five fucking hours, and we still don't have any answers. You're the one with the resources. The one who promised me identifying these people would be easy to do the minute we got the phone call."

"I did." Neil nodded. "And it usually is. You know that. This time, however, we've run into a little...problem."

"Problem?" Darius raised an eyebrow. "Like what?"

"For one thing, no word yet on who owns that hangar or the plane inside. For another, we haven't identified the men she was with today. Not the one she met at the hangar or the two who came to where her car crashed." Neil studied Darius. "And nothing on either of the cars at the accident scene. You should just be damned glad I put a tail on her to see when her car zeroed out. A tail, by the way, who had to make himself blend into the scenery. He had no trouble following her out to the hangar, but that accident was lucky for us or we wouldn't have known who she was meeting with. And we still don't know who they are. We can't just stand around with our dicks in our hands."

"How long before Sanchez started the search using the license plates?"

"He got right on it." Neil repeated it for the tenth time. "He's just having an unexpected problem with it."

"So you said." Darius frowned. "What kind of problem? I don't understand. This should be a very simple records search. You've got the license plates and the address. He's always been the best at this. There's nothing and no one he can't trace. So tell me again what the problem is with getting these particular pieces of information."

"They're dead ends. They lead to shell companies which disappear into thin air. It's as if these people just do not exist."

"Impossible." Darius snapped the word. "If they're breathing, they exist. Now this whole thing has become unbelievably complicated." He shook his head. "Today turned into a major fuckup which we have to find a way to fix."

"Obviously neither of us expected what happened, so we have to regroup." Neil rubbed his jaw, watching his friend. "With all your money, how the hell did you get yourself into this situation? Aren't you smart enough to have avoided this? Have you lost all control?"

"It wasn't intentional," Darius told him. "Believe me. More like bad luck. And my control is just fine."

"Apparently not." Neil cocked a brow. "We make our own luck. Isn't that what you're always saying? So how did yours run out this time? And in such a spectacular way."

Darius drained his glass and rose to refill it.

"Bad weather and bad timing."

Neil snorted. "Bad timing? You never should have been there in the first place. You pick the wrong places and the wrong women to indulge your special activities. If you hadn't lost your control and gotten carried away in the first place, we wouldn't even be here discussing this."

"Oh, like you've never made a little mistake that I helped you cover over?"

Neil stared at the other man. "A little mistake? Killing a woman under the guise of sex?"

"I told you, it was an accident. A fucking accident."

"And doing it in a place with others around, for god's sake? Nearly getting caught with the body in your car?"

"You're no lily white yourself," Darius snapped at him. "You have your own little habits."

"That aren't the kind to injure anyone or anything. Keep that in mind. Shit happens. Accidents happen. Except this was more than an accident. I grant you neither of us expected something like this to happen, but you overreacted and now we have to fix it. And to tell the truth, I'm not at all happy about it."

Darius took a cigar from a humidor on the small table, snipped off the end, put the cigar in his mouth then lit it. Then he carefully blew out a perfect smoke ring.

"Ah, yes." Darius leaned back and drew on his cigar again. "Fix it. The body's been disposed of, we've covered things over at the club, so what's left?"

"You're sure your driver isn't going to be available? Discovered?" Neil pushed.

"Yes, damn it. Joel's got enough money to live two lives as long as it's under a different name and someplace far away from here." Darius shook his head. "I wish I'd had the guts to eliminate him, too, but I'm not a murderer."

Neil barked a laugh. "Yeah? Is that so?"

"It was a fucking accident," Darius snapped. "An accident. My whole life could be disrupted because of it."

"I'll let that pass for the moment. Okay, I took care of the car for you. It's gone. Dismantled and scrapped, so there's nothing left to tie you to a murder no one knows about. I just wish we hadn't gone to such drastic lengths to make sure Jeremy Hunt was out of commission. The architect," Neil reminded him, "who may or may not have seen you and the body in the car. Who may or may not remember anything more. And who apparently, along with his sister, is impossible to get rid of. He should be out of options by this time. I just think we made a mistake doing what we did."

"I don't like to take chances," Darius told him. He rubbed his jaw. "I owe you big time for your help on this one."

"Fine. Then let's just do what we can to put it behind us and hope we've heard the last about Jeremy Hunt."

"We should have gotten rid of Sierra Hunt first to begin with," Darius snapped. "She's the one who has kept pushing this thing. Who knew she had so much determination or so many contacts? Or so much money."

"For god's sake. She has a high-paying job with a powerful firm," Neil snapped. "She's not some inept idiot. We can't talk to her firm about reining her in without raising some unwanted interest. If people on our level didn't have their own secrets to hide, we'd never have been able to pull this off as much as we have."

"What I'd like to know is how she just came at this out of the blue." Darius frowned then looked at Neil. "Didn't you do a thorough study on the two of them, so we'd be prepared?"

"Of course I did. All my resources turned up was she worked at a computer design firm and he had a quiet girlfriend. No warning bells from either of those women."

Darius shook his head. "We couldn't have dug any deeper without being questioned. But damn! I had her followed for a week and the report came back on a person so boring she faded into the woodwork."

"She must be one of those people who turns into a wonder woman if someone close to her is threatened."

"Well, whatever the situation, we've got to get it under control." Darius drew on his cigar again. "What did you find out about those people she was with today?"

He was damn glad they'd decided to have someone continue to follow her after the brake line was tampered with. Their intention was to have someone watching when the brake finally gave way and an accident happened. That way they could be confident she was at least temporarily sidelined. And permanently, if they were lucky. That was already down the drain now and bringing a new set of problems.

"I had someone following her again from the time she got back from New Orleans," Neil reminded him. "When she drove to that hangar outside of the city, he sent me the address so I could check and see who owns it."

"And you found nothing." Darius frowned.

"Like I said. A shell corporation. A dead end."

"Damn it."

Darius pushed himself to his feet and began to pace. He was a tall man, over six feet, muscular and without an ounce of fat on him. For a man of sixty, he was in better shape than a lot of men younger than he was. It was a matter of ego that he looked good to the women—hookers, really—he "played" with. This whole new world of carnal games had spiced up his sex life and he had no intention of letting it go.

He still couldn't figure out how the hell it had all come to this. He was just indulging himself in his particular source of pleasure. His latest "partner" had seemed so enthusiastic in the beginning, into anything he wanted, no matter how extreme. He found his cock staying hard longer and his orgasms more frequent, with only a little medicinal help. The high he got from the games they played was better than any alcohol or drugs.

But then she'd begun to change her mind, and he had no idea why. He was pissed that she wanted to end their so-called relationship and had let his anger get the best of him. That little fender bender, because some stupid schmuck wasn't paying enough attention on a rainy night—who could have planned for that? He certainly couldn't have left Scarlet—was that even her real name?—behind and could only hope that with the rain and darkness no one would see her in the car.

He still didn't know whose fault the accident was, but it didn't matter anymore. Fate was fucking with him and this whole disaster had come about as a result.

He suddenly realized Neil was speaking to him.

"Did you hear me? Where did you go there? Darius?'"

He gave himself a mental shake. He had to stay in control. He couldn't lose it. "Sorry. I was just thinking what a rotten piece of luck this whole thing has turned out to be."

Neil actually laughed.

"Luck? Not hardly, my friend. You made a deliberate choice and now Queen Fate is laughing her ass off."

Darius tightened his hands into fists and reached for his control. It would not help his situation at all to antagonize his oldest and closest friend. The only one with whom he could share the secret parts of his life. He was about to say something to him when Neil's cell phone rang and he picked it up.

"I hope you're calling to tell me you finally have something." He listened for a long moment, nodding his head, but the muscles of his face were as tight as a rubber band. "Okay. Email that to me on our secure line and I'll get back to you."

"What did you find out?" Darius demanded. "I can tell by the look on your face it's beyond bad, so let me have it."

"Not nearly what I would like. It's only bad because I can't find out a fucking thing. We have to regroup."

"What do you mean, regroup? We have to make sure she's out of options where her brother is concerned and that she has no more resources."

"And if she was your average person," Neil told him, "we could do that. But we need to figure out a new approach now."

"And fast." Darius poured his own drink refill. "When these guys — whoever they are — don't help her, she'll finally give up."

"That's what I'm telling you, my asshole friend. People that mysterious could very well help her. So we have to start covering our tracks and making that impossible. And we have to do it fast."

Darius stared at the dark amber liquid in his glass, and for the first time the taste of fear invading his mouth.

"God damn it."

He tossed the glass across the room where it shattered, leaving the liquor dripping down his wall.

Fuck, fuck. Fuck.

Chapter Seven

Eagle came awake slowly, aware of a lassitude in his muscles, an unfamiliar feeling of satisfaction and relaxation. But beneath that was the tension he was used to when he was involved in an active mission. The next thing he became aware of was the soft bundle of woman curled into him and the faint, lingering scent of the body wash they'd used in the shower.

He noted that Sierra fit perfectly against him, her legs bent slightly at the knees, her ass nestled softly against his hardening dick, one breast fitting perfectly into his palm. He couldn't resist pinching the hard nipple and giving it a little squeeze.

"Mmmm." She wiggled her ass and pressed it more firmly against him.

Little arrows of heat stabbed at his balls.

And just like that, the last forty-eight hours came to life in his brain.

Eagle Bodine had certainly had his share of great sex and probably a lot of other people's, too. Adventurous sex. There was very little that he didn't enjoy, no matter how off-the-charts. But in all honesty, he had to admit that none of it held a candle to what he and Sierra shared. Just looking at her gave him a hard-on, for god's sake, and the slick, tight feel of his cock in her pussy was permanently lodged in his mind.

He tucked stray curls behind her ear and kissed the edge of the lobe before brushing the hair aside and taking little nips of her neck. She pressed the sweet cheeks of her ass against his cock again and wiggled them just a little bit.

"You're playing with fire there, darlin'," he murmured in her ear.

"So are you. And I think it's getting hotter."

She'd slept in one of Eagle's T-shirts the night before but without any panties. He stroked her bare skin with a lazy caress and wondered if she was getting as turned on as fast as he was.

"Yes," she said in a soft voice, adding a sexy little chuckle.

"Yes, what?"

"Whatever you want." She wriggled her butt against his dick. "Anything."

Her words sent heat straight to his balls, making them ache with need.

"How about this?"

He slid his hand beneath the edge of the T-shirt and cupped one bare cheek, giving it a gentle squeeze. She hummed softly and pushed back against his touch. Easing his hand to the other cheek, he did the same, then gave each a little pinch. He waited to see how she'd react to the little bite of pain, but instead of trying to pull away from him, she writhed enticingly against his fingers.

Damn!

"That sweet ass was just made for spanking," he murmured in her ear. "One of these nights I'd like to bend you over the bed and redden that delicious flesh. Think you'd like that?"

When she didn't answer him, he brushed his fingers against the skin in a soothing motion.

"It's okay, darlin'." He brushed the curls back from her face and placed a little kiss on her neck. "I'll take whatever you want to give me."

She pressed her face into her shoulder and mumbled something.

"Can't understand you." He made his voice as calm and smooth as possible. "Just spit it out. Whatever it is, it's okay."

"I said…" She still leaned her head into the pillow. "I said I might like having you spank me."

Well, holy shit!

At her words his cock immediately swelled, hardened and tried to break its way out of his boxer briefs.

"You sure, darlin'? You might want to give it some thought. It's not for everyone."

"I, um, read about it and… You like to do it, right?"

"I do."

"And it turns you on." A statement, not a question. "Then I want to try it."

He squeezed one cheek gently. "Then that's what we'll do. But not now. I don't want to squeeze your first time with it into a few minutes."

"You sure?" she asked.

"Positive. There's something else I'd rather do right now."

He hiked up the T-shirt so she was bare below the waist and slid one hand between her thighs. When he touched her pussy, he felt it already soaked with her juices. He slid one finger in, then two, and began a slow, easy, in-and-out glide.

"You like it when I finger-fuck you, sugar?"

"Mm-hmm." She wiggled a little, seating his fingers more firmly inside her.

"More?" He bit the lobe of her ear.

"Oh, yes, please." She pushed back again.

He set up a steady rhythm with his fingers, slow at first, then increasing the pace. She began to rock back against him, making his dick swell even more. He moved the arm that was beneath her so he could reach his fingers down and pinch her clit between the knuckles of two fingers, tugging on it.

Her little moan made him even harder, which he hadn't thought possible.

"Feel good?" He had his mouth close to her ear.

"Real good." She began moving her hips back and forth, rocking against his fingers.

He kept up the movement with all his digits, his strong arm holding her in place, while she rode his touch. The little sounds she made were so delicious he was afraid he'd come just from listening to them. He pressed hard against her clit as he added a third finger inside her wet heat and in seconds she came, her sweet pussy clenching his fingers, sexy little moans rolling from her lips. She dug her fingernails into one forearm, her body jackknifing as she surrendered to the spasms.

As she lay in his arms, panting slightly, catching her breath, he reached over her to his nightstand drawer and pulled out one of the condoms he kept there. The funny thing is, since he'd moved into this place, he hadn't brought a single woman home with him. Now he was glad, because it meant that only Sierra would have her imprint on it.

"Hold on, darlin'."

He kissed her temple then shifted both of them so he could roll the condom on his very desperate dick. Then, lifting one leg, he slid into her pussy from behind, his thick length filling every inch of her. In this position he could achieve deep, deep penetration. He sucked in a breath at the heat that shot through him, the feel of her wet flesh electrifying every nerve. He had to exert massive control to steady himself or it would have been all over for him.

He wrapped one arm around her, his hand cupping her breast, his fingers squeezing her taut nipple. With the other bracing her leg, he began a steady motion in and out of her hot, wet pussy, the sensations spreading right on his aching balls. In and out, in and out. He closed his eyes, intensifying the feel of her, images of what it would be like to paddle that sweet ass heightening his feelings.

"Just hold on," he murmured, "because we're going for a hot ride."

He splayed his hand on her stomach, holding her firmly in place, while he fucked her thoroughly, his dick hitting that sweet spot in her cunt with every in-and-out movement.

Oh, sweet Jesus!

Everything fell away then, except this incredible woman in his arms, her slick flesh clamping down on his dick and the insane pleasure consuming him. He pumped into her, harder and faster, stroking her clit again and again, gritting his teeth for control until he felt her second orgasm grab hold, the spasms rocketing through her, bathing his cock with her juices and squeezing him again and again and again.

Nothing existed for him except this woman, this heat that was consuming them, these incredible sensations as his cock throbbed inside her. The spasms rocked them, each one more intense than the last until finally they slowed then, at last, subsided. He could feel Sierra's heartbeat as it thudded beneath his hand that was still cupping her left breast. His own heart still thudded from the intensity of the orgasm and his breathing was raspy and uneven.

Holy fucking shit!

He'd kind of thought to treat them both to a quiet little orgasm before they got out of bed, but this one was so intense it shook his entire body.

He lay there with Sierra nestled against him, his cock still firmly inside her sweet pussy, his hand still cupping her breast until both of their heartbeats had settled somewhere close to normal. Gripping the rim of the condom, he eased himself from the heat of her body and maneuvered off the bed. When he'd disposed of the rubber, he slid back onto the bed and pulled her into his arms.

"How is it possible we only met forty-eight hours ago?" he asked, kissing the edge of her ear.

"I don't know." She hummed with satisfaction. "I feel the same way."

When she tensed in his arms, he turned her onto her back so he could see her face.

"What is it? What's wrong?"

"Nothing. I'm just as stunned as you are that we've only known each other for two days, yet here we are."

"Yes, indeed, here we are."

He pressed his mouth to hers for a moment then gently licked her lips.

"Sometimes the best things happen at the worst moments," he told her. "I learned that in the SEALs. We're going to save your brother and we're going to have an us. Take my word for it."

"Speaking of my brother—"

His cell phone rang, cutting off the rest of her sentence. The number showed the call was from Blaze.

"Yeah?"

Blaze chuckled. "Well, hello to you, too. Everything okay there?"

"Yeah, fine, but we need to get together again and see what everyone's managed to find."

"My thoughts exactly," Blaze agreed. "We've each dug up some information and we all have a list of questions that we're running out of time to answer."

"No shit."

"And we want to drop off Sierra's suitcase, plus give you a report on the alarm system and what's up there. Half an hour good for you?"

Eagle wanted to tell him three hours wouldn't be enough but business first.

"Yeah, that's good."

"Peyton says we need sugar for energy so I'm stopping by the bakery on the way. Put the coffee on."

"See you in thirty." He clicked off.

Sierra stretched in a lazy, languid motion. "Was that Blaze? Was Peyton able to get some things for me?"

"Yeah, he's bringing a suitcase, which should be here before you finish with your shower." He brushed strands of hair back from her forehead. "Then we get back to work."

But he treated himself to one last kiss before he swung his legs out of bed.

Chapter Eight

Sierra showered quickly, blow drying her hair and brushing it back into an uncomplicated ponytail. Peyton had done a great job packing things for her, including a variety of clothing plus all her personal items.

Bless you, Peyton.

She pulled on jeans and a simple T-shirt, shoved her feet into a pair of flats then headed toward the main part of the house. Everyone was already gathered in the dining room—laptops open on the table. Eagle had explained yesterday they were vital in planning missions, because every bit of information was out there at the click of a key. They were already deep in conversation when she entered the room.

The man himself jumped up as she walked into the room and pulled out a chair for her.

"Sit. Please. Let me grab coffee and muffins for you."

"I can get them myself," she protested.

"The guys have some questions," he told her. "So sit. I'll be right back."

"Blaze, please thank Peyton for me for getting my things. She did a great job and I really appreciate it."

He grinned. "You can tell her yourself tomorrow night. We're all having dinner together."

"Oh, wow. Great. But thank her anyway."

"I will. Oh, and Danny's at your place, installing your 'cable' system. He'll text me all the codes when he's done. Eagle will have them, too."

"Oh. Um, well, thanks. Uh, how much is the bill for this?"

"It's included in our fee."

"But—" She frowned. "You said you aren't charging me anything."

"Right. That's right."

"So..."

She looked around the table. The other men acknowledged her with smiles, but their faces were dead serious. And before she could say anything else, they rolled into the meeting.

Wow! was all she could think.

"I'll go first," Viper said, clicking his mouse. "I did a search of the area where you said your brother had his accident, Sierra. I wanted to see what was around there. Do you know what he was doing at that particular spot at that hour that night?"

She tamped down her impatience. Nobody had been interested in that before now and she had no idea what it had to do with the murder. Why were they wasting their time with it? But she had to believe they knew what they were doing, that every tiny incident might have some kind of clue, so she answered him.

"He had just taken Cheryl home after a late dinner. He stayed over at her place a lot, but he had an early morning appointment the next day and it was pouring with rain. He just wanted to get home so he could prepare sensibly for the next day."

"Was that his usual route from her place?" This from Rocket.

"I don't know." She took a swallow of coffee. "To tell the truth, I never thought much about it. I have no idea what relationship it has to the main subject here. He had a fender bender in the pouring rain. The other guy was obviously in a hurry to get home and in that weather, who could blame him? I still don't understand why you're focusing on this."

"In every situation," he told her, "we're trained to look for things out of the ordinary. Sometimes they mean nothing, but when a situation doesn't make sense, like this one, those are the things you go after. I pulled down some satellite imagery of the area last night. Let me send it to everyone here. Sierra, you want to get your own laptop or share Eagle's?"

"She'll share mine," he answered for her, hitching his chair closer to hers and sliding his computer over so they both could see the screen.

Sierra studied the scene that came up.

"There's The Library," Rocket explained. "I don't know much about it except it's a very private club for uber wealthy people. As you can see, it's really three buildings. I'm trying to get photos or something to give me a visual on the place. It's in a very exclusive area."

Sierra nodded. "It is. I don't know a lot about it. It's so private and the membership is so rich nobody talks about it. I understand there weren't this many residences for a long time, but land became valuable, and people wanted an exclusive address."

"I checked the address the other day," Blaze told them. "The entire property, including all three buildings, has a listed value of twenty-five million dollars. When it was built, the listed value was fifteen million, but that was a few decades ago, and Bayshore Boulevard has escalated in value."

"But what on earth would a centuries-old private club have to do with anything?" Sierra still had trouble wrapping her head around it. "Neither Jeremy nor I know anyone who belongs there. Oh. Wait." She snapped her fingers. "It's possible one or two of his clients does. But if it was a client in the other car, he would have said so and handled the whole thing differently."

"Unless there was something in the car he didn't want anyone to see."

"It's an anomaly," Rocket pointed out. "It may turn out to be nothing, but it has to be checked out."

"Absolutely," Eagle agreed.

"I'm going to pull every bit of information on the place I can find. I don't know if I can get the list of members, but I'm going to try. And just in case there's weird shit there, I'm going to search on the dark web and see if there's anything. I just have a feeling there's some dirt under the rug that set this off. Jeremy Hunt is clean, so this entire situation makes no sense at all. I'll get on it now."

"Good," Eagle nodded, "because we're short on time here."

Beneath the table, he reached for Sierra's hand and gave it a reassuring squeeze. It eased the tension gripping her just a little.

"Let me just ask this before we move on to something else." She looked around the table. "Just so I know I'm not missing anything. You think it's possible there was something about the accident that caused my brother to be framed for murder? That's what started this whole nightmare?"

Blaze nodded. "I know it sounds farfetched, but at the moment it's all we've got, and it's the only thing that doesn't fit. Meanwhile, let's look at some other things." He tapped keys on his laptop. "I dug into the background of Rose Aitken." He glanced around the table. "She's the woman who was murdered."

"I'm sure I'll never forget her name," Sierra said, glad that Eagle was still holding her hand. "I don't think I'll ever get the pictures of her body out of my head."

"Copy that," Eagle told her.

"I couldn't find anything on her," she added. "I mean nothing. Not even where she worked or anything. It's almost as if she didn't exist, except of course she did. I tried to find out more about her online, but she didn't even have social media accounts."

"Which," Rocket told her, "I find very off kilter in this day and age when people spend their whole lives on social media."

"No shit," Eagle agreed. "Sierra, do you have anything in your files we might have missed?"

"No." She shook her head. "Nothing. Nothing at all. If I did, it would be in there."

"And none of the attorneys you hired thought that odd?"

"You don't understand. After the first one I hired, only two others agreed to even look at the case. They skimmed the material I brought them then they both turned me down. Said the evidence against Jeremy was too strong." She saw the men all exchange looks. "What? What did I miss?"

Eagle was still holding her hand and he gave it another gentle squeeze.

"Sierra, where did you get these attorneys?"

"I, uh, did some research online. Not one person I knew had ever hired a criminal attorney, so I looked for those who had clients in similar cases." She shook her head. "They weren't cheap, either."

For the next fifteen minutes, she took them through doing her research then being turned down by the first two. The third one had started out optimistic, but by the time the trial was over, he told her the evidence was just too strong and there were no grounds for appeal.

"Two more attorneys after that told me the same thing. No one else would even touch it. The attorney I went to see in New Orleans was polite and respectful but flat-out told me there was nothing in the case that offered grounds for appeal."

Again the men all exchanged looks.

"What?" She studied them each in turn. "What's going on?"

"There is something very fishy here," Eagle told her. "None of this played out the way it should. You and your brother are getting screwed, and we have to find out why."

"And I bet money that accident has something to do with it," Rocket added. "Maybe it's even at the root of everything. I'll get right on it, pull everything I can from the Internet then take a recon trip to the area."

He began clicking the keys on his computer again.

"I'm going to see what I can find out about the murdered woman," Viper told them. "Her whole identity seems to be phony, and I want to know who created it and why."

Sierra stared at him. "You can do that from your computer?"

He grinned. "I can do anything from my computer. Just watch me." He winked at her and began clicking keys.

"When was the last time you spoke to your brother?" Blaze asked.

"Two days ago, after I met with the last attorney. We had set up a time for him to call me. Since incoming calls are not allowed." She rubbed her face. "That was a call I really hated. He sounded so depressed." She shook her head. "And frightened."

"I bet." This from Eagle. He looked around the table. "What do you all think about my taking Sierra to see her brother? I can assess his situation and hopefully assure him that we'll get the job done. Then, once I get a reading on him, we can get Tom's help in hiring a new attorney for him. One that's not obligated to anyone else., which I think all of these were."

"A new attorney?" Her pulse stuttered with a faint flicker of hope. "Are you sure you can find one who won't turn it down?"

"Darlin'," Eagle said to her, "if we vouch for him, there won't be a problem. But I think it's time for us to talk to the man himself."

"I hate to give him hope without knowing for sure that you can fix this."

Ignoring the other men at the table, Eagle cupped her chin and turned her face toward his.

"Sierra. Galaxy *never* loses. Timelines don't matter. Impossible and hopeless situations are our specialty.

We need to let him know we're all in his corner. Giving him something to hope with."

"If you're sure this isn't going to be just another disappointment. I mean, this is his life."

Eagle nodded. "And we're going to get it back on track. So what do we have to do to set this up? I'd like to take the trip this afternoon. What's the distance from here to Raiford?"

It depressed her that Jeremy was incarcerated in Florida State Prison, in Raiford, the toughest prison in the state. The more she visited him, the more depressed she became.

"Less than three hours," Sierra told him. "But visiting hours are only from nine a.m. to three p.m. Saturday and Sunday. Not on weekdays except for an attorney meeting."

"Well," Eagle grinned, trying to ease her tension, "it just so happens we have an attorney who might be able to pull some strings for us. Right, Blaze?"

The man nodded and glanced over at Sierra.

"Tom Hernandez has been a part of the group from the beginning. He did all the legal work to set up Galaxy and handles a number of other things for us. He can pull strings just about anywhere." He pushed his chair back and stood up. "Let me give him a call and see what he can set up. I'm hoping for this afternoon but if not then tomorrow for sure."

Sierra stared at him. "But they have very strict rules."

Blaze nodded. "Except for attorneys. Let's see what he can do and if he's available. Be right back."

He grabbed his cell phone and wandered into the living room.

Rocket cleared his throat. "Meanwhile, cut me out of any conversation for the moment while I do research on The Library and the history of the area where it's located. But first I need a coffee refill. Anyone else?"

"We can handle ours," Eagle told him.

"Okay, then." He grabbed his mug and headed for the kitchen.

Sierra and Eagle got their own refills and returned to the table. Viper opted to switch to water. By the time everyone was seated again, Blaze was finished with his call.

"Tom says he'll take care of it," he told them. "He's making the calls right now and we should hear back from him within the next hour."

"He can do that?" Sierra asked.

Blaze grinned at her. "Tom can do just about anything. That's one reason we keep him around."

"That," Viper added, "and the fact that he likes hanging out with former SEALs."

Blaze nodded. "Tom injured his leg when he was a lot younger. You'd never know it now, but it was enough to keep him out of the military. He kind of thinks of himself as a SEAL by association."

"He's a really good guy," Rocket added. "We're proud to have him be part of the team."

For the next hour or so, everyone was busy on their laptops, doing their assigned research. Viper did a deep dive on the police report of the death, looking for anything that wasn't in the reports that Sierra had. Every so often he'd ask her a question, but she had no information to give him. She and Eagle did an intense search on the architectural firm where Jeremy worked, just in case someone there had it in for him for some reason. But no matter where they searched, there was nothing to find.

"What puzzles me," he said, leaning back in his chair, "is your brother is Mr. Squeaky Clean. He is definitely not the type to hook up with a call girl, even a high-class one. Unless he didn't realize she was a working girl."

"That's what I kept trying to tell everyone. Jeremy was devoted to Cheryl, his girlfriend. All I heard was you never know what another person will do in any given situation. I wanted to scream and hit someone every time I heard that."

"I'll bet."

Eagle gave her a brief hug which the others made it obvious they were ignoring, just as Blaze walked back into the room.

"We're good to go," he told them. "Four o'clock this afternoon."

Sierra stared at him. "B-But—"

"Give it up," Eagle told her. "Our specialty is working miracles."

"Let's hope it carries through this whole thing. So it's all set?"

Blaze nodded. "We should get going pretty soon. Tom said they're pretty bitchy about procedure."

"They are indeed," Sierra agreed. "Will Tom have to come in with us?"

"No. I'll be Jeremy's legal rep." He winked. "I even have a nice leather briefcase. Tom will keep working on your list of attorneys, but he says it might take until tomorrow. He's run into some bumps in the road."

"Oh?" Sierra frowned. "Is it a big problem?"

"No, and even if it was, he'll handle it. Okay, kids. We'd better leave in about thirty, so do whatever you need and let's get on the road."

Sierra thought about giving him a hug but then decided that would be too forward. Instead, she'd give Eagle a big hug later. She hurried to the master suite to change into more businesslike attire, thankful that Peyton had thought to add some clothes in that style.

Oh, god, please let this work. Otherwise, we're out of options.

* * * *

"It's as if they don't exist."

Neil dropped into the chair in the conversation area of Darius' office.

"What do you mean?" Darius frowned. "Of course they exist."

"Not so you can find. Every trail I follow leads back to nothing. I used different software to track the license plates and they still come back to that address where the plane is hangered. The owner is listed as some shell corporation named Skylift, of all the damn things."

"That's impossible." Darius went to reach for the humidor on the coffee table before he remembered he'd removed it. Too many fucking people complained about the cigar smoke. If he couldn't resolve this problem, he'd smoke a hundred cigars and blow smoke at everyone. Because that would be all he had left.

"What about Steel? They have every resource in the world. We've paid for a lot of them."

"They are working on it," Neil assured him. "But the Steel agents are not your ordinary dark agents, or whatever they are. They've been trained somewhere and trained very well. And they don't come cheap."

Darius ground his teeth. "Do you think I'm worried about cost when this entire plan could fall apart if the right steps aren't taken?"

Neil poured coffee for himself from the setup on the credenza and carried it to the big floor-to-ceiling window that looked down out at Tampa's constantly evolving skyline.

"I don't like people saying I told you so," he said in an even voice, "but if you recall, I did point out that your, um, peculiarities might end up getting you in trouble. I was with you when you got the call from Matthias, remember?"

Yes, he fucking remembered. He'd had an insane urge to drive to The Library, find the manager and choke the life out of him. But that would only prove the man's point—that Darius had a temper that he often found it difficult to restrain. One that got him in trouble too many times.

"I just need to get some answers," he ground out. "Make people understand what's necessary."

Neil laughed. "You mean 'encourage' them to do what we want, right?"

"Call it what you want, but it's been part of the key to our success. Whoever these people are, I am not going to let them bring down everything we've spent years building up." He looked at his watch. "I don't think it's too early for a little liquid courage, do you?"

"Just don't let it get the best of you," Neil warned.

"Have I ever?" He dropped two ice cubes in his glass and poured a small amount of golden liquid over them. "Why didn't your guy at least get pictures of these guys at the scene of the fender bender?"

"You're kidding, right? He said they must have taken a class in how to avoid being photographed, because they managed every minute to have the view of their faces and most of their bodies disrupted by others. I'm telling you, he said it was eerie."

"And he couldn't figure out a way to just grab an image with his cell phone?"

Neil glared at him. "I only use the best. If he said a picture was impossible, I believe him. Let's move on."

"That's exactly what I'd like to do, but I can't while there are still people out there determined to fuck up my carefully structured plans."

"We've dealt with it before and we will again," Neil reminded him. "There's no way Hunt is getting out of prison—we've arranged things so his appeals are continuously denied, and no attorney is going to take on his case at this point, so—"

"So all we have to do is make sure Sierra Hunt and these weird strangers she's managed to hook up with don't interfere with our plans," Darius finished for him. "And to do that, we have to find out who these people are. We don't even know where the fuck the Hunt woman is at this point. These men she's managed to connect with must have her tucked away somewhere. Why didn't your man follow the Hunt woman and whoever she left with?"

"He tried to when he realized he wasn't going to get anything from the two men left at the site. As soon as he ran the two license plates through his database and came up to a blank wall, he realized that was a useless exercise until he had more resources. He left when the Hunt woman and the man she was with drove off, but he obviously was ready for it, because he took so many twists and turns my guy lost him."

"Fuck." Darius slammed his hand on the arm of the chair. "We have to find out who these people are and figure out how to stop them. If they have enough clout to get the investigation reopened —"

"I know, I know. We're in deep shit."

"I'm glad you said *we* because the outcome of this affects you, too."

"Yes." Neil snapped the word out. "Believe me. I know."

"So now what?" Darius asked. "We can't just sit here and wait for the world to fall on our heads."

"I'm going to meet with two of the men from Steel," Neil told him. "Meet me for dinner about seven o'clock. I'll have more to tell you then. Meanwhile, you'd do well to keep a low profile. It's taken a lot of work and exerting pressure to bury this as deep as possible. Let's not muck it up."

"Fine." Darius wanted to smack someone, but he had to admit, however reluctantly, that he'd gotten himself into this by not controlling his darkest desires. "Let's meet at Donato's. I could use some good Italian food tonight. It's quiet there, and we can ask for one of the alcoves."

"Good idea." Neil pushed himself out of his chair. "See you at seven."

Chapter Nine

"That was exhausting."

Sierra leaned back in her seat, yanked off the ball cap that partially obscured her face and took her hair down from the knot she'd curled it into on top of her head. The guys had done their best to camouflage her just in case someone other than people in the prison somehow spotted her and did their best to follow her.

But it had gone smoothly, and Blaze had done some masterful evasive driving.

Seeing Jeremy was always emotionally draining. When this whole nightmare had begun, her brother, at six feet, had been an athletic man with well-defined muscles, a healthy complexion and dark eyes that always carried a hint of humor and a great attitude. He'd had a fabulous career and was engaged to the woman of his dreams. Looking at him today made her want to cry. His complexion was pale, even pasty. His eyes were dull, without even a glimmer of hope. He had lost weight to the point where he could almost be called skinny. And the love of his life had died unexpectedly of the flu.

But his good manners were still in place. He shook hands with Blaze and Eagle, thanked everyone for coming and, knowing everything they said could be heard, followed the lead of the two men.

Sierra was impressed at the way Blaze, the 'attorney,' let him know what was happening without giving anything away. He extracted every bit of information with skillfully framed questions. When he was finished, he shook Jeremy's hand and said he'd be back in touch shortly but not to give up hope. Sierra hugged him so hard he worried she might break a rib then she slipped a note into his pants pocket. Now they were on the way back to Eagle's to sort everything out.

"What do you think?" She couldn't stop herself from asking.

"I think he's a good guy who got royally screwed for some unknown reason," Blaze answered. "He's definitely not guilty. He impressed me and not many people do. I'm calling Tom when we get back to Eagle's place, giving him my assessment and telling him to find the best attorney he can. We'll get this done."

Sierra almost cried with relief. She was so afraid to hope, but Senator Kane had been right. These guys could do things no one else could.

They had driven in Blaze's truck and now, exhausted, Sierra was happy to just lean back in her seat while the men conversed in low tones in the front.

"You okay back there, darlin'?" Eagle asked, turning in his seat.

"Drained but okay," she assured him. "Thank you both so much for doing this."

"This is only step one," Blaze assured her. "I have to tell you, your brother impressed me. After all he's been through, to keep his shit together the way he did? Not a lot of people can do that."

"What is your assessment of what he told you? What do you think?"

"We've got a lot more digging to do and a very short window to do it, but at least I have some ideas. You listened to his story about the accident that night?"

"Yes." She rubbed her forehead. "I've heard it so many times I could recite it from memory. You still think that has something to do with this?"

"I think it has to. Before that night his life was great. After that night, it fell apart. Eagle, we've got to find out more about what happened. Sierra, didn't anyone check for security cameras on the buildings near that spot?"

"I was told they did, but they didn't show anything because the rain was so heavy." She took a steadying breath and let it out slowly. "I asked his attorney about it several times, but he kept telling me the police had checked all the surrounding buildings and got nothing."

Eagle turned in his seat. "He didn't check himself?"

She shrugged. "I guess not. He had me convinced the police had done a thorough job." She saw Eagle look over at Blaze. "What?"

"Any defense attorney worth his salt would have done his own investigation," Blaze told her. "He'd never just accept what the prosecuting attorney gave him access to."

"Okay, we'll table that for now," Eagle said. He slid his arm over the console between the seats and held out his hand to her. "But we'll do our own investigation. Tom has many resources he can tap into."

Sierra hated the idea that this knowledge caused yesterday to pop into her brain.

"But that would mean this was a conspiracy. That everyone from the cops to the prosecutor's office would have had to be in on it. How is that even possible?"

Blaze made a disparaging sound. "You'd be amazed at what's possible. I am, on a daily basis."

"And that's a good indication," Eagle added, "that there's a major, major conspiracy involved. Someone with a huge amount of clout is pulling the strings."

"The more we hear," Blaze said, "the more I'm convinced the root cause is something in that little fender bender Jeremy had. It's just too much of a coincidence."

"But you heard him today," she reminded the men. "He remembers almost nothing about it. He doesn't even know who was in the car because the only person he saw was the driver."

"I know," he agreed. "But that doesn't mean whoever it was isn't still worried that Jeremy might remember some tiny thing about what happened. We're going to have to really dig deep on this, but we can absolutely do it."

"I feel as if I'm living in a nightmare." She looked at him and then away. "One minute my brother and I are enjoying life. In the next it's all going to hell. Why? That's what I want to know."

"And we're going to get you the answers," Eagle assured her.

"Thank you." She wanted so much to believe him.

Then she leaned back and closed her eyes, mentally exhausted by the tension of the situation. She couldn't believe she'd fallen asleep until a hand touched her knee and gave her a gentle shake. She pried her eyes open and saw Eagle smiling at her from the front seat.

"Good nap?" His smile was tender.

"I guess." She rubbed her face, trying to wake herself up.

"Let's get inside, check in with the others and send Blaze on his way."

As soon as Blaze left, Eagle reset the house security system, took Sierra's hand and led her down the hallway.

"You need to get rid of some of that tension," he told her. "Galaxy is on the job, and I promise whatever it takes we will get it done. Come on."

"I think I could use a drink," she told him. "Could we do that first?"

"You can have one when we're finished." He grinned. "That is, if you still want one." He cradled her face in his palms and brushed his lips over hers. "But I think I can promise you that you won't even be thinking about a drink when I'm finished...relaxing you." He teased the seam of her lips with his tongue. "Trust me. Okay?"

She just nodded, somehow unable to form proper words. How had they reached this point in just a couple of days? What was it about this man that turned her body and her emotions upside down?

He tugged her into the bathroom where he turned on the water in the big shower, stripped off both their clothes with incredible efficiency and positioned her under the rain-style showerhead.

"We're taking a shower?" She lifted an eyebrow,

"Mm-hmm, so just enjoy it. Tip your head back and feel how soft that spray is on your skin. Just close your eyes and don't think about anything except my hands on your body." He brushed a kiss over her lips. "I have very talented hands."

As stressed as she was, still, a tiny thrill wriggled through her. She knew exactly how talented those hands were. And he was right about the shower. The water was a gentle spray, warm, and the feel of it was very soothing. As he had the night before, Eagle lathered his hands with body wash and in slow, careful, methodical movements, spread the foam over every inch of her body. And while he paid diligent attention to her breasts and her nipples, his touch was more to relax her than sexual. Even when he spread the scented foam over her pussy and eased his fingers inside her. She clenched down on them, stunned that her body could respond to him this way after the day she'd had.

He spent only a few seconds lathering his own body and rinsing it off before drying them both and carrying her into the bedroom, where only a bedside lamp was turned on low.

"Just relax," he told her in that deep, warm voice she'd come to love so much in just two short days. "Let me do all the work. I want you to make your mind a blank. Shut everything out except the touch of my hands and the pleasure they bring to you. I do bring you pleasure, right?"

"Mm-hmm." He had no idea just how much.

When he had her arranged on the bed to his satisfaction, he straddled her and layered a string of kisses down her spine. It was so soothing she almost forgot what kind of day she'd just had.

"Is this an add-on to your massages?"

"Only for you, darlin'."

He did it again and again, nothing but a scattering of butterfly kisses, a light pressure of his lips…until he drew a line with his tongue from the nape of her neck to the dimple just above the cleft of her ass. Then he proceeded to massage every muscle in her arms and shoulders and back. His very talented hands kneaded and rubbed until she felt like a limp noodle floating on an air mattress.

"Your skin is so soft," he murmured. "I could stroke it and rub it forever."

"And I think I could let you." She hummed with satisfaction.

Her muscles turned to even softer spaghetti as he continued to work on her back and shoulders and arms. His hands were strong and his touch sure, finding every pressure point and every twisted knot. She thought she could lie here like this forever, shutting out the world and letting him sooth her body.

Then he slid a little lower and began to work on her ass, on its curve, massaging the muscles and easing his hands over the arc of her cheeks. He moved his body so he was between her legs, moving a hand up the inside of one thigh and down the other. A shiver raced over her, and she wished he could touch her every place, inside and out, all at the same time.

And suddenly this became more than just a plain old massage.

She forced herself to lie still while his hands continued to coast over her, soothing her jangled nerves. But then, out of nowhere, the image of Jeremy in prison popped into her brain and every muscle tightened.

"Uh-oh." Eagle placed a kiss on each swell of her ass. "Someone started thinking."

She had to laugh because that was exactly what she'd done.

"No thinking allowed. Hold on a sec and don't move. And keep your eyes closed."

She closed her eyes again and felt him climb off the bed. He was only gone for seconds then he was back again, stroking her shoulders and her spine and running his fingers through her hair.

"Eyes still closed," he reminded her.

The next thing she felt was him gently lifting her head and sliding something silken between her face and the pillow.

"Want to try something new?" he asked.

New?

"Well, like what?' She studied his face.

"Ever been blindfolded when you were having sex?"

Sierra sucked in a breath. Could she tell him it had always been one of her secret fantasies, along with others she read about in the romance novels she was addicted to? They were her relief from the intense pressure of her job and often she had laid in bed at night, pleasuring herself while she read a particularly explicit section. A tiny thrill of anticipation wriggled through her, and a pulse throbbed deep in her pussy. She had to squeeze her thighs together to control it.

"Um, no. I haven't."

He brushed a kiss over her mouth. "You'd be amazed at how much better it makes things. Shuts out everything that's bad so all you have to think about is what you're feeling."

She thought for a moment.

"So, do you do that a lot?"

His laugh was low and husky and made the walls of her pussy spasm with need and hunger.

"Only when I want my lady to enjoy herself without restraint. And right now, I think you need that. If I blindfold you, darlin', you can actually block everything out and concentrate only on what your body is feeling. It makes everything so much more intense." He paused. "Do you trust me, Sierra?"

And strangely enough, although she'd known him for such a short time, she did. Completely. She knew he'd never do anything to hurt her. And the idea of being wrapped in the dark while he fucked her thoroughly was so arousing she was afraid she might come just from the thought of it.

"If it starts to bother you," Eagle whispered, "just tell me and I'll take it off. Okay?"

Oh, god!

The idea of it was so erotic that it actually made her nipples tingle.

When she nodded, he tied the ends of the silken material behind her head just tight enough to shut out all the light but not enough to hurt.

"One more thing and we'll be all set," he told her. "Deep, slow breaths. Block everything else out of your mind." His voice lowered. "I've got this great body oil that melts every muscle and tells your brain to stop thinking."

Oil? What kind of oil? What did he use it for? Did he bring home a lot of women and give them a massage? She startled when he stroked his fingers through the cleft in her ass. *Oh, god!* Was he going to touch her *there*?

Apparently so, as he lightly stroked the delicate skin. In an instant, her nipples hardened, and the muscles in her cunt clenched in need. What in god's name was happening to her?

"Now," he said, his voice deep and—oh, yes—erotic, "don't move and don't think about anything but my hands and how they make you feel."

Sierra shivered in anticipation as Eagle climbed back onto the bed and straddled her again. Then his hands were touching her body, lightly, stroking, before he returned to massaging her shoulders and her back. The oil was warm and slick, and it let his hands coast easily over her skin. He kneaded it into her muscles, plying them like he was molding clay. He was right. With the world shut out, with his fingers slick on her skin, she fell into a warm, dark place where nothing was bad, and everything felt good.

Then he eased back down her body and resumed kneading the muscles below her shoulder blades and at her waist. Every so often he would stop, and she knew he was pouring more oil into his hands because when he touched her again, his skin was slicker than before.

When he inched a hand between her thighs and eased up to her cunt, she sucked in a breath. But then his busy fingers were caressing her sensitive flesh, and she forgot about anything else, just as he'd told her to. She'd never had the lips of her pussy massaged like this before, but that was exactly what Eagle was doing. He rubbed them lightly with the tips of his fingers, stroking them, not sliding inside her, which made the sensations all the more erotic.

Both hands rubbed the lips of her sex, gently, lightly, just enough to send tiny shivers through her inner flesh. He did it over and over again, barely brushing her clit, just enough to ignite shivers and send them racing through her. Eagle was right. The dark made it so much better, intensifying every sensation. Tiny little spasms rippled through the walls of her cunt, her inner muscles clutching in need. Her nipples ached for his touch, and she wanted to feel his cock filling her.

But at the same time she loved what his hands were doing to her, the way he stroked her pussy, barely brushing her clit but lighting up her nerve endings. Being cocooned in darkness just intensified every sensation, every feeling.

When she felt the touch of his lips on her ass, she was stunned for a moment, her muscles tensing, but then she realized how much and how unexpectedly she loved it. It shocked her, but wrapped in the darkness, she could indulge herself and give herself over to it.

"I love the taste of you," Eagle told her. "Everywhere. All over. Every inch of your body. Here." He ran his palms down her back. "And here." He stroked the lips of her cunt. "And here."

He slipped two fingers between the cheeks of her ass and found her tight opening, circling it with the tips of his fingers. The vibrations that slid through her made the inner walls of her pussy clench. She tried to squeeze her thighs together to contain the sensations cascading through her.

Although she'd never been much of one for anal sex, right now she wanted to scream at him to slide those fingers inside her. She heard a low, guttural moan and was shocked to realize it was coming from her.

"I knew you'd like that, darlin'." He placed light kisses on the curve of her ass again. "You have the sexiest butt I've ever seen. One of these days I'm going to fuck you here and make you come like you never have before in your life." He kissed each cheek again. "Think you can handle that, darlin'?"

"I, um, don't know."

But something dark and sensuous and erotic began to wiggle its way through her, a sexual hunger she'd never felt before, and every nerve ending lit up

Eagle laughed, a deep, sensual sound that ramped up her desire even more.

"Oh, I think you do. Yes, I really think you do."

At first, she'd been a little skeptical about the blindfold, but as he continued to touch her and massage her, arousing her in a subtle way that was more intense than anything she'd ever felt, a hunger began to grow deep inside her.

He moved his hands again, she was sure to apply more oil, then knelt between her thighs. The feel of him moving against her and with her accelerated everything else. When he slid the edge of his hand into the crease in her buttocks, a warmth spread through the rest of her body. But then he eased those two fingers in there again, pressing against her opening, and this time he eased one inside her.

Holyfuckingshit!

She had to clamp her teeth together to keep from coming right then and there.

Ohmigod! Ohmigod! Ohmigod!

As he slid a second finger inside her, she sucked in her breath and pushed back against his touch.

"That's it. That's the way, darlin'. Before long I'm gonna slide my cock right into your dark heat and fuck you until neither of us can breathe."

Ohmigod!

"Oh," was all she could manage. The feelings consuming her blocked everything else out of her mind. She had never allowed this intimacy before, but with Eagle it seemed so natural. All her invisible boundaries disappeared, along with the tension that had gripped her. She hummed her satisfaction, drawing a dark, sensuous laugh from Eagle.

"Oh? I'd say, oh, yeah."

He continued to move his fingers in that steady rhythm in and out of her ass. But then, just when he had brought her to a peak, he removed his hand.

"No," she protested. "More." She couldn't believe she was saying that.

"Oh, don't worry." He kissed an ass cheek again. "I'm not finished yet."

He turned her over gently, checking to make sure the blindfold was still securely in place. Then he bent her legs at the knees, placing her feet securely on the bed but situating her so the entire area of her pussy was wide open and exposed. She'd never thought she'd beg a man to fuck her in the ass, but she was so aroused she was ready to spit the words out. She lay there in a state of intense expectancy, waiting to see what he would do next, when she felt his fingers around her wrists. He'd apparently pulled out another scarf, because in a moment, he held her wrists together and wound the wrap around them.

"Don't move them," he told her. "Keep them right where they are, clasped together on your chest. Just don't move them."

She'd always thought being restrained would frighten her, but not the way Eagle did it. It only aroused her more. The bed dipped as he climbed onto it again and she tried to imagine what he would do next.

She didn't have long to wait.

She felt him settle himself between her outspread thighs and begin to tease her clit with his fingers. Just her clit. Her ass still tingled from his teasing exploration, making her entire body hum with sexual need and desire. Again she realized how much the blindfold and now the scarf around her wrists intensified every feeling. And in the soft darkness that surrounded her, she could give in to every response and every desire.

She uttered a tiny moan of protest when Eagle moved his hand away from her cunt and began to stroke the inside of her thighs. Shudders raced over her body even as her internal muscles pulsed with hunger and need. The touch of his fingers, now here, now there, now sliding up her body to pinch her nipples. Dancing over the surface of her skin. Driving her crazy.

By now every nerve in her body was doing a crazy dance, enhanced by the cloak of darkness. She could think of nothing but this man, his touch, his scent, his voice. She wanted to scream *Fuck me!* but the only sounds she seemed able to make were those of pleasure. Eagle touched her everywhere, gliding his fingers into her then stroking them over every inch of sensitive skin.

By the time he moved them between her thighs again, her body was screaming with need and hunger. She felt his knees on either side of her, heard a faint sound that she thought was the snap of latex then he was over her, his body heat like an erotic blanket. His voice, when he spoke again, was deep and thick with hunger and passion.

"I'm going to bury myself in you," he murmured, "so deep you won't be able to tell where you stop and I begin. Then I'm going to fuck you until neither of us can breathe anymore."

His words were like little matches lighting her nerve endings, and every pulse point in her body began pounding.

"Yes." She could barely whisper the word because her body was so on fire. "Please."

He entered her slowly, his thick cock stretching the walls of her slick cunt until he was fully inside her. As he eased in, he brushed the hot spot in her inner walls, making her wrap her legs around him to intensify the contact. Heat like she'd never felt before shot through her and without any warning, her orgasm exploded, her cunt gripping him again and again as spasm after spasm consumed her. And with her wrapped in the darkness, every beat, every throb was intensified.

Eagle wrapped his arms around her, holding her against him as she came with a force that gripped every muscle in her body. When the last spasm subsided, she drew a deep breath and let it out slowly. Eagle scattered kisses along her jawline and her collar bone, following the kisses with little nips of her flesh that unbelievably ignited her nerves again.

"Didn't think we were finished, did you?" That low, deep voice set her alight again and, unbelievably, she felt the walls of her pussy beginning to flex again.

"That's it." He put his mouth close to her ear. "Yes. Here we go again."

This time he moved with her, slow strokes in and out at first, then speeding up. And again the darkness was like an aphrodisiac, igniting a response she could have sworn she didn't have. His strokes were steady and deep, increasing in speed a little at a time. He slipped one hand between them, found her clit and began to massage it and pluck at it and tug at it.

"That's it," he said again. "Ride with me, darlin'. Just like this."

He moved faster, thrust deeper, and unbelievably another orgasm rumbled up from deep inside her.

"Now." His voice was hoarse and guttural. "Now, Sierra. Come now."

They exploded, her pussy squeezing his cock, milking it as they came and came and came. She lost all sense of time and place as everything faded except the welcoming darkness and the thick cock throbbing inside her.

She had no idea how long it went on, only that at some point the pulsing slowed then faded, and she let her legs fall limply to the side. Eagle managed to reach the scarf binding her hands and untie it so their slick bodies were touching. His heart beat against hers, thudding heavily at first, then slowing as hers did the same.

And, finally, he removed the blindfold. She blinked, glad the light in the room was limited to the nightstand lamp. When she looked at Eagle, he was smiling at her, and his eyes were filled with some kind of emotion.

"How you feeling now, darlin'?"

Her laugh was soft and breathy.

"You were right about the blindfold." She wet her lips. "You were right about everything." She blew out a soft breath. "How did this happen so fast?"

"I asked one of my partners the same thing, and he told me when it's right, it's right and you shouldn't take a chance on missing out on it." The look in his eyes was serious now. "He's right. All my partners met their women in situations something like this and it worked. I want that for us. Tell me you do, too."

She swallowed. "I do. I really do."

And she totally believed it."

His smile was all she needed. "Then let's grab another shower and get some sleep. I have a feeling tomorrow is going to be another busy day for us."

Chapter Ten

"We need to start with The Library."

Blaze had refilled his mug and carried it to the dining room table, dropping back into his chair across from Eagle. He'd arrived shortly after eight, bringing breakfast and his laptop.

"I agree." Eagle clicked a few keys on his laptop and brought up a document. "You read the same thing I did. Right?" he asked Blaze.

"Yes. The most detailed history of the place I could find, but it isn't very much."

"What kind of place is it?" Sierra asked.

She was feeling more than well sated after the incredible sex she and Eagle had experienced. Her body ached in a number of places, but it was a good ache, and she was satisfied as she'd never been in her life before. When Eagle reached for her hand and gave it a squeeze, she saw Blaze look from one to the other then swallow a smile.

"It's okay," he told Sierra. "Eagle was the last one left. We didn't want to be dragging him around as a fifth wheel."

"Hey." Eagle creased his forehead in a mock scowl. "I was just being picky, waiting for the right woman." He winked at Sierra. "Thank god I found her." Then his smile disappeared. "Okay, let's get down to it. I live in this city, but I don't know a lot about The Library except it's some kind of private club."

"One of the last ones left," Blaze told him. "The others are all specific, like strip clubs or gay clubs. I'm sending it to your laptop, Eagle. You and Sierra can share."

"Are the others coming today, also?" she asked.

Blaze shook his head. "Rocket is with Tom. They're going through your list of former attorneys. Tom's helping profile them. They're trying to figure out the common denominator that made them all turn away from an appeal. Tom seems to know everything about everyone. But along with that, he's helping identify the best attorney to take on Jeremy's case."

"Tom is the best there is," Eagle told her. "And he's a good friend besides. If he practiced criminal law, he'd jump on this right away. But since he doesn't, he's going to get you the best there is."

"I thought that was what I was doing when I went to New Orleans."

"And that's something else we need to look into," he pointed out to her. "What would make an attorney who doesn't even live in Tampa just summarily refuse to take the case?"

"I sure hope he can find some answers," she told him. "And Viper?"

"He's setting up a special project." Blaze grinned. "Hannah, his fiancée, is a brilliant drone engineer. Has her own firm, as a matter of fact. That's a story we'll share with you at some point. Anyway, she has a new prototype she wants to test, so she's letting us be the guinea pigs."

Sierra's eyebrows shot up. "You're using a drone to track something?"

"Well, sort of. This camera is supposed to transmit up to eight miles and has a camera life of fourteen hours. Early this morning, Viper set it up in a tree right by The Library where hopefully this will get pictures of vehicles pulling in so we can see their license plates. It's transmitting back to Hannah's control room where she'll monitor it and download the video. Every time I go through all these documents, I'm more and more convinced this disaster started with The Library and whoever was in that car coming from it. And Hannah jumped at the chance to give her new design a test run."

Sierra felt her jaw drop.

"She must be incredibly brilliant."

Eagle chuckled. "That she is. And she has a hatred for people who use their power wrongly. She was a victim, which is how she and Viper met."

"What happens when the battery dies?"

"Viper will replace it," Blaze told her. "We'll keep reloading and checking the license plates until we hit paydirt."

"Do they get much traffic during the day?"

"From what I've been able to find out, while the bulk of activity is at night, they have a pretty active lunch hour in the restaurant," he explained.

Sierra could hardly believe it. "Please thank her a lot for me."

"Will do. Okay, then. Let's get started." He pulled up a document on his laptop. "The Library itself is actually a very old house whose owner had built an incredible library. He was a booklover, collected rare editions and wanted to properly house and display them. When he sold the property several years ago, the people who bought it decided The Library would be a good name for it."

"I can understand that," Sierra told them. "I'm a book addict myself.

"Yes, well, it's one of those massive houses on Bayshore Boulevard that was sold ages ago. Then the owner decided to buy the two adjoining houses and set it up as a private club. He also reconfigured the iron fencing to contain all three buildings." He checked his notes. "I understand one of them is used as a private inn and one of the others has a small restaurant in it. It sits way back off the street and most of the property is heavy with mature trees."

Sierra frowned. "I've driven past it a lot, but I never paid much attention to it. I don't think anyone I know even discusses it, except to mention its name and the rumor that the collective membership could buy and sell small countries."

"From the little bit I found," Blaze said, "it's open only to the members. Any parties held there are only attended by members and rigorously vetted guests. Some of whom, by the way, are from other countries."

Eagle shook his head. "Maybe it has to do with politics or…I don't know. It's just too weird, is all."

"There's no published list that I can find," Blaze continued, "and I've tried a number of different search engines. I can't pull it up anywhere. I did discover members are vetted six different ways and there's very little discussion about what goes on there."

Sierra frowned. "You think these people might be criminals of some kind?"

Blaze's laugh held little humor. "It would be easier if they were."

"I bet there's no way to get anyone inside any of the buildings," Eagle mused, "to see if something off the wall is going on there."

"That's what I'm trying to find out. But privacy and security are mild words for that situation. I learned even the staff is investigated more than the president's security detail."

Sierra frowned. "And none of you were able to hack into their computer system?"

Blaze actually laughed. "I think the government would celebrate if it could achieve this kind of secrecy."

"So what do we do? I agree with all of you. That's the only event that's an anomaly in Jeremy's life, so something about that fender bender triggered this. But what?"

"I was finally able to find the name of the corporation that owns it," Blaze went on, "but much like Galaxy, it's a dead end. It's buried under layers of shell companies. I'm thinking I'll pass this along to Tom, also. He has way more resources to search for this stuff than I do."

"God." Sierra brushed a stray hair back from her forehead. "Who are these people, anyway? And why would they do this to Jeremy? And why do they need so many layers of secrecy?"

Eagle leaned closer to her. "We're all asking the same question. There was something or someone in that car that they don't want discovered. Afraid enough to set up this elaborate charade. But I promise we're going to find out who and what."

Blaze tapped his keyboard again. "Meanwhile, I'm trying to narrow down the list of what I'm calling the Top Untouchables in the area. People insulated by money and position who might be doing something at The Library that they feel they have to hide."

"Any luck yet?" Sierra asked.

"A little, but I'm really just getting started. Yesterday, if you remember, I got a list of Jeremy's clients from him so right now I'm doing a deep dive on them. It would help, however, if you could go over the list with me and tell me anything you might know about any of them. You know, just from living here and hearing or reading things."

"I'll do anything you need," she assured him. "That's the most puzzling bit about this whole situation. Someone has gone to great lengths to frame Jeremy for something, and I know you're already sick of hearing me say this, but I still can't imagine why. This is a nightmare I can't seem to wake up from."

For the rest of the morning, Blaze and Eagle took her through everything she could remember about Jeremy's client list, his personal life, his friends. By the time they'd finished she was drained and wondered if there was even a scrap of information in all that.

She got up to fix another cup of coffee for herself and noticed that her hands were shaking. She put the mug down, twisted her hands together and took a deep breath then let it out slowly.

Eagle came up behind her and now put his arm around her, giving her a hug.

"We can take a break."

She leaned back against him, taking comfort from the feel of his body.

"I'll be okay. It's just…" She blew out a breath. "I haven't even allowed myself a minute to let down since this happened. I couldn't because I was the only one Jeremy had fighting for him except Cheryl. Both our parents are dead. The architectural agency he worked for politely told me that while they believed this was all a horrible mistake, they would have to separate themselves from this until it was resolved."

"It's lousy," he agreed, "but I understand their position. With the case against Jeremy, they had to think of their clients."

"I know, I know, but damn. It just sucks."

"Hey, guys." Blaze hollered at them from the dining room. "Come back. We need to look at this."

Sierra almost sloshed her coffee over the rim of her mug as she hurried back into the dining room.

"What is it?" She slid into the chair next to Blaze and looked at his computer screen. All she saw was a document. "What am I looking at?"

"Okay, I'm going to tell you something that does not leave this room. I was able to hack into the police computers, and—"

"What?" Her eyebrows nearly rose to her hairline. "How can you do that?"

"A skill I developed with the SEALs when we needed to see what the enemy was up to. I use it sparingly," he assured her, "but I've been damn curious about the woman who was killed. If she drugged your brother, it's possible she was a call girl and someone hired her. That someone could also be the one who killed her to frame your brother. The big question is why."

"Do you mean Rose Aitkin?"

"Yup. There's nothing in here that says where she came from, where she lived, what she did for a living if anything. All I could get was a head shot that showed me a nice-looking woman with a lot of makeup, but not one other stitch of information."

"I know!" Sierra nodded. "That's just so weird. I kept asking about it, but the attorney I retained just said none was available. He said it was obvious Jeremy had either just met her at the hotel bar or knew her from someplace and asked her to meet him there. But from where? He was so much in love with Cheryl. He wasn't the type of person who picked up women, and I say that not just because I'm his sister."

"What did the people at the architectural firm have to say?" Blaze asked.

"They said they knew nothing about her. That Jeremy didn't seem the type to hook up with a stranger, but you didn't always know the people you worked with that well." She pressed her fingers to her eyelids for a moment, trying to remember anything else she'd learned. "It was just so strange that everyone was so willing to accept the obvious without questioning anything."

She frowned as Blaze and Eagle exchanged glances.

"What? What are you thinking?"

"I'm thinking that this whole thing is just too fucking neat. Too well packaged. Everyone from the cops to the prosecutor to the defense attorney you hired just took it at face value. Nobody did any investigating."

"Our attorney did, or so he said. I paid for a private investigator to look into it, but the attorney told me they hadn't found anything?"

"What's the investigator's name?" Blaze clicked his mouse and brought up another document. "I don't see it here."

"I believe it was Hawthorne Investigations, but there should be a copy of their invoice as well as a listing on the final expense sheet. I scanned everything into the folder I emailed you."

Blaze click-clicked through pager after page, scanning each one then going back to those that required more attention. At the end he just shrugged.

"Sierra, I hate to tell you, but I see no actual report in here, nor a separate statement. There's just a line item in the summary bill for investigations for fifteen hundred dollars."

Sierra waited while Eagle pulled it up on his own computer then scrolled to the documents he wanted. He did this a few times, just as Blaze had, before shrugging his shoulders.

"I don't know, darlin'. There had to be more proof of billing than this. You're too smart to pay that money without proper documentation."

"I had it," she insisted. "In fact, I not only had all the files emailed to me but also scanned to my hard drive. There's something wrong here."

"That's an understatement," Blaze agreed. "I'll say this, Sierra. The attorney you hired — what's his name? Geoffrey Bendell? — did a good job faking this report."

A sick feeling rumbled up and caught in her throat. "This whole thing was one big sham, wasn't it?"

"Yes." Blaze nodded. "I'm sorry to tell you, but you're right."

"But can't he be disbarred for that?"

"Under normal circumstances I'd say yes. But these are definitely not normal circumstances. Not by a long shot. The fix was in from day one and by some very, very powerful people. That's the only way this could have played out the way it did and so extensively."

Sierra didn't know whether to cry or throw up. Or kill someone. She had suspected as much for a long time but didn't have the resources to prove it. If she hadn't been directed to Senator Kane, she and Jeremy would still be facing disaster.

Eagle slid his arm around her and gave her a gentle hug.

"We've got this, darlin'," he told her in his deep voice. "We're on it and we're going to get it taken care of."

"Whoever was in the car Jeremy had the little collision with is at the root of it," Blaze told her. "And it has to be someone very powerful. Which lines up with The Library and what it is and what its members are."

"And is why we need to focus hard on getting the member list," Eagle added.

Sierra gave a short laugh. "Yeah, right. Good luck with that."

Eagle gave her shoulder a light squeeze. "Darlin', aren't you getting the idea by now that there isn't anything Galaxy can't do? We eliminated the word 'impossible' from our vocabulary."

"Okay, but where do we start? Blaze, you already said you can't crack their membership list."

"I'm going to reach out to Rocket and see if he and Tom have come up with anything regarding all the attorneys you contacted. There may be a clue there someplace. But we need to kick this into overdrive."

* * * *

Darius refilled his coffee cup, silently noting to himself that he was liable to have a caffeine hangover by the time this episode in their lives was resolved. Assuming, of course, that it was, because otherwise he might just as well commit suicide. His body was rigid, and he was sure his heart rate had accelerated. Nothing was going their way. Nothing at all.

Anna Lisa, his admin, brought in breakfast rolls from the bakery in the lobby of the building, and he grabbed one from the box. Maybe an infusion of sugar would help.

He was just taking the time to allow him to savor the taste of the pastry when Neil arrived, filled his own cup and sat in one of the big chairs.

"Well?" Darius asked.

"Well, what?" Neil demanded.

"Could you please tell me why we can't find out who the fuck these people are who have erected an invisible wall around Sierra Hunt? Why she's not at her home, and we can't find her anywhere? Why she chose this particular time to install a cable system? And what the fuck is going on? And now how are we going to get rid of this woman if we can't find her?"

"That's a lot of questions. Where do you want me to start?"

"I want you to start with answers." Darius ground his teeth.

"The most interesting and aggravating answer I can give you is whoever these men are that Jeremy Hunt's sister has hooked up with, they have a longer reach than we do. We may be in trouble here."

"No!" He practically shouted the word. Then he took a breath and pulled himself together. "No little nobody is going to destroy my life. I will not allow it."

"Then we'd better figure out who these people are and how to stop them without making things worse."

Darius glared at him. "Have you gotten any further in your search?"

"Unfortunately, no. I'd love to know the name of their attorney. Their paperwork is impeccable. You can't tell who anyone is."

"Well." Darius shook his head. "We'd damn well better find out soon. What about Sierra Hunt? Any word on her yet?"

"It's the damnedest fucking thing," Neil told him. "She seems to have just disappeared off the grid."

"That doesn't make sense. One minute she's all over the place looking for attorneys to file an appeal. The next she disappears altogether."

"After she hooked up with these people," Neil reminded him.

"But for what purpose? Everything's in place to shut down an attempt for an appeal. You think she's planning to break him out of Raiford? That's why she's hired these guys?"

"I think she knows that would be a disaster. However, not knowing what she's up to makes me very nervous."

"Me, too," Darius agreed. "Very edgy. I don't like being in the dark."

Neil studied him. "I hope you haven't been to The Library while all of this is going on. You need to find another way to soothe your nerves right now."

Darius frowned. "Why not? It's the best place for me to indulge in anonymity and work off a little frustration."

"Yeah, well." Neil shook his head. "You'd better not be indulging in anything for a while, not with these strangers digging up everything they can about everyone associated with the situation."

"But they have no idea I'm connected," he protested. God, he wanted a drink.

"But how long do you think it will take them to start digging into everything involved with Jeremy Hunt's life? To look into that stupid accident?"

"It was raining," Darius protested. "You could hardly see your hand in front of your face. He couldn't see anything inside the car. He has nothing to tell."

"Don't be so sure," Neil argued. "I have a bad feeling these people, whoever they are, stick like leeches."

"Then find out who the fuck they are and how we get rid of them."

"I hate to tell you this." Neil walked to the big window, hands in his pockets, as he looked out at the brand-new revitalized Tampa Waterfront District. "For the first time in all the years we've known each other and after all the things we've done together, I'm actually feeling a little nervous."

Darius forced himself to take another bite of the sweet roll and chew it slowly. Swallow. Take a sip of coffee. Losing it wasn't going to help one single bit.

"And exactly what is it that makes you nervous? My friend, we have the goods on many people in this town. We control a lot of destinies. Nobody's going to fuck with us. Nobody."

Neil snorted a laugh. "I'm glad you're so confident. Yesterday you were skating on the edge of insanity."

And I still am, but I can't afford to show it. Not even to you, my friend.

"We have to be confident," Darius told him. "We have to believe there's no trail to me. But...we still have to find out who these people are. We have to be in control of the situation."

"Well, I hate to tell you, but I still don't have a clue. And I am beyond frustrated."

Darius nodded. "As am I, and I have a question for you. How many people can we trust with confidential activities?"

Neil turned to face him.

"Why? What do you have in mind?"

"For one thing, I want to put someone on the location of that plane. Two someones, so there's always an open pair of eyes. I want to know if anyone even walks up the driveway."

"Assuming there's a place to sequester themselves without being seen," Neil added.

"We'll have it checked out. And..."

"And what?" Neil prompted.

"Do we still have our connection to get into the CCTV traffic videos?"

Neil let out a slow whistle."

"Jesus. What do you have in mind?"

"I'd like to find video from the other day and see if we can track them. Sierra Hunt and the man she was with are probably a lost cause. But there were two other men there who may not have been as cautious when they left the alley. If we're lucky, we can narrow down where they went after they had the car towed. We just need a copy of that video."

He watched his friend run the idea around in his brain.

"I don't know if there's anything to see," Neil said at last. "There may not be cameras where they went after leaving the crash scene. We'd have to do this very carefully and it would cost a whole lot of cash."

"That, my friend, is something we have no shortage of. See what you can do."

Neil rubbed the back of his neck, an unconscious gesture of frustration. "And I know I said to stay away from The Library until this is settled, but I changed my mind. I think If we stay away, there will be questions we don't want to answer. I'm sure you managed this so no one even knew what was happening but there's always a chance we missed something. And that something could come back to bite me in the ass."

"Fine. Let's have dinner there tonight. We can check things out."

Neil nodded. "Probably a smart move."

"Meantime, reach out to your contact in the city and give him a fat bunch of money to look at the CCTV footage. Tell him you want everything from that section of the city during that time frame."

"All right." Neil pulled out his cell and made a note to himself.

"Then get back on your info line and keep right on looking to see who these people are that seem to have swooped into Sierra Hunt's life. And where they came from. How did she get in touch with them, because I'm telling you, I have so much info on her I even know what time she goes to bed at night? Yet I can't find out who these people are. Find them, we find her, and we can get rid of her. Because if we don't, she'll haunt us and cause trouble forever. She's not going to let this thing rest."

"There's something funny here," Neil told him. "And it gives me a very uneasy feeling."

"It does? Think how it makes me feel."

"Okay. I get it. I really do and I've reached out to all my contacts to see what we might have missed. But there also has to be someone you know, with all your stratospheric connections. Someone who you can tap that might identify them. Get busy on it, and I'll see you at dinner tonight."

Darius nodded but he wasn't sure he'd have any appetite for dinner if they didn't get somewhere on this. In the future, he needed to get a better handle on his self-control.

Chapter Eleven

He knew it was stupid, he knew it was idiotic, and most of all he knew it was dangerous. But after Neil had left, Darius was too edgy to stay in his office. After battling with himself for ten minutes, he grabbed his suit jacket and headed out of his office, stopping at Anna Lisa's desk.

"Call Champion and cancel this afternoon's meeting," he told her. "Reschedule for next week."

She raised an eyebrow. Anna Lisa had worked for him for ten years and by now knew almost as much about Standard International as he did.

"They'll be upset," she reminded him. "Today was the meeting to go over the final contract details. You know they were looking forward to it."

"Yes, well, it won't kill them to wait another week. They came to us if you remember. If they annoy me too much, I'll lower the offer."

She smiled. "They always come to you when they're desperate because they know they'll at least get something. They're so grateful by that time they take whatever you offer."

"Smart woman," he told her.

"What time should I expect you back?"

"I may be gone the rest of the day," he told her. "Tell everyone I was called away to a meeting and take messages. I'll have my cell with me if anything dire pops up."

She just nodded and went back to her work. Once again, he blessed the day he'd hired her.

He just needed to get out of here today. His situation was beginning to choke him. He didn't feel comfortable in most places and some Neil had suggested that he stay away from.

Like The Library.

God, how he missed that place. The one place in his life where he could truly be himself. Where he could discuss private matters, eat the expensive food he loved and drink the expensive liquor he enjoyed. And where he could satisfy his other needs without anyone being the wiser.

Everyone knew about the private rooms, of course. They were never discussed and arrangements for them were made with the utmost discretion. For some of the men, it was the most private place to spend time with their mistresses. For others, a chance to indulge their needs without the world knowing. And arrivals and departures were always arranged to occur with the utmost secrecy. No one ever knew who was using any of the other rooms and no one ever saw the women — or men — who guests brought to the very private rooms. *Thank god for that.*

Except Armand, the night manager, of course.

Darius didn't want to stay away from The Library too long. People might ask questions about his health or situation. He and Neil were having dinner there tonight—that was certainly safe, and he could get a sense of things there as they regarded him. But right now, he had other things to attend to. He needed to make his phone calls then be doing something while he waited for people to call him back.

He headed to his house, glad no one was home today. His wife had seldom been here in the last years of their marriage, preferring the company of her friends to that of her husband, which had been fine with him. The housekeeper was apparently off doing some errands. Both of his kids were away at college. He could slip in and out without having to answer any questions, and he had an itch he just had to scratch.

First, he took care of making his phone calls, telling each person he needed action and results yesterday. Then he changed clothes, to something more innocuous. Khakis, a crew neck sweater and a ball cap without any logo. Then he went to the back yard where their Sheltie, Boris, was running around. The dog was important because it would be good camouflage, and Boris danced around on two legs, excited to be going somewhere.

He had parked his car, the one he usually drove, in the garage when he got home instead of in the driveway. It was quietly ostentatious, broadcasting the fact it belonged to someone of wealth. But instead of firing it up, he climbed into what he called his 'spare', a very generic sedan that he used when he wanted to remain as anonymous as possible.

And that was what he needed now because he'd decided to drive by Sierra Hunt's house again. He wasn't sure if he wanted the woman to be home or not. Except, once he finally knew where she was, he could stop being edgy about it. He urged Boris into the car and backed it out of the garage.

He thought the odds of her being home were pretty good. The man he'd had do a drive-by the other night said it looked like she had a power problem that was being fixed and the next day a cable company had a truck in her driveway. She wouldn't be worried about those things if she wasn't going to be home, right?

But what if any of those men were with her now?

Darius felt more unsettled than at any time in his life, even when he was working his first deals and Standard International was just a startup. He'd vowed never to let someone else be in control, but it seemed that was exactly what was happening. Whoever these people were Sierra Hunt had hooked up with had turned everything upside down.

Normally he would tell himself this was a wasted trip. It was the middle of the afternoon, and she wasn't likely to be home. But with things the way they were, he might get lucky and find she'd come home to reorganize herself.

He parked one street over. Then, clipping Boris' leash to his collar, he locked the car and began a leisurely stroll. The neighborhood was a quiet one in an older but well-maintained part of the city, peaceful, a place where probably nothing ever happened. Well, he hoped he could keep it that way.

Most of the houses were in the distinctive Craftsman bungalow style, with neatly mowed lawns and well-cared-for landscaping. At two of them, he saw women working in the flower beds. At another an older man was sitting on the front porch, reading something.

The last thing he wanted was to call attention to himself. If Sierra Hunt was home, he'd get a couple of the men he used to grab her out of the house with no fuss and take it from there.

When he reached her bungalow, he saw there were no vehicles in the driveway. Glancing casually around, he acted as if the dog wanted to sniff his way up the driveway and gave him his head. He hoped to anyone noticing him they'd think he was just a neighbor out walking his dog.

There was a light on inside the house even though it was only late afternoon, and he thought that might mean she was home. He stood on the sidewalk a few moments, studying the house, trying to decide if he should move closer, then changed his mind.

Luckily, Boris decided just then to pee at the edge of the driveway, which gave him a few more minutes to study the area.

He had to be careful, because he didn't know if she had a security system in place. Although, he told himself, with everything going on regarding her brother, he wouldn't be surprised. But then he had to ask how sophisticated it would be.

Fortunately, Boris decided he needed to pee again and spent some time sniffing the grass. That gave Darius more time to look around. He had a feeling he was missing something, but what?

He heard a car come down the street and turned to see it pull into the driveway across from Sierra's. The woman who climbed out of the car glanced over at him for a long moment before going into her house. Okay. Time to leave. He looked away from her, tugged on Boris' leash and as nonchalantly as possible, began to stroll back down the street.

It wasn't until he was in his car again and pulling out of the neighborhood that he began to breathe more easily. Something was out of whack at that house, and he just couldn't figure out what. But he knew he'd better if he was going to stay protected and get out of this — whatever this was turning out to be — with his life intact.

Time to jab at the people who were supposed to be getting information for him.

* * * *

Eagle knew Sierra was going stir crazy. Who wouldn't if they were cooped up in one place and shut away from everyone and everything in their life? He would have liked to join Rocket at Tom's office to discuss the list of attorneys and pick apart their lives, and also look at alternatives. He didn't, however, want to risk taking Sierra out where anyone might see her.

He was about to turn on the hot tub and see if that would relax her when his cell phone rang. He looked at the readout. Blaze.

"Tell me you have something," he said, "so I can peel Sierra off the wall."

He faked a groan when she poked him with her elbow.

"I have something."

"Good. Let's have it."

"Our security guy just called me," Blaze told him. "You know, we've had him monitoring the feed from the cameras he installed outside Sierra's house.

"He got something?" Eagle did his best to contain the excitement in his voice. He didn't want to give

Sierra false hopes if it turned out to be nothing. "Let's have it."

"First, ask your lady if she has a neighbor that walks a little Sheltie."

"Okay." He repeated what Blaze had said.

Sierra's eyes widened and she shook her head.

"Not unless it's someone from several streets over or a new pet acquisition by someone in the past two days. Why?"

"She says no and why?"

"Cal said he just got video of some guy strolling past her house with his dog. He walked a little ways up the driveway, let his dog pee on the lawn then did his best to look nonchalant while he visually scanned the area."

"And?"

"And it was obvious he was trying to figure out whether Sierra was home or not. I think he might even have tried to get closer and maybe peep in the windows, but one of the cameras picked up a neighbor across the street getting home. She got out of her car and looked over at whoever this guy was in Sierra's drive."

"What did he do?" Eagle asked.

"Just tugged his dog and led him back onto the sidewalk. Then he continued on down the block. There's no more footage of him so I'm going to assume he parked his car elsewhere and strolled over to Sierra's street. Ask her if she's familiar with her neighbors on the streets on either side of hers."

She shook her head when Eagle asked her about it.

"I've been pretty much a loner in the neighborhood. My job takes a lot of my time, and since Jeremy was arrested, that's all I've been focused on. I think the only people I'd recognize are those on either side of me."

"Okay." Eagle passed that on to Blaze. "What's next?"

"I'll be heading your way in a couple of hours. Cal is turning several of the screen shots into stills and sending them to my computer and my phone. I'll shoot one of them to you but I'm going to print out all the others and bring them with me so we can all look at them. We're all coming for dinner tonight anyway. You remember?"

"I do. I'll get the grill set up. You guys are bringing the food, right?"

"All taken care of," Blaze assured him. "See you in a while."

"That gives me such a creepy feeling," Sierra told him when he related everything to her. "Someone is sneaking around my house? Who on earth could it be?"

"That's what we're going to find out," Eagle assured her. "Whoever this is can't get to you as long as you're here."

"I can't stay here forever, Eagle."

He reached out and pulled her against him, cradling her face in his palms and looking at her with such heat and hunger in his eyes her entire body turned hot.

"You will if I have anything to say about it."

Sierra swallowed but said nothing.

Suddenly he worried that she might think things were moving too fast. That she was getting involved too soon. But there was such a rightness about the connection that he just couldn't deny it. It was totally unexpected, but he didn't want to screw it up. He had never met a woman he linked with on such a deep emotional level as he did with Sierra. And it was a lot more than just fantastic sex.

He thought about the things they had done, the instant physical bond that had formed, the way their bodies responded to each other and knew he'd never found that with anyone else. He glanced at his watch.

"We've got two hours before the horde descends, and I already had an idea how to settle those nerves of yours."

She lifted an eyebrow. "And exactly what would that be?"

"Come with me."

He took her hand and led her through the house to the pool and hot tub.

"Look," he told her. "Magic."

"But this is fantastic!"

The tub was oval and deeper than average. Eagle crouched down and pressed a button in its side. At once a muted hum vibrated through the air and the water began to bubble and froth.

"Hold on one second," Eagle told her.

He stripped off his clothes in an instant, tossing them onto a lounge chair. Then he drew her close to him and slowly removed every article of her clothing. He eased her jeans over her hips, helped her step out of them then flung them to the side. After kissing each knee, he ran his thumbs up the inside of each thigh, the tips meeting where the barely their scrap of lace panties covered her sweet, sweet pussy. He flicked his tongue lightly over that tiny piece of fabric before sliding it down her legs and discarding it.

As he exposed each part of her body, he kissed and teased it. He swirled his tongue around each nipple, taking a moment to gently close his teeth over them. He trailed kisses along her neck and along her collarbone then strung little nips between her breasts.

"I think the water's just about at the optimum temperature. Let's get wet." He slid the edge of his hand between the lips of her cunt. "Oh, wait. You already are."

He nipped her bottom lip before lifting her in his arms and carrying her into the hot tub. *Oh, yeah, exactly the right temperature.* He eased himself onto the little ledge that ran around the inside of the tub. When he was settled, he arranged Sierra in his lap, leaned back with his hands beneath her arms, cupped her breasts, and breathed a sigh of satisfaction.

"You doing okay?" Tension still zipped through her body, so he deliberately made his voice warm and soothing.

"I am now."

She wriggled herself back against him. When her ass brushed back and forth over his cock, he had to bite the inside of his cheek to maintain some sense of control.

"You okay?" she asked.

"I will be." His mouth was soft on her earlobe, and his voice as gentle as a caress. "Let me adjust you here a little bit."

He dialed the control for the jets to the intensity he wanted as they pulsed into the water, the froth filling the surface around her. At this rate, he might die of pleasure before he turned fifty.

But what a way to go.

"Eagle?" Sierra's voice pierced his consciousness. "Did I lose you there? I'm starting to feel really good."

She pressed against his very swollen cock, and he was afraid he might lose it right there.

"Still here, darlin'. I think you need some real relaxing."

Adjusting her position against him, he coasted his hands over her shoulders and down her arms. Jesus! She was tighter than coiled wire. He couldn't blame her, though. In her position, he wouldn't be any different. Okay, he'd have to fix this. No, he *wanted* to fix this.

With a gentle touch, he went back to rubbing and lightly squeezing the muscles of her shoulders and upper arms. As the tension began to slip from her body, he swept her hair aside and planted nibbling kisses along the nape of her neck. Again she hummed her satisfaction and nestled her sweet little ass against his body, trapping his cock between them.

Holy sweet Jesus!

God give me strength.

But then he shifted her slightly, breaking the rhythm of his hands and her muscles tightened again.

"Stop thinking," he told her. "You have permission not to think for the next half hour."

Her laugh was anything but humorous.

"If only. I swear, Eagle, it feels as if I've been trying to help Jeremy forever."

"I'm sure it does, but let me help you take a breath and get rid of some of that tension."

She hummed with satisfaction as he continued his massage. He worked the muscles in her shoulders and arms, feeling them relax one tiny bit at a time. Finally, when she was limp in his arms, he took a tiny nip of her ear.

"I think you're ready for a little treat I have for you."

"A treat? Should I guess what it is?"

His laugh rumbled in his chest. "I don't think you'll guess this one. It's something to take your mind off this mess for a little while and get rid of some of that stress."

He spread her legs wide, arranging them on either side of his knees so she was wide open. Punching the button to increase the force of the jets, he shifted her until one of them bubbled directly onto her clit.

"Oh, god!" The word came out on an uneven breath.

She tried to push herself harder against the force of the bubbles, but Eagle banded his arm around her waist. If he kept it up, he'd come before another second went by, and he'd miss all the good stuff.

And good it was, with this woman, who lit him up like the Fourth of July. He was still shocked at how his body responded to her, but even more at the unexpected emotional connection. Suddenly all the terrific sex he'd had in his life seemed so plain and uninteresting.

Sierra was still rotating her hips, so he pressed his knees harder against the inside of her thigh, reached down and captured her clit between two fingers. She began to rock her body, seeking the magic of the bubbles and his fingers.

"Feel good, darlin'?" He breathed the words into her ear even as he pinched her little nub of sensitive flesh even harder. And tugged on it.

She gasped her pleasure.

"Should I stop?"

"No!"

She almost shouted the word, and he laughed low and soft.

He shifted both of them so he could ease the tips of two fingers inside her, lightly stroking the rim of her opening. She rubbed against him even as she arched into his touch.

He increased the pressure of his legs against the inside of her thighs, opening her even more. Now she was in constant motion, her body begging for something in that sweet, sweet channel. The more he tugged on her clit and skated his fingertips around her opening, the more frantic she became.

Then, without warning, he removed his hands and slid them beneath her body. Still using his legs to keep her wide open, with the stream of water pounding against her very aroused pussy, he eased two fingers into the cleft of her ass. As soon as they touched her, he began to rub those fingers back and forth in a teasing manner. Hot little sounds burst from her mouth as she worked hard to find relief.

He was having a problem himself, his swollen cock screaming for mercy, demanding to lose itself in her hot little cunt, wanting to feel her inner muscles squeezing around him.

But he gritted his teeth. This was for her. All for her. His goal was to give her more pleasure than she'd ever had, and he was going to do it.

As he massaged her rear opening, he placed his mouth close to her ear, taking a moment to gently nibble on the lobe.

"We were talking about spanking, darlin', but what about being handcuffed? Restrained? Ordered to kneel while you were blindfolded, and your ass was gently flogged? You should try it. You might like it."

She was gasping for breath as she wriggled in his grasp.

"Oh, god."

"What was that?" He nipped her ear again. "You said you'd love it? Especially the handcuffs part?"

"Do you do that a lot?" She was breathing so hard now the words came out in bursts. "The handcuffs?" She blew out another breath. "The blindfold?"

How should he answer that?

"Not a lot, but if I said I liked it, would you decide I was all wrong for you?"

He waited, barely drawing a breath, for her to answer him.

"No." She was still breathing hard. "I-I think I'd like to try it." Another pause. "With you."

He could tell she was still teetering on the edge of uncertainty, but the more he stroked her, the more he teased her, the more he could feel her respond. Feel the hunger and desire surging through her.

He reached into a little box right next to the hot tub, hoping Sierra didn't get turned off because he kept a supply of condoms there. He shifted her body so she was kneeling between his thighs while he rolled on the condom, then arranged her, trembling now with need, so she was leaning on the rim of the hot tub, poised on her knees. He really wanted to fuck her in the ass, but he'd wait for that. This would do for now.

Still, he couldn't resist running his hands over the curves of her body, and whispering in her ear, "One day before too long I'm going to take you here."

Then, kneeling between her outspread thighs, he gripped his cock and slowly, slowly eased it inside her. When he was fully seated, he had to suck in his breath and hold it to steady himself. From this angle he could plunge himself in deeper, her inner walls gripping him like a vise. He nipped the lobe of her ear, licked it then whispered, "Get ready for a hot ride, darlin'."

As he began to move, plunging in and out, he hoped he could last long enough to bring her to orgasm. Jesus, she just did it for him, in a way no other woman ever had. Whatever it took, he was going to make this work.

He moved slowly at first but then sped up the pace as his need intensified. He reached around her, sliding one hand down over her cunt to find her clit and manipulate it with the tips of his fingers. Sierra was making the most delicious noises now, moving in rhythm with him and, as he picked up the pace, so did she. He gritted his teeth, reaching for control, and felt the first tremors in her inner walls, growing into spasms that clutched at his dick.

He increased his pace again, plunging even deeper, rubbing that hot nub of flesh, pounding into her. And then…and then…the tremors increased, and he let go, taking them both to an explosive climax that had them shaking with the force of it.

He had no idea how long it took before all the spasms finally faded and they could breathe again. He managed to ease himself from the clasp of Sierra's body and removed the condom with great care. Then he tugged her so she was sideways in his arms, the jets at a lower speed again doing their work on her body.

He studied her face, which looked relaxed for the first time since the moment he'd met her. The pinched look was gone, and hot satisfaction shone in her eyes. He was sure he could stay this way with her forever, except the water would probably turn them into prunes. Besides, he had his people coming for dinner and both he and Sierra needed to make themselves presentable.

"All good?" he asked, smiling at her.

"Mmm. Better than good."

He carried her out of the hot tub and stood her on the tiles surrounding it. After that he wrapped her in a towel and led her inside.

"I think we've just got time for a shower," he told her. "But we'd better make it a quick one."

"Well…" She looked down then back up at him. "Not too quick."

Chapter Twelve

Darius was not a man given to emotional reactions. He'd built up a multimillion-dollar business and created an international niche for himself by always being in control. Even when events threatened to turn against him, he never lost it. But right at this particular moment, he could cheerfully have grabbed someone's neck and broken it.

He had to admit it had been stupid to check out Sierra Hunt's house, but damn it! The man he'd hired to find her, who was the best in the business, couldn't get a scent of her. The one who was trying to identify the men with her the other day wasn't having any better luck, and it was driving him out of his mind.

His people had tried everything, and they had the manpower and equipment to do it. They had scanned her face into the computer and ran it through facial recognition software although he had no idea why, since they already knew who she was. They tried the same thing with the pictures his man had taken with his phone of the men with the Hunt woman the other day, but without success. These were well-trained individuals who knew how to keep their faces away from cameras and not to be identified.

The only thing that gave him even a tiny sense of safety was the conviction that no one had his picture or the details of the accident. *Yeah, the fucking accident.* Neil had told him enough times that his arrogance would be his undoing. He pointed out that was exactly what had happened that rainy night. Darius had taken his 'games' too far and the woman he was 'playing' with had ended up dead.

Every detail of that night still lived in stark clarity in his mind.

Thank god for Joel, his driver, who had helped him sneak the body off The Library's premises. It had been easy to tell Armand, who aided him in getting her out to the car, that the woman had had too much to drink and could barely stand up. As the night manager, Armand had seen many things in his years at The Library and very little flustered him.

Between them, they'd been able to settle the body in the car without calling attention to it.

Everything would have been fine if not for the fucking rain. He still didn't know which car caused the fender bender, his exiting the gate at The Library or the man he now knew was Jeremy Hunt sliding on the wet street outside the property's fencing. But shoving money at him seemed to make the situation go away without calling the cops.

Then Darius gave Joel the address of a rental property he owned that was vacant and said to take them there. Of course, as always, Joel asked no questions.

After that he called Neil and dragged him out in the rain.

Using Neil's car, they took the body to a place where they could easily dispose of it and went home. Finally, he called Joel again, suggested the man might want to go on a long vacation and arranged to meet him to give him a fat handout. Joel was no fool. He'd rather have the money and disappear than get caught up in something he wanted no part of.

Darius knew having more money than god was always helpful.

But he had fretted every second after that, waiting for the other shoe to drop, even though he'd been sure it was impossible to see into the car what with the rain. But he wasn't a man who liked loose ends, so he set his usual people on it. He still worried about it, but finding a way to neutralize Jeremy Hunt hadn't been easy. The guy was so clean he shone, and there wasn't a single person who had a bad thing to say about him.

That meant setting him up in a way to get rid of him and controlling the people who could manipulate that situation. It also meant using the one thing he had plenty of — money — to create a situation and either pay people off or blackmail others into going along with it. Sure, it was elaborate, but he'd had to do something that would work. It just meant convincing people that the oh-so-clean Jeremy Hunt could kill a woman and think he could get away with it.

The scene was arranged and set meticulously, and the right people were paid off. Except there was always the possibility of someone questioning it, or some asshole deciding Hunt's situation was too well arranged. Or any number of things that could screw this all up. And making sure no attorney would file an appeal once the verdict was in. He probably should have let the whole thing go, assuming Hunt never knew who was in the car or what had happened. He'd just been so fucking undone about the whole thing that he'd gone overboard. He knew that but there was nothing he could do about it now.

He absolutely had to get hold of himself. There was too much at stake here to lose control. And he had to figure out what to tell Neil. He held nothing back from him, as a matter of course. It was one of the things that cemented their friendship and also allowed them to help each other out of, well, difficult circumstances. He hoped they had a table in a private alcove for dinner because this was not a conversation for anyone to overhear.

He supposed he could call Neil and tell him he wanted to eat somewhere else, except he knew his friend was already at The Library by now, having a drink while he waited for Darius to arrive, maybe even chatting with one or two of the members. If he got up and left suddenly, before even eating dinner, that could call attention to things best hidden.

By the time he finished the conversation with himself he was at The Library, under the portico by the front door of the main building, and one of the staff was opening his car door.

"Good evening, sir. Charlotte will show you to your table."

So he already had a table. That meant that Neil was there. Good. He hoped the table wasn't in the middle of the room.

"Nice to see you, sir," the hostess who greeted him told him. "We haven't had the pleasure of your company for a while."

Great. Just what he needed. Something to call extra attention to himself. The key to membership here was anonymity. Everything crossed the threshold here from international finance to international shenanigans to cheating spouses to extreme sex and more. The reason people felt so free was because no one gossiped and no one stood out for their behavior. But this was probably on him. He'd been so hellbent on staying in the background as long as Sierra Hunt was chumming the waters that he'd probably called attention to himself with his absence.

"I've been traveling a lot," he told her. "Internationally."

"Well, we're certainly glad to see you again. Please let your attendant know if there's anything special you require."

Oh, yeah, something very special. But not tonight. Not until all this finally goes away.

When he followed the hostess through the main dining room, he took a moment to admire the quiet luxury of the place. Thick carpeting that silenced footsteps. Hand-carved molding at the top of the ceilings and antique crystal chandeliers. The place whispered money and a lot of it, which was good, Darius always thought. It emphasized the exclusive environment of the place.

He saw that Neil was waiting for him in a corner alcove, one of those reserved for intimate business discussions. The manager, who'd been conversing with Neil, backed away with a deferential bow. Darious frowned. He detested the annoying man who always seemed to be lurking around corners and popping up where he didn't belong.

"You look like you could use a drink," his friend commented, studying him through narrowed eyes. "Or maybe ten. What's up now?"

"You mean besides still hitting a wall in the search for those men hanging around Sierra Hunt? And why?"

"You know why," Neil told him. "Somehow she's found people she thinks are going to help her free her brother. She's been on that kick for months. That's not news. It's why she took that trip to New Orleans. So what's going on?"

"Outside the fact that these people she's hooked up with are buried deeper than the dinosaurs?"

"Yes." Neil took a swallow of his drink. "Outside that. But we may get some help identifying them. A copy of the CCTV video for that day in that area will be emailed to me, hopefully tonight. My contact has to wait for the opportunity to search for it and copy it."

"Thank god." Darius felt the tension ease slightly.

He signaled the waiter and ordered a Pappy Van Winkle, a special twenty-five-year-old bourbon on the rocks for himself. To his credit, Neil sat quietly, watching, until Darius had taken a healthy swallow of his own drink before asking anything else.

"You think you can tell me what's going on now? It must be damn awful for you to need that alcohol before telling me."

Darius took one more tiny swallow, put his glass down and leaned across the table.

"I went to Sierra Hunt's house this afternoon."

He could see the tremendous self-control Neil was using to keep from reaching across the table and strangling him.

"So let me get this straight. After all the effort and money that have gone into keeping you completely out of this outrageous fiasco caused, I might add, by your ridiculous arrogance and lack of control — you then do something to put yourself right in the middle of the picture. Am I right?"

Darius took another swallow of Pappy Van Winkle, although he wondered if even drinking the entire bottle would help.

"I was very circumspect about it." He leaned forward and described the entire episode, not leaving out one detail.

"We have to hope the woman across the street wasn't curious about a stranger she had probably never seen before walking his dog in front of Sierra Hunt's house."

"I think we'll be fine." Darius took another swallow of his drink. "Just a neighbor walking his dog. I didn't peer in any windows or anything." He attempted a smile. "Boris can vouch for me."

Neil shook his head. "Boris will? I don't know whether to laugh or cry. All right, what happened?"

"Well, nothing, really. It's a very quiet neighborhood. You'd think there weren't any live people there." He took another sip of his drink. "Except for the woman across the street, but she barely got a look at me. And I had my cap pulled down," he added. "I didn't look anything like myself."

"Jesus, you idiot." Neil stared at him, his pupils like bullets. "Unbelievable. Just unbelievable. For a very smart man, you can be incredibly stupid. Did you at least get any information?"

"Well, I couldn't exactly go house to house asking questions now, could I?" He paused. "I'm more concerned about the unavailability of information on those men Sierra Hunt disappeared with. Who in the fucking hell could they be? And where are they hiding her?"

"The bigger question," Neil said, "is how would she come into contact with people like that?"

"Do you realize we've reached out to every one of our sources and nobody could identify them?"

Neil shook his head. "Not all of them."

Darius frowned. "What do you mean? Of course we did."

"Do you remember when you had a 'ghost' pressuring you where Standard International is concerned? And none of our usual sources could find out who it was? And it was a lot more than a paper trail."

Darius thought for a moment, his mind a blank. Then it came to him.

"Of course. Sprague. He and his guys could find anyone, no matter what." Then he frowned. "But we haven't been in touch with them in a long time. You think they're still active? Maybe we should have had them keeping an eye on the Hunt woman."

"People like that are always active," Neil assured him. "Let me quietly check it out. Very quietly. So quietly even I won't know I'm doing it. Meanwhile, have another drink and let's order dinner."

"Dinner." Darius shook his head. "I never thought I'd be in a situation where I lost my appetite. Fuck it all, anyway. I've spent years building an empire, creating a life I can control, an image that no one can see behind. Jesus." He looked across the table at his friend. "Jesus. People trembled when I spoke."

Neil nodded. "And now some nobody is in a position to bring it all down. But we have to be sensible about it. You just can't run around eliminating people, at least not without a foolproof plan."

"I thought I had one," Darius ground out.

"We need to make some changes. For the first time ever I see you reacting on emotion."

"If we don't find this woman and get rid of her," Darius growled, "my entire life could implode. We can't just do nothing."

"I agree, but let's be sensible. You hear?"

"I hear."

"Okay, my friend. We're not going to let the worst happen. You have my word. Without the sister, there's nothing driving this."

"What about the men she's hooked up with? It looks like they could be big trouble, too."

"Let me think about that. Now about that drink and some excellent dinner."

But Darius knew in this world there really weren't any guarantees and the knowledge made him nauseous. He'd apparently become so arrogant that he thought he could get away with anything and people would bend to his will. He had to figure out what to do to stop this runaway train.

God damn it all anyway.

Chapter Thirteen

Sierra dressed carefully for dinner. She realized it was just casual, and she'd met all the men, as well as Peyton. But she also knew how important the approval of the women was, all of them, if she and Eagle were going to be a thing. And after this afternoon, she was pretty sure they were.

Every bit of her body still tingled from their activities in the hot tub. She'd never imagined being that uninhibited with anyone, but Eagle just seemed to melt all her barriers and reservations. It hardly seemed possible that four days ago she hadn't even met him.

While Eagle set up everything for the barbecue on the lower porch, she took her time dressing. Nothing fancy. Just jeans and a nice casual blouse. Sandals. She tried her hair in a ponytail but then decided to just clip it at the nape of her neck with a large barrette.

She had no idea why she was so nervous, except that this was a social event as well as business. Rocket had been meeting with Tom about the attorney situation and she was fidgety, waiting to hear what they had come up with.

She knew all the men except Tom, but of the women she'd only met Peyton. Who, by the way, was one of the nicest people she'd ever come into contact with. But that was before she realized this thing with Eagle was going to be something more than temporary. And in such a short time! It both excited and terrified her. Here was the sexiest man she'd ever met in her life who could probably have any woman he wanted, yet for whatever reason he'd chosen her. Would Peyton look at her differently? Judge her differently? Judge whether she fit into the group?

What are you, sixteen? Just be yourself and it will be fine.

As she was putting the finishing touches on a light application of makeup, she heard people arriving in the living area. She gave herself one last look in the mirror.

Okay, kiddo. Show them you can be part of this group. Family, actually. The bond between the four men was stronger than any she'd ever seen and her little contact with Peyton had told her it was the same with the women.

Taking a breath, she hurried down the hallway and into the kitchen, where everyone seemed to be gathered. Blaze, who she'd discovered was the de facto leader of the team, made her feel comfortable at once.

"And here she is now," he told everyone. "The woman of the hour. Eagle better be taking good care of you." He grinned.

"No complaints yet," she joked.

One of the women, with light brown chin-length hair and hazel eyes, turned from the counter and held out a hand.

"Hannah Modell. Welcome to insanity."

"The drone genius. Thanks for what you're doing."

"I actually have some video we can check out, believe it or not. I figured after dinner we'd see if there was anything important on it."

Sierra frowned. "After dinner?"

"Yes." She nodded. "And I'm happy to help. I haven't even sorted it out yet, so let's get some food in our stomachs."

"Good idea," Blaze said, "because I've got the photos from the security cameras at your house, too, Sierra. It seems you had a visitor this afternoon. Danny Tardello is running it through a sophisticated facial rec system as we speak, but so far no results. There wasn't a lot of the face to see, unfortunately. But he's putting together a video clip and some stills for you to look at."

"Then let's—"

"He's still putting it together," Blaze continued, "so after dinner we'll check it out. Take a deep breath, eat, have a glass of wine then we'll get to it. I know how anxious you are to do this, but we'll get it done, believe me."

"Thank you again. You have no idea how much I appreciate this."

"Oh, no, you don't get all the credit." A woman of medium height, with thick, glossy chestnut hair and dark green eyes elbowed Hannah. "Mallory Kane. My sister is the one who hooked you up with these guys."

"For which I am more grateful than I can tell you. But I can't figure out who left me her name and phone number and helped me make the connection."

"Let's just say she has her finger on a lot of pulses and was sufficiently outraged by what was happening to you and your brother to reach out. If you want more than that, you'll have to get it from her." She winked.

"But don't hold your breath. Anyway, we're all happy to welcome you to our little group. These are some special guys, and if Eagle chose you, you have to be a pretty special person."

Heat crept up Sierra's cheeks.

"Oh. Well. I mean…"

Peyton laughed. "Yeah, we've all been there. It's like you don't know what hit you then suddenly you're there." She gave Sierra a hug. "But trust me. It's a good place to be."

Blaze walked over to her and gave her a sideways squeeze. "It won't be too good if we don't get some food pretty soon."

"Just like a man." Hannah shook her head. "Always thinking of his stomach. Sierra, think you could finish chopping the veggies here?"

And just like that she felt at home and comfortable. Nobody asked her questions. Nobody treated her like a stranger. They just made her feel an important part of the Galaxy family. If she was with Eagle, that was good enough for them. When this was all over—and hopefully with a positive ending—she would ask Mallory Kane what she could do for her sister to show her huge appreciation.

Smiling to herself, she attacked the salad veggies.

Even with no one giving directions, the preparation of dinner was a well-coordinated event. In less than thirty minutes, they were all seated at the table and digging into the food. Sierra was surprised at how hungry she was. Eating had not been a priority for her for weeks except to keep up her strength.

She could feel the warmth from Eagle's body as he sat next to her and again the scenes from the hot tub flashed in her brain. And it wasn't just the sex, which astonished her. There was a connection between them she'd never had with anyone else. The speed with which it happened shocked her, but it was so unexpectedly strong there was no way she was letting it go.

Rocket walked in from the living room, stashing his phone in his pocket.

"Tom will be here after dinner," he told them. "He had some business to get out of the way first, but he says he'll definitely be here."

Like a well-trained team, once dinner was over the dishes were cleared, everything was cleaned up and everyone was back at the table with mugs of coffee. She'd seen beer in the refrigerator but when she asked Hannah if they should serve it to the guys, the other woman shook her head.

"After we take care of business tonight. Just because these guys aren't active duty any more doesn't mean they aren't still SEALs. They go after this stuff just like any mission they've been on."

And once they began, Sierra could see what she meant. First Hannah took her laptop into the kitchen and set it up on the breakfast bar.

"Let's see if the video that surveillance camera fed to my system caught any license plates," she told them. "You all go on with the pictures Blaze has, and I'll bring this over once I've checked it out."

As soon as the laptops were open, Blaze rapidly clicked a few keys. In a moment he had four photos up on his screen and he handed out copies of photos around the table. But studying them, either on the computer or in hard copy, did no good. The man's face was mostly hidden by the ball cap he wore, and he never looked directly at where the cameras were.

"Almost as if he knew," Mallory said.

"But if he knew there might be cameras there," Peyton said, "why did he even go over there?"

"A good question." Sierra looked around the table. "But just as screwy as the rest of this whole situation."

"I have videos from the side exit of The Library," Hannah called, carrying in her laptop. "I clipped certain frames that had discernible license plates. The way the cars pull in most of the plate is obscured by the decorative fencing and the shrubbery, but at least we have a starting place."

"Thanks for the effort." Viper hugged Hannah and kissed her forehead. "We all really appreciate it."

Hannah set her laptop in the middle of the table so everyone could gather on one side to watch, but they had to agree with her. The Library was designed and maintained to give everyone maximum privacy. They had to hope that the next video would be more useful. They had gone through about a minute's worth of frames when there was a knock at the back door.

"That's Tom." Rocket headed to answer it. "I'll let him in."

Tom Hernandez walked into the room and shook hands with everyone. He was as tall as the Galaxy men, with thick inky lashes and ebony-black eyes that could see right through her. She thought that was probably a good skill for an attorney to have. Yet, although she'd certainly seen her share of them in the past several months, none of them had the same skewering look. She was certainly glad he was on her side.

"Let's hear what Tom has to say," Viper suggested to Hannah. "We'll get back to these afterwards."

"Okay. No problem," she told him.

"Thanks for working on this." Eagle appeared grateful on Sierra's behalf for the attorney's involvement. "As Rocket told you, we're trying to get Sierra's brother out of a very sticky frameup."

"Yeah, no kidding. I read all the files, Sierra, and it's obvious someone's been working overtime on this."

"You have no idea how grateful I am," she told him.

"I've looked over all the information and the kindest thing I can say is you got a raw deal," he told her in a deep voice.

"Oh?" She swallowed, hard. "And what's the worst?"

"You got royally screwed and somewhere in there is the framework of a massive coverup of something someone needs to have in place."

Breath whooshed from her. At last! A legal brain who believed the same thing she did.

Thank you, Galaxy.

"So you don't think I'm nuts?"

He shook his head. "Not at all. And I have some points to discuss with you. Can we take a moment and go over this?"

When they were all seated again and everyone who wanted coffee had a full mug, Tom pulled out his cell phone and scrolled to the notes section.

"First of all," he began, "this took a lot of searches and made me glad we have some special software designed for our firm. It identifies key words and components that tie different files together."

"So it recognizes, for example, if, say, all the men have black hair?" Eagle asked.

"Only the best of them," Tom joked, running his hand over his own thick hair. "Seriously, it can pinpoint specific characteristics, activities, different things that define people if you're trying to group them together. You just electronically feed files on them into a program, and it segregates by certain characteristics. For attorneys, we can look for commonality in court cases or types of filings."

"That sounds like some program," Rocket commented. "Is it available commercially?"

Tom grinned. "There may be some like it, but this one my computer whiz designed. She's incredible. Anyway, as to what she found. The list of lawyers you provided, Sierra?"

"Yes?"

"All had one thing in common. Every one of them had some connection to The Library."

In the sudden silence, everyone shared a look.

"That's a pretty specific thing," Eagle finally said. "Is it illegal to get that kind of info?"

"Depends on how you get it." Tom shrugged. "Don't ask, and you can plead plausible deniability."

"But what kind of connection could it be?" Sierra finally asked. The information shocked her almost as much as the fact that Tom was able to get it. "These are all criminal attorneys. Right?"

"Yes." He nodded his agreement. "But that could be something as small as getting a traffic ticket dismissed or handling a case for a relative. Not all that stuff makes it to the media. And I think it all goes back to that fender bender your brother had. He never had any use for an attorney before."

"Which means," Rocket added, "it started with the first attorney who passed but recommended the next. That one also turned you down but suggested another and so on and so on. It's very obvious that someone was passing the word to stay away from this case. Someone with a lot of clout."

Sierra buried her face in her hands. She felt as if she were choking, trapped in a net not of her own making with no way out. Except, of course, now she had Galaxy.

"No wonder none of them would take the case," she said at last. "But that means each of them had to be suggested as possibilities and they were all given their marching orders. I can't believe all the time I wasted getting nowhere."

"Did you ever just do your own research and find an attorney not recommended?" Tom asked.

"Of course. But each one I called asked who had handled the case before so they could try and get notes. Whatever information they got wasn't good, because they turned me down, also."

"Because someone with immense power was pulling the strings."

"God." She rubbed her forehead, pressing against the edge of a headache. "No wonder I couldn't get anywhere."

"But that's come to a stop," Eagle reminded her, "now that we have this information. Tom, what else?"

"With your permission, Sierra, I'm going to contact an old friend of mine from law school. We keep in touch socially and fortunately in this situation he's a top-notch, nationally known criminal attorney who itches to take cases like this."

"But he must be incredibly expensive." Her stomach knotted as she wondered where she'd get the money. There wasn't a lot left of her dwindling resources. "And what about your fee? I mean, I'll do anything to get Jeremy freed, but I need to know what kind of dollars we're talking about here. What amount I should expect the bill to be."

From everything she'd learned about him, he had to be very expensive.

"There won't be one," he told her

She stared at him. "I don't understand. I don't want to be a charity case and I don't want Galaxy to absorb your fee. It's bad enough they aren't charging me anything."

Hernandez laughed. "One of the benefits of being disgustingly rich." Then he winked and pointed to Eagle and his partners. "I meant them, of course." Then he sobered. "But it does give us flexibility, especially when we feel someone has been thoroughly screwed over the way you have. Let's just get this done then we'll worry about any charges."

"And your friend?"

"Well, see, there's where you're in luck." He smiled. "He absolutely is death on attorneys who did what was done to you. The opportunity to destroy them and remove them from the practice of law is all he wants. Believe me, he's not hurting for money."

Her eyes widened. "He's not charging me anything, either? Where do you guys all come from?"

"Places where we don't like to see people taken advantage of," Eagle told her. He put his arm around her and gave her a gentle squeeze.

"What's his name?" Sierra asked.

"Myles Fairfax."

Sierra's jaw nearly dropped. "Are you kidding me? I think the entire *world* knows who he is. He's the top criminal law attorney in the country. Every major personality and corporation runs for him when they have even the tiniest bit of trouble in that area."

Tom chuckled. "True, but he is scrupulous about who he takes on as clients. He has to be convinced of their innocence. Which is probably why they usually never get convicted."

"Yes. An article I once read about him was very definite about that. My god. You know him personally?"

Tom nodded. "I even dated his sister Rebecca for a while, but we decided we were better as friends than lovers. So I'm going to reach out to him. He'll set up a meeting with Jeremy and we'll go from there."

"I can't believe this." She shook her head. "Two days ago, I would have thought this was all hopeless."

"We're getting it done, darlin'." Eagle squeezed her hand. "We're moving in the right direction."

Thank god.

Although she knew who Myles Fairfax was, his willingness to look into Jeremy's case stunned her. Tom had brought information on Fairfax, even though he was one of the most sought-after defense attorneys.

"He knows the warden and he's going to ask the man to have Jeremy call you first thing in the morning. As you know, he'll call collect so be ready to accept the call. Once that's done, Myles will also arrange the meeting and take it from there."

"I'd like to meet him, too, if possible," Sierra said.

"Of course." Tom nodded. "Actually, guys, if you could have Saint pick him up first thing in the morning and fly him here, that would be great."

"Text me all his information," Blaze said. "Then I'll call Saint and after I make the arrangements, you can send them on to Fairfax. One of us will pick him up in the morning. And I have a suggestion about where to take him."

Viper lifted an eyebrow. "And where would that be?"

"He usually has a suite he works out of at a small but expensive hotel. However, considering how intent these people are on contacting Sierra, or getting rid of her, just in case he catches someone's eyes, I think we should put him up at your place, Viper. Easier to protect."

"You think he'll be good with it?" Rocket asked.

"I wouldn't suggest it otherwise."

"I've got his info now, so let me call Saint." Blaze stepped away from the table to make his call.

"Ask him how early he can make the pickup," Tom called after him. "Myles said he'd be ready very early."

Blaze waved a hand in acknowledgment.

"Sure. Then I'd like to discuss Myles with all of you and give you more background on how he operates."

"I just hope you know how much I appreciate this." Sierra wanted to make sure he was aware of that.

"I do."

"We're all set." Blaze walked back into the room and took his seat again. "Tom, I texted you the info to send along to Fairfax. And cc'd everyone on it. You'll pick him up at the hangar and bring him to Viper's, and again, I think everyone should be at this meeting. Agreed?"

"Yes." Tom nodded. "I'd thought about taking him to breakfast, but I don't want to draw attention to us, so meeting here works the best. I'll pick up breakfast goodies on the way to get him."

Sierra could hardly believe this was all happening so quickly.

"Why is he even doing this?" she asked Tom. "Are the two of you such good friends? I mean, this is a really big deal."

"I think I'll let him tell you."

Hannah, meanwhile, had been busy moving her laptop and hooking it up to Eagle's big television set. That way everyone had a good view of the screen.

"We're all set here," she told them when she was ready. "Grab a seat or whatever so you can see the video. Here we go."

The thing Sierra realized as the first shots popped up on the screen was how much the iron fencing and shrubbery camouflaged the cars as they drove in. She explained there hadn't been trees at the corner where the entrance to the drive was to hide a camera, so the best they could hope for was shot as each vehicle was parked by an attendant. But there was a lot of shrubbery and trees on the path they drove so the best they got was glimpses of the license plates.

"Damn shrubbery makes the plates difficult to see," Rocket pointed out. "The best thing we can do is write down whatever we can see of each plate then get Tom to run them through the Department of Motor Vehicles database. We'll get way more than we need but maybe we can narrow the list down."

"Another thing we have to figure out." This from Blaze. "Who in hell is a member of The Library who has this much power? I mean, he controlled every attorney Sierra went to see. It's evident now he controlled the elements of the trial. And he made the victim virtually anonymous."

"We can do it," Tom assured them. "It will just take some effort on our part. And I know you're not keen on taking Sierra out of here until we catch this bastard."

"You're right."

"Can you tell us any more about your connection to Myles?" Peyton coaxed.

"We've been friends for years," Tom said, "since we were kids growing up next door to each other. He has his own reason for taking on cases like this. I'm going to let him tell you what it is because I think it's more effective coming from him."

"Sounds good," Blaze agreed. "In that case, I think we're ready to call it a night."

Right after Tom left, the others gathered their things to leave, also. Each of the women exchanged cell numbers with Sierra.

"Call any time," Peyton told her. "Whenever. If you need to talk or bitch or whatever. We've all been here, Sierra, and we'll do anything we can to help."

The others all said the same thing. She was honored at how easily these women had accepted her into their group.

"If Eagle chose you," Hannah told her, "you have to be pretty special. We're the ones who're honored."

By the time everyone left Sierra was exhausted, both mentally and physically. One of the last things she'd ever expected was to be caught in a trap as complex and extensive as this one. If only she could wave a magic wand and make the whole thing go away.

But then I never would have met Eagle.

After they were all gone, Eagle locked up the house and checked the security system. Then he held out his hand to Sierra.

"Big day, darlin'."

"You haven't the faintest idea how grateful I am for all of this. For every one of you. And for those wonderful women who act like I'm part of the family."

"You are," he told her. "The Galaxy family. We take good care of our own. Now, how about coming to bed? We have a big day tomorrow. I could tell you're all wound up about it and I think I have a way to relax you."

And just like that, the stress began to roll away and the pulse in her pussy started to flutter.

Chapter Fourteen

"We seem to spend a lot of time in my den," Darius commented as he poured drinks for both of them.

"We could always move to the living room," Neil joked. "There's no one in the house to disturb us."

"That's true, but I feel more secure in this room. I just wish the things I needed to feel secure about now didn't involve my life coming apart at the seams."

"It hasn't come apart yet," Neil pointed out.

"No, but my intuition, which I've learned to respect, tells me that until we find out who these guys are and where Sierra Hunt is and eliminate all of them, it's right on the verge."

"Eliminate?" Neil's eyebrows hiked to his hairline. "You can't be serious. Isn't one dead body enough for you? Look at what's happened because of it."

Darius glared at him. "If you had been the one in the car with a dead person, you'd be doing the same thing."

"I never would have been in that spot." He shook his head. "I'm not criticizing your lifestyle. There is nothing wrong with BDSM when it's performed properly and with all the safeguards. Didn't I go with you to that club in Thailand? And the one in Brazil?"

"Yes." Darius raked his hand through his hair. "Yes, you did. But—"

"But arguing over it isn't going to fix it. From now on, stay away from erotic asphyxiation. Even experts are very careful with it. We need to get these people off our tail so we can go back to burying the whole incident. But we can't do that until we find out who they are and know what we're dealing with. Please, god, the CCTV videos will tell us something."

"I have an idea." Darius rubbed his jaw. "I know you'll tell me I'm crazy, but I think we're at the point where crazy is probably the only thing that will work. And don't have a fit until you hear me out."

"Okay. Okay." Neil refilled his coffee cup then sat back down in his chair.

"We need something to flush them out, right? Something that will bring them out of wherever they are?"

Neil nodded. "And we can do this how?"

"We don't know where they live," Darius reminded him, "but we do know where they keep their plane because we were following Sierra Hunt. So what if we created a crisis on that property? Don't you think that would bring them out?"

Neil stared at him. "What kind of crazy idea have you come up with now?"

"We can't get onto the property," Darius agreed, "but what if we shoot a Molotov cocktail over the fence onto it? They'll have to call the fire department, plus the mystery men will want to check the damage for themselves. Then we'll follow them."

He forced himself to wait patiently while Neil, staring at him as if he'd lost his mind, processed what he'd said.

"You've done some crazy things," Neil told him, "but this is nuts. Set fire to someone's property? That's really out there."

"We won't be anywhere near it. We'll get the right people to be watching. These guys are sure to show up."

"And tell me this. What will be different this time?" Neil asked. "The license plates will still come back with some shell company's name. Following these men won't be any easier than it already has been because they obviously know evasive tactics. Because…"

"Because what?"

Neil held up a hand. "I'm reaching out to Sprague. Nobody's trickier than he is. He ran some of the blackest of black operations. Nobody can fool him."

Darius knew that Sprague could do anything and had served them well before. He had to be the right choice for this.

"I don't know. This is too far out there. So many things can go wrong. How about we get him to set up surveillance? There's a couple of places with a view of that property where someone can make themselves invisible. And nobody's better at following someone than he is. We should have used him to begin with."

"Who the fuck knew these guys would be like ghosts? Like a black ops team? Who knew the sister would even know people like that?"

"But we can fix that now, right?" Darius wanted to know. "I sure as fucking hell hope you're right because I don't like the way this is going. Go ahead. Have Sprague put the whole operation together and we'll—"

Neil's cell phone rang, interrupting them and making his forehead crease in annoyance.

"It's my guy at Raiford. I sure as fuck hope nothing's wrong up there." He punched the answer button. "What?" He listened for a moment, then anger and something else flashed over his face. "And you're just telling me now? Well, maybe you should stop taking days off, for the money we're paying you. Uh-huh. Uh-huh. Damn it all to fucking hell, anyway. Okay, call me if you get anything else."

He punched off the phone and for a moment looked like he was going to throw it across the room.

"What now?" Darius was getting a bad feeling about this.

"Well, more bad news. Our guy at Raiford had his day off yesterday, so first of all the news is twenty-four hours old, and second, he wasn't there to get a look at the people. So he got it all second-hand."

"Got what?" Darius snapped.

"Jeremy Hunt's sister paid him a visit yesterday."

"What?" Darius leaned forward in his chair. "She came out of wherever she's been hiding? But family is only allowed in the weekends."

"Well, someone got her special dispensation," Neil pointed out.

"What the hell was so important that she arranged this? Or got someone to arrange it for her."

"You aren't going to like this. My guy says she brought a new attorney with her and another guy. And they both looked like they could destroy a country singlehandedly. They had *don't mess with me* all over their faces."

Darius felt a thread of fear wriggle through him.

"They have to be part of this group she's hooked up with. Where did they get an attorney like that, if that's what he is? And how the hell does your contact even know all this?"

Neil shrugged. "Prison gossip. Apparently not many people have gone through as many attorneys as Hunt has without any success. Guys who have been in there for some time are always looking for someone new to help them, but Hunt's not giving out any names. All he'd say was his sister told him these people were going to get him out, and he believes her."

"Who the fuck could it be?" Darius ran his hands through his hair. "Shit, Neil. We have to fix this. I mean, *god*. We can buy and sell small countries, yet we can't fix this mess? And who are these people who can get her an attorney that can turn the whole thing upside down? I thought we had it all fixed."

Neil just shook his head.

"We like to think of ourselves as two very powerful people, probably you even more than me. You head an international conglomerate, can fund any world organization and know enough personal secrets to blackmail half the universe." Neil raked his fingers through his hair, a sign of his frustration. "How is it we can't get a handle on who these people are and find out why, for the love of god, they even care about what happens to Sierra Hunt?"

"I don't like doing this," Neil told him, "but I'm calling Sprague and getting this thing started. Just don't lose your shit now. We'll get this taken care of."

"I hear you." Darius studied the other man. "Listen. We've been friends for a very long time. Decades. We've weathered a lot together. Right?"

Neil nodded. "Yes, we have. Since college. You've made me a very rich man with a great deal of my own power. I am not going to let you down."

"I'm taking you at your word. I want those fuckers flushed out and eliminated. As for Sierra Hunt, I want her to disappear forever."

"I'm on it. We'll get it done."

Chapter Fifteen

Eagle went through his nightly routine of checking every lock and every sensor connected to the security system. He felt encouraged that they were getting closer to identifying the person or persons behind this whole debacle. He was really glad that Tom had chosen to take an active part in this. Tom had his fingers in just about every pie in the pastry shop, plus he had access to things Galaxy did not. Databases. Files. Information most people didn't even know existed.

Sierra had gone down the hall to the bedrooms a few minutes earlier, and as he entered the master suite, he heard the water running in the bathroom. Thinking of her with her naked body slick with water, droplets clinging to her sweet nipples and the trimmed thatch of hair neatly covering her mound made his dick suddenly spring painfully to life. Showering with her had become one of his favorite things to do and they'd only known each other for a couple of days.

A couple of days?

Shit, it felt like they'd known each other for years and they'd hardly even talked about their backgrounds or families. The Galaxy women had welcomed her at once and watching her bond with them had given him a really great feeling. He'd ask how it was possible to feel the way he did after two days — well, three, if he counted New Orleans — but the same thing had happened to each of his partners.

As he passed the bathroom, he saw the door was open and through the fog on the shower door, he could see the image of Sierra's wet, naked body. Would she think he was just a lech if he wanted sex with her again? Shower sex? Any kind of sex? How would she react if he added some of the elements of BDSM into this? Maybe tonight he could distract her even more with the pleasures of spanking and see how she reacted. Just the thought of his hand reddening her ass made his balls ache.

Five years had passed since he was first introduced to the pleasures of BDSM. He'd been on a night out with other members of his platoon. Two of them had guest passes to a local private dungeon and wangled them for others who wanted to visit.

At first he'd just watched, out of curiosity, trying to decide if this was for him. The more he'd watched, however, the harder and more excited his dick became. He was pretty sure he wasn't someone who could immerse himself in the lifestyle, but enough elements interested and aroused him that he wanted to incorporate them into his personal life. Finally, when the dungeon master had quietly asked if he'd like a session with an experienced Mistress who could give him a basic introduction, he hadn't been able to resist.

Holy fuck!

A whole new world had opened up to him.

He'd always enjoyed all kinds of sex, but that had taken things to a whole new level. He'd done a search for Top dungeons, which were not always that easy to find. But from then on, whenever his team was home, or someplace for more than two minutes, he did his best to score an invite to one of them. He always asked for a session with an experienced Mistress, intent on learning everything he could before introducing it to his life outside of the clubs.

One thing he'd needed to be specific on. He wanted the elements to spice up his sex life but did not see himself living the lifestyle. She'd assured him there were thousands of people in that category and had praised him for wanting to get it all correct, even if it was just for play.

By now he knew exactly what he liked and what he didn't, what kind of spice he enjoyed in his sex life. He didn't have to live the BDSM lifestyle to get pleasure from parts of it. He'd tested some of what he'd learned in his playtime with a few of the women he dated. He knew which things aroused him to a high level and which ones didn't. And which ones gave pleasure to women. He was very careful about choosing which women he experimented with. And he especially liked being able to control their pleasure.

But he'd always felt that, despite a great sex life, there was something missing. The last thing he'd been looking for was something permanent, but now he realized it was because the right woman had not come along, like it had for his partners. Maybe it was all coming together now that he had Sierra in his life. His desire for her was on a whole different level than it had ever been with any other woman.

Maybe.

Remember, this isn't a date. It's much more. I can feel it and I don't want to fuck it up. Please don't let me fuck it up.

He stripped off his clothes and stepped into the shower with her.

"I wondered if you'd be joining me."

He noticed that while she attempted to be nonchalant, there was a tiny note of uncertainty in her voice. Well, he had to figure out how to get rid of that and fast.

Turning her to face him, he cradled her face in his hands.

"I always want to be with you, in the shower and out of it. If neither of us had other obligations, I'd want to be with you twenty-four seven. Once again, it might have happened fast, but I'm all in, Sierra. And that's no load of bull. So put that at the top of your list of things not to worry about."

She studied his eyes for a long moment, then nodded.

"Okay. I'll do my best, but—" She nibbled her lower lip. "But I feel like I've had to keep such a tight control on myself for so long. Now that it looks like we might be turning the corner, I'm so worried this might not work. Do you think you could do wild things to my body so I can shove everything to the back of my brain? At least for tonight?"

Could I? Holy shit! Talk about opening a door.

"Darlin', I promise tonight I can make you forget everything. All you have to do is close your eyes and feel. Can you do that for me?"

"I can." She whispered the words.

"Good." He nipped her lower lip then soothed it with his tongue. "Because I'm going to fuck you until all you can think about is my mouth, my hands, my cock."

Another shiver skittered over her, as the water continued to pour over them in a light rain shower fall.

He took her nipples between thumbs and forefingers and rolled them, squeezing then pinching, then pinching them hard.

"Ohhh." She threw her head back.

"Too much?" he asked, testing her limits.

"No. No, it's good. Really good."

He eased back on the pressure, then squeezed again, this time pulling on the nipple, also. Still holding those swollen buds, he covered her mouth with his, thrusting his tongue deep inside. She hummed with pleasure as his tongue danced with hers, and he felt it to the soles of his feet.

Lifting his mouth, he cupped her breasts and kneaded them, loving the lush weight in his hands. Every so often, just to test her, he'd pinch her nipples, very hard, then back off at once. At first, she gasped as she'd done before, but then as he did it fiercer and faster, she moaned and tried to push her breasts more into his touch.

He laughed, low in his throat. The water was starting to cool, and they needed to get out of there soon, but he had one thing he wanted to do before that.

"Do you remember when I said I'd love to spank you?"

She nodded, eyes closed, the pulse beat at her throat accelerating.

Excitement coursed through him, and his balls ached as if caught in a vise.

"Let's pretend you've been a bad girl, and I have to punish you. I'll give you a little taste, and you can tell me if you like it."

Please like it.

He turned her so she was facing the shower wall, rearranging her arms so she leaned against them.

"Bad girl," he whispered. "I think you've been very bad."

Then flattening out his hand, he brought his palm down on one sweet ass cheek.

Smack!

She made a little mewling sound as her body jerked, but she didn't tell him to stop.

Thank fuck!

He did it again, this time on the other cheek, with the same results.

Fuck! He was getting so turned on he might just come before he even got them dried off.

He put his mouth close to her ear.

"When I get you out of this shower, I'm going to blindfold you so all you can concentrate on is what's in your head and what I'm doing to your body. I'm going to tie your hands so you can't grab mine or push me away. I'm going to spank that sweet ass until it is a beautiful shade of red. Then I'm going to fuck you, pounding into you until you scream the house down when you come. Think you'll like that?"

She shivered and nodded.

"Say, 'yes, Sir'," he whispered, his voice teasing.

He'd never brought that up with another woman because it hadn't mattered. And again, he didn't want the kind of definition in their relationship, but the use of it in intimacy was an extra thrill. Would she give him a hard time about the title? Then, beneath his touch, he felt her shiver. It must have been a good sensation, because she didn't try to pull away from him.

"Yes, Sir."

"And I'm in control. Right?"

Until he wanted to give it to her, which also appealed to him.

Again, she nodded.

"If it gets too intense, say yellow and I'll slow down. Red, and I immediately stop."

Her gulp was audible, but she moved impatiently, restlessly against him.

The feeling surpassed anything he'd ever know. This wasn't just hot sex, or even hot sex with BDSM elements. This was anticipation and pleasure and connection like he'd never experienced. He couldn't wait to give her commands.

In seconds he had the water off and both of them out of the shower and dried. Only slightly nervous, he carried her into the bedroom, ripped back the covers and placed her facedown on the bed, but with her feet on the floor. He took a moment to place a string of soft kisses down the length of her spine and one on each tempting ass cheek. She wriggled a little and a tiny moan drifted from her lips, but she didn't try to pull away.

Good. Very good.

He took the two scarves he'd used before from the drawer where he kept them and used the first to blindfold her.

"You liked this," he reminded her. "Remember?"

"Mm-hmm?"

"Still good?" He waited for her answer.

"Yes."

He saw her lips curve in a smile and had to tell his dick to take a break.

Next, he brought her hands behind her to the base of her spine and tied them with the other scarf. He waited to see if she objected to having them restrained behind her instead of in front but again, he got that little hum of satisfaction. And she actually wiggled her butt at him.

He decided to see just how ready she was for him with practically no foreplay

He drew in a deep breath, held it for a moment, then let it out slowly. Sliding one hand up the inside of her thighs, he reached her pussy and stroked it with the tips of his fingers. And she was already wet.

Holy sweet Jesus!

When he slid just the tips of those fingers inside her, she hummed with pleasure and tried to push back against them.

He laughed and pulled his hand back. "Not yet."

He debated about taking the paddle he liked from the drawer but decided to work his way up to it. He'd get her used to his hand, first.

At the first smack, she hitched a little, a normal reaction. He smoothed the warmed spot and smacked again, on the other cheek. The he fell into a slow rhythm, one side then the other.

At first Sierra just lay there, cocooned in her darkness, obviously enjoying the slide of heat over her body, just twitching slightly each time his palm made contact with her skin. But when he stopped for a moment, she wriggled her hips, which he took as silent encouragement. When he touched the lips of her pussy again, he found them even wetter than before and when he slid two fingers into her, she clamped hard on them with her inner muscles.

Holy shit!

He resumed the spanking, keeping a steady rhythm, encouraged by the sexy little sounds she was making. Of course by now his cock was so hard he was sure he could pound nails with it, but he forced himself not to rush it. One of the first lessons he'd learned from his Mistresses was to keep things slow and steady in the beginning. Build up the sensations and reactions, especially for someone new to it. The intensity and desire would steadily build.

"*The idea*," one of his Mistresses had told him, "*is to make the sub beg for more*."

Well, damn, he hoped that was what he was doing with Sierra.

The cheeks of her ass had turned a pretty shade of red, and she kept clenching the muscles. When he slid his hands between her thighs again, he found her cunt dripping wet, even more than before.

Eagle inhaled a steadying breath and let it out slowly. He gave each ass cheek a tiny pinch then lifted Sierra and positioned her on her hands and knees. He carefully placed pillows beneath her chest, piled in a way she could rest her cheek, also, and made sure she was propped in a kneeling pose, bent at the waist. Then he nudged her thighs apart, exposing her pussy to his exploration.

Fuck, that looks sweet!

He moved to stand behind her so that he could see every inch of her, the wet pink flesh of her cunt making his mouth water. He stroked his palms over her ass, down her legs and up the inside of her thighs, reaching to tease her clit with two fingers.

"Oh! Oh! Oh!"

She rocked on her knees, pushing herself back against him. He continued to tease her cunt with one hand while he resumed the spankings with the other. He kept it up, warmed by her response, the tiny little sounds she was making, the flutter in her inner walls.

Sierra rocked harder, now begging him for more.

"Please," she cried. "Please, please, please."

He moved to the side so he could lean over her and place kisses along her spine.

"Please what, darlin'?"

"Please…anything. More. Just more."

"Tell me what you want. My cock inside you?"

"Yes, yes, yes, yes."

He was at that point himself, in fact, almost past it. He grabbed a condom from the nightstand and rolled it on with hands he suddenly realized were shaking. Moving her so she was at the edge of the bed, he gripped his shaft and slowly eased it into her hot, wet, welcoming cunt.

Oh, god!

He'd died and gone to heaven. It seemed every time he was inside her, it just got better and better. He gave each cheek one last smack, let out his breath and began the ride of his life. In and out, his dick hugged by her inner walls, her little sounds continuing to drive him crazy.

He reached a point where he had almost tipped over the edge.

"Get ready, darlin'."

He pounded into her harder, the clench of her muscles around his dick growing stronger and stronger. When he was about to detonate, he reached beneath her to find her clit and rubbed and pulled it hard.

She exploded and he was right there with her. The orgasm was like nothing else he'd ever experienced, intense and draining. He held on to her hips for dear life while the last pulses throbbed in his dick and his heart rate returned to something close to normal. He finally eased his cock from her tight hold and disposed of the condom. Then he removed the scarf binding her wrists, tossed it to the side and eased her down to her stomach. Last came the blindfold.

He brushed her hair back behind her ear and kissed her cheek.

"Don't move," he told her, although she looked like moving was the last thing on her mind.

He had a bottle of special lotion he kept in the bathroom with his 'just in case' items. A Mistress had told him it was great to soothe the skin. Lifting Sierra, he carried her into the shower, which seemed to be getting a lot of use these days, and held her under the stream of warm water.

When he was finished, he dried her with a towel from the warm towel rail, carried her back to bed and stretched her out on her stomach. Then he poured some of the lotion into his hand, letting his palm warm it before applying it to the reddened skin of her ass. He massaged it gently, lightly, until the reddened areas were completely covered.

By the time he'd finished, she was almost asleep. Certainly fully relaxed, which was what he wanted. He climbed into bed next to her and spooned her, pulling her back against his body. He didn't know what gods of good fortune had brought her into his life, but he gave silent thanks to them.

"Did you enjoy that?" he asked.

She was silent for a moment, enough to make him think he'd somehow fucked up. But then she spoke again.

"Yes, Sir."

"Excellent. Time to fall asleep."

He hoped Myles Fairfax was the answer to her brother's problem and they could free him from this nightmare. After that, he was going to talk to her about the life he wanted them to share. Smiling, he closed his eyes and drifted off to sleep.

Chapter Sixteen

Sierra had not expected to sleep well the night before. Even when Eagle had joined her in the shower, she wasn't sure shower sex would take the edge off enough. She'd certainly had no idea what Eagle had in mind for her.

None of the men she'd ever been with had had any interest in any kind of BDSM play, at least not that they'd ever let on to her. And she wasn't sure that she'd have been into it with any of them. But with Eagle, somehow it seemed so natural. No, not just natural but enticing. Exciting. Arousing. And many more words.

She had slept better than in a very long time. Since before the crisis with Jeremy.

And now, as she slowly opened her eyes, she felt a lassitude in her body that was totally unfamiliar. She didn't ever remember being this relaxed in her entire life.

The feel of Eagle's warm, hard body curled against her was certainly a factor. He spooned her, one arm around her with his hand cradling a breast. His cock nudged at the cleft of her ass, and she wondered if this man was perpetually hard. Just the feel of him wedged against her made her inner walls quiver with desire for the feel of him.

"You awake?"

The warmth of his breath stirred against her neck.

"Reluctantly," she told him.

He kissed his way down her neck to her shoulder. "You sure taste good in the morning. Wish I could taste you all over right now."

"Mmm. Me, too." Then it all came back to her, and she sat up so fact she nearly bumped Eagle with her elbow. "Ohmigod, I am so sorry."

He laughed, that low warm sound that singed her nerves.

"No problem. I'd say you have to kiss it all better, but we need to get up and about."

At that moment his cell phone rang, and the present came running at her.

"Morning," Eagle said into his cell. "Blaze? Where we at? Uh-huh. Uh-huh. Good. Okay. We'll be ready."

He disconnected the call and rolled over to face Sierra.

"What did Blaze have to say?" she asked.

"Saint is on his way back with Myles Fairfax. They should land in an hour, and he'll bring him directly to Blaze's house."

"Not here?" She frowned. "I thought the whole thing was to keep me hidden, but I'll be out in the open when we drive there."

"It still is. But we'll camouflage you for the ride and go from my garage to Viper's. He has a full guest suite, which gives Fairfax a private place to work." He cupped her chin and turned her head so she was looking directly into his eyes. "I promise you, nothing is going to happen to you. You have my word on it. And the word of Galaxy. Do you believe me?"

She blew out a breath. "I do. If I trust anyone it's you. It's just…if these people could construct the complicated frame against Jeremy that they did, and cut the gas line in my car, I just think they could do anything."

"We're one step ahead of them now. Well, as much as I'd love to start my day by worshiping your body, I think we need to hold off until tonight." He winked. "But it will be hard on my part."

She giggled. Actually giggled. "*Hard* does really describe it, right?"

He gave her ass a playful swap, but then in the next second his expression turned serious again and a questioning look appeared in his eyes.

"One more thing before we get up."

She frowned. "What would that be?"

"Last night. I want to be sure…I mean, not everyone is into what we did."

"You mean the spanking?"

He nodded. "Was that okay? The blindfold? All of it?"

She brushed his hair back from his forehead, even as a faint pink warmed her cheeks.

"Eagle, last night was the best sex of my life, and that's no lie. I've never been into that stuff before. Maybe it was just doing it with you, because I trusted you not to take anything too far. To always ask my approval." She smiled, her blush heating, and she whispered, "I can't wait to do it again."

"Then let's get up and see how fast we can clean up this mess so we can get back to it." He brushed a kiss over her lips then gave her ass a playful tap. "And just so you know, it was the best for me, too."

A feeling of warmth…and something else…surged through her. *Okay, then.*

Just as she swung her legs over the side of the bed, Eagle's cell phone rang again.

"It's Tom," he told her, looking at the screen. "Yeah, man. What's the latest? Uh-huh. Uh-huh. Yup. Got it. Thanks a lot for this. Really."

"What?" she asked when he disconnected.

"In fifteen minutes, you're going to get a call on your cell phone. Answer it. It's your brother. Now that Fairfax is on his way, you can tell Jeremy and also let him know to expect a visit tomorrow."

"I thought he was going to see him today?" she interrupted.

"He was, but Tom says he wants to spend a full day with us, making sure he's gotten every piece of information he can to flesh out the files and reports."

"Oh." She blew out a breath. "Okay."

"This is the number the call will come from, and it won't be collect."

"Where is it?"

"The warden's office at Raiford."

Suddenly her hands began to shake as she realized exactly how powerful these men were and that her brother might actually get out of prison.

"I can't believe this is really happening," she told Eagle.

"What did I tell you? For Galaxy, the sky is the limit. We can make anything happen. Let me get you some coffee."

She had just taken her first sip when her cell rang and there was the number on the screen. She hit the Answer button.

"H-Hello?"

"Is this Sierra Hunt?" The voice was unfamiliar.

"Yes, it is. Who am I speaking to?"

"The warden at Raiford. I have your brother here waiting to speak to you. I tell you, Miss Hunt, this is not our usual method of operation. You have some very powerful people on your side. I'm surprised." He paused. "And impressed. Here's your brother."

Myles Fairfax, she thought. *And Tom Hernandez. Galaxy is a powerhouse.*

"Sierra?" It was Jeremy's voice, and it was filled with a mixture of fear and hope.

"Yes, it's me. Are you okay?"

"I might be if I knew what was going on. Why am I in the warden's office? What's happening? Is something wrong? Although I don't know how much worse it could be. Those men who came to see me with you…are they going to help?"

She made her voice as calm as possible.

"Yes, and they already are. You're getting a visitor tomorrow. A man named Myles Fairfax, who—"

"Myles Fairfax?" he broke in. "Are you kidding me? I know who he is. Anyone who watches or reads the news knows who Myles Fairfax is. There are guys here who say if they'd had the money to hire him, they wouldn't be in here at all. Are you saying he's coming here? To see me? Are you sure? This isn't just some bad joke?"

"Yes, he is definitely coming to see you and he's going to represent you."

"I can't believe—" He stopped. "Oh, god, Sierra." His voice broke, and she knew he was taking a minute to compose himself. "But listen. I've heard this guy charges fees equal to the national debt. Who's paying for this?"

"It's a long story, which I'll tell you when you get out of there. Meanwhile, just tell Fairfax every single thing he wants to know. Answer all his questions. We're going to make this happen."

"I—oh, god, I—" He stopped. "Okay, the warden says I have to hang up now. They had to sneak me into his office so there wouldn't be gossip about it."

"I'll be talking to you soon," she promised and hung up.

She threw herself at Eagle and hugged him as hard as she could. Then she turned her brain to meeting Myles Fairfax.

Eagle reminded her that they were positive the people after her had not identified anyone from Galaxy yet, but he wasn't taking any chances. She pulled on the baseball cap she'd worn the other day, her hair concealed in a topknot. Then she put on one of Eagle's jackets, zipping it up to the top and finished off with an oversize pair of sunglasses.

When they reached Viper's place, she watched Eagle press a code into an electronic box in the gateway to the area. He did the same when they pulled up to a gorgeous house set on the water, surrounded by a fence. Then he texted Viper, the garage door rolled up, and they pulled into a three-car garage. As soon as they were inside, the door rolled down. The whole entrance process had taken less than two minutes. Again, Sierra was impressed.

"Lord. How many people live here?"

Eagle grinned. "Two. Viper and Hannah. But he likes his space."

"I guess."

It seemed everyone was in the kitchen, either filling mugs or helping themselves to pastries from the huge platters on the counter. The women were all here, too.

"We thought you could use a little more moral support," Peyton whispered. "Is it okay?"

Warmth surged through Sierra. She'd had a lot of different friends, a few for some time now, but she was astonished at how easily she'd connected with these women and how they'd instantly accepted her. One more thing to give silent thanks to Senator Alicia Kane for, as well as the person who'd hooked them up.

"More than okay." She impulsively hugged the other woman. "I am so grateful for all of you."

"We're just glad Eagle has found someone that deserves him. He's an incredible man."

"Yes, he is. But you don't know anything about me."

Mallory, who was just serving herself from one of the platters, chuckled.

"Oh, honey, the minute Eagle accepted you as a Galaxy client, all the guys did a deep info drive. Even though my sister recommended you, they leave nothing to chance."

The only stranger in the group was a man as tall as the others and just as lean and muscular. He wore a collared shirt and slacks along with hand-tooled loafers that she estimated cost her a week's pay. His dark hair was perfectly trimmed as was his close-cut beard and he looked freshly washed and fluffed. The best word she could find to describe his presence was powerful, which said a lot since the room was filled with men whose very aura spelled power.

This had to be Myles Fairfax.

"Thank you for doing this." She shook his hand, which was strong and firm. "Even if nothing works, you'll never know how much I appreciate this."

"Oh, it's going to work," he assured her. Warmth flickered in his eyes and a smile notched creases on either side of his mouth. "I never lose, and I don't intend to now. We'll get it done." He looked at Tom. "I think we should get started. I have a lot of questions to ask Miss Hunt."

"Sierra," she corrected. "Please."

He nodded. "Sierra it is. And let me make a suggestion. I had planned to meet with your brother this afternoon, but I want to make sure I'm fully prepared. I know you're the only one with personal contact with him, although Blaze and Eagle did go to see him to assess the situation."

"That's correct. Does that make a difference?"

"No." He shook his head. "But Tom gave me the feedback on this, and I want to be fully prepared before I meet with Jeremy. Let's take a minute while you fill me in from your point of view."

Fifteen minutes later Fairfax told her he was satisfied with what she had to tell, and they all took seats at the table. Fairfax opened the conversation.

"You all know why I'm here, but you don't know the reason behind it. Tom said under the circumstances you'd want to know, and I could trust you with the information. I don't exactly broadcast it."

Tom nodded. "I explained it would be a good idea."

"I grew up in a modest, middle-income family in a midwestern town. We lived in a great neighborhood and most of the families were either friends or good acquaintances."

He stopped to take a sip of his coffee.

"One of my best friends lived next door. We were friends starting in the third grade and were even planning to attend the same university. The night before we were leaving, he went out to pick up pizza and got into an accident. Now here's where it gets weird."

He paused, as if gathering his thoughts.

"The other car in the accident was driven by an obscenely rich and powerful man in the area. It was rumored that everyone who was anyone was in his pocket. The police report said the accident was my friend's fault, that he was drunk. But the weird thing was, he didn't drink. Couldn't. He was allergic to alcohol."

"But didn't that come out at the trial?" Sierra asked.

"No. In fact, the trial was so fast, and his attorney convinced him to take a plea deal because the evidence against him was so strong. We know now some of it was just swept under the rug." He looked around. "Not to mention the fact his parents were convinced the judge and the prosecutor had been paid off by the man with unlimited resources."

"I know the feeling," Sierra told him.

"I'm sure you do. Anyway, long story short, my friend went to prison and no other attorney would file an appeal. He spent ten years in jail until I graduated law school and passed the bar. I managed to get a job with a firm that took cases like this. Within a year, my friend was out of jail and a lot of other people were either in or on their way." He shook his head. "But it definitely took its toll on him, although he's doing a lot better now."

"What's he doing with his life?" Eagle asked.

"He studied law while he was in prison, and graduated and passed the bar after he was released. He works for a family law practice now." Myles grinned. "And he's married to my sister, Rebecca."

"Wow!" Sierra stared at him. "That sounds like a television movie."

"Some say it should be. Anyway, I vowed to do whatever I could to make sure that didn't happen to other people. I know I can't save the world, but I can try to save a little piece of it now and then. I know finances are worrying you, so let me assure you of this. I make more than enough money on my other cases to do these pro bono. So we're squared. Okay?"

She blew out a breath, still stunned by the story. She'd thought people like this only existed in books and on television shows. Now she realized why Tom had wanted the man to tell his story himself.

"Well, yes, of course. And I am most grateful." She managed a smile. "Both to you and your rich clients."

"Good. Then let's get to work. I asked Tom to have everyone participate. I know you aren't aware of the details of the crime, but you might have oblique knowledge of any of the attorneys involved. Plus, with all of us looking on the Internet we just might find a nugget or two."

"Good point," Tom agreed.

"But first, some questions and these are for you, Sierra. The woman who was killed. I don't find any background information on her. How did Jeremy meet her? Was he the type of man to cheat on his girlfriend?"

She drew a breath.

"Okay, in order. There was none. I even offered to hire an investigator to research her, but the attorney of the moment said the police had already done that. She supposedly was an office manager for a temp agency with no family or friends. No one knew how they met. And he would never, ever cheat on Cheryl. They were very much in love, and he was about to give her an engagement ring. I could tell no one believed me."

"After going over all the files, which by the way are way thinner than I would have expected, the absence of that information was a red flag."

"I kept trying to tell people that," she cried, "but every lawyer I spoke to, including the first idiot, said the police had done their job and basically it was what it was. Period. Accept the situation."

"That falls in line with what I've got." He pulled up a document on his laptop. "I put one of my best researchers on it as soon as I got off the phone with Tom. She can literally find the needle in the proverbial haystack. She said if Jeremy really was seeing this woman, he concealed it so well he could get a job with the CIA."

For the first time Sierra felt hope surging through her.

"So what does that mean?"

"It means someone with more money than god is pulling the strings. That's the only kind of person who could make this happen."

"So what can we do?"

"I'll keep my team on it, but I also have research work for everyone here." He looked around the table. "Tom assured me you were all in to doing what you could. So if you're ready, here's what I need."

Myles sent his file to each of them, they activated their existing ones and they were in business. Sierra was impressed at the methodical way Myles Fairfax went through each item and document, line by line.

He must have spent hours studying these, she thought, to have such detailed notes on everything. It gave her a strong feeling of reassurance that finally someone would be representing Jeremy who knew what the hell they were doing and who wasn't on someone else's payroll.

Lunch was delivered, and they ate as they worked. By late afternoon, Myles finally sat back in his chair and looked around.

"I've got what I need, at least for now. And I think I have people I can reach out to about membership at The Library."

"You can?" Sierra stared at him. "I thought that was more secret than the CIA."

"There's a way into everything," Myles assured her. "You just need a road map, and I think we may have one. I need to make some phone calls, if you'll all excuse me for a moment? After that we'll review what we went over today." He pushed away from the table. "Viper, I snuck a couple of bottles of Jameson's onto your bar. I think these good folks have earned a drink. Why don't you pour, and I'll be back in a few."

He picked up his laptop and headed toward the wing where the bedrooms were.

"Well." Tom leaned back in his chair. "I told you he'd shake things up."

"I'd like to know how he thinks he can get information on The Library's super-secret membership list." Sierra wanted to believe they could accomplish the impossible, but her brother's life was at stake if they failed. Part of her was afraid to hope.

"I've learned over the years never to ask how or why. Just accept it. Meanwhile, as he hinted, we've all earned a drink." Tom strode to the bar and twisted open the bottle to pour a round for everyone.

Chapter Seventeen

Darius had just stepped out of the shower when his cell phone rang.

"Fuck."

He'd chosen to stay the night at The Inn at The Library, the high class European-style bed-and-breakfast that was part of the facility. He didn't socialize, uninterested in seeing anyone, and had his meals sent to his suite. Even though his current disaster had begun here, it was the one place where he could be insulated from the world and where no one would disturb him.

Except by phone.

He saw that it was Neil and pressed the Accept button.

"Please tell me that you've located Sierra Hunt. Or at least learned who these people are she's hooked herself up with. Or at least gotten a copy of the CCTV video."

"Not so much on the first one," Neil told him. "We ran facial recog on the video but the only face that was identifiable is Sierra Hunt. These guys know how to stay invisible. The next one you're going to like even less. And worse than that, I have news that's going to completely ruin your day."

A combination of rage and fear cycled through him. If Neil said it was bad, it was more than bad. How the hell had this happened to him? He'd worked his ass off to reach the position of power he had, the control over other lives as well as his own. People feared him and respected him, although if he had to choose, he'd pick fear. Now one careless moment, one accidental slip, and his entire life was slowly disintegrating.

When he took the time to go over in his mind what had happened that night, he had to admit that using erotic asphyxiation might not have been the best ideas with Scarlet, or whatever her real name was. That was the first time he'd used it with her, and it produced such a fantastic orgasm that he had to do it again, Unfortunately, he misread her protests for drama rather than reality.

"Darius?" The voice shouted from the phone. "You there?"

Darius shook himself and put the phone to his ear.

"Sorry. I'm here. What's the big emergency?"

"Where are you? We need to get together. Now. And someplace private."

Not here, he thought. This was the one place he wanted to keep everything away from. The one place where his position of power was unquestioned.

"Meet me at my house in half an hour."

He disconnected before Neil could answer him.

Well, so much for a leisurely breakfast before he had to plunge back into the day. He couldn't begin to imagine what the hell kind of emergency this was that had Neil so wound up. He dressed quickly, pulling on the slacks and sweater he'd worn the night before. He had a feeling whatever Neil wanted to discuss wasn't a suit-and-tie kind of thing.

He called for his car to be brought around to the side entrance and headed down to the main floor. Fifteen minutes later, he pulled into his own driveway, where Neil already waited for him. When he pulled into the garage, Neil followed him, and they walked into the house together.

"Coffee?" he asked Neil. "I didn't even have time for breakfast."

"This will kill your appetite," Neil told him. "But coffee is a necessity."

They carried their filled mugs into the den. Darius stood at the window for a moment, allowing himself the pleasure of a long sip, before turning back to Neil.

"Okay, let's have it. What can be so bad?"

"We have a new visitor in town," Neil told him. "You don't know him, but you know who he is. I think everyone in the country does."

"Enough, already," Darius snapped. "Who the hell is it?"

"Myles Fairfax."

Darius choked on his coffee, spewing it all over his sweater and down onto the carpet. Grabbing his handkerchief from his pocket, he mopped himself as best he could before turning to his friend.

"What. The. Hell. *Myles Fairfax?* Big legal asshole Myles Fairfax?"

"Yeah, well…" Neil made a snorting sound. "You might want to amend that to big legal always wins asshole. Because he does."

"Who could he possibly be here to see? There's no big headline case going on right now in Tampa. No high-profile person in trouble. I didn't miss something, did I?"

"You're not going to like this one bit," Neil told him, "so brace yourself. He was flown in early this morning on the private jet that belongs to our mysterious friends."

"What?" Darius stared at him, every bit of saliva in his mouth drying up. "Are you crazy? How is that possible? And how do you even know this?"

"I sent Sprague out to the area of the hangar yesterday as soon as we finished our conversation. There's a spot where he can conceal himself to keep an eye on the place. I told him to take pictures of any activity and that's what he did. The plane left very early this morning, returning about two hours later. A man had driven onto the property and was waiting for them. Sprague had no idea who any of the people were, but he just sent along pictures of everything as I'd asked him to."

"And?" Darius was getting impatient.

"And Fairfax was picked up at the hangar by Tom Hernandez. You know who he is, right?"

"Hernandez." Darius frowned. "Big-shot attorney — although I have to point out not as big as me — who has a lot of clout in this town."

"Right. The one good thing that came out of this is I remember hearing a little nugget of news about him a few years ago."

"And what was that?" Darius raked his fingers through his hair. "Jesus, spit it out already."

"I only know this because I was having coffee with a friend of his, trying to get some information. Anyway, this guy likes to puff himself up, so he enjoyed telling me about a little secret he'd discovered. Bragged that he knew it, because he said it's hush-hush."

"For fuck's sake," Darlen exploded. "Will you tell me already?"

"He says Hernandez is very close friends with four men who are all former SEALs. They left the service, won the Powerball lottery and started their own private black ops business. You can't ask questions about them because people stop talking to you and you have to be recommended for them to take you on as a client. They don't even have an office."

"What—"

"Our guy had to pull some hidden strings to get this information and it's not good." Neil cleared his throat. "The plane is owned by a company called Galaxy. Four former SEALs who take jobs that are too tough for most security agencies. They do hostage rescue, high-level investigations, stuff like that. Their last mission was rescuing a woman from a drug cartel. Our guy is good. He dug deep and provided quite a bit of information on these guys, including the women in their lives."

"Shit." Darius jammed his cigar into the big ashtray.

"Yeah, no kidding." Neil refilled his coffee cup. "Apparently they also know twenty different ways to kill someone without leaving a trace."

"How did the Hunt woman get involved with them? We checked her out. She's not in a relationship with anyone that fits that profile, so how did she connect with them? And how is it that none of this turned up when you had her checked out?"

"Damn it, you asshole." A muscle in Neil's cheek twitched. "These men have gone to great lengths to bury who they are and what they do. I'm not sure even the FBI could have found out. But that changes everything here."

Darius stared at him. "What do you mean?"

"They have such a black ops rep that all their meetings with clients are held on that plane the Hunt woman took a trip on. Darius, that means she's a client of these guys, and they don't mess around."

"Neither do we. Did he say what kind of things they do?"

Neil blew out a breath. "You won't like this, either. I reached out to a couple of people who would know stuff like this before calling you. Remember the big scandal in the Kendrick law firm? Owen, the son, got in trouble gambling and one of the younger attorneys in the firm discovered it. Owen's life was about to fall apart, and his wife was in a panic. So she decided the answer was to kill the other attorney. She ran him down one night, along with his wife. He died, the wife was in a coma for weeks. She happens to be the sister of the woman now engaged to one of the SEALs."

"Shit."

"Uh-huh. They tore the city apart looking for answers," Darius said. "If you remember Owen, his wife and his father were all arrested. I also heard rumors that some kind of black ops group was behind the takedown of Lowden Tactical. Remember that drone that dumped its payload of explosives on a senator instead of a terrorist? They tried to blame it on the drone engineer, but this group blew that plot all to hell, if you'll pardon the metaphor. I'm pretty sure now it was them since the engineer is now engaged to another of the SEALs."

"Jesus. This just gets worse and worse." Darius was afraid he might throw up. "Is that all?"

As if that's not enough.

"One more little bedtime story. They also rescued the sister of Senator Alicia Kane from a drug cartel and destroyed the cartel while doing it. The sister is now with another of the SEALs."

Darius squeezed his cell so hard he was afraid the case would crack.

"Please tell me that's all."

"Almost. If that's who Sierra Hunt hooked up with, and if they're the connection to Fairfax, we have some huge problems here."

Darius suddenly felt very ill. If Myles Fairfax and his team were taking Jeremy Hunt's case, he was going to lose everything he had. *Everything.*

"We have to stop this," he told Neil. "Stop Fairfax. And get rid of that woman."

Neil's laugh held no humor. "Good luck with that. The man is a force of nature. Anyone who's ever taken him on regretted it for a long time. These men are not your average bears, my friend. They'll dig into everything, and I mean everything. We have to regroup on this."

"Okay." Darius began to pace, raking his fingers through his hair. "We need a plan. The first thing we need to do is verify if this is all true. And pay whoever to make sure this is what he's here for."

"That ought to be fairly easy," Neil told him. "But we also need to find out where these people have stashed the Hunt woman and where Fairfax is staying."

"My guess is not a hotel," Darius mused. "They'll want to keep everything under wraps. Remember, they don't know that we've been keeping an eye on things."

"You hope they don't," Neil said.

"There's no way they could. I believe that. So. Fairfax would want to set up shop someplace both convenient and sequestered."

"Yeah, so where would that be?"

"Don't know, but one person who knows should be easy to find."

Darius frowned. "Yeah? Who's that?"

"Tom Hernandez. He can't exactly hide, which means we can track him." Neil rubbed his forehead, obviously thinking. "Okay, let's get a tracker on Hernandez's car and also put a team on him. He's going to lead us to the others, but only if we're practically invisible. I'll get hold of Sprague and have him take care of it."

"Then what?" Darius asked. "You can bet Fairfax will be out at Raiford introducing himself to Jeremy Hunt and telling him he's his new attorney."

"And also putting his staff to work on the list of the attorneys who turned Hunt down to find reasons for their disbarment."

"Jesus Christ!"

Darius began pacing again. This was worse than anything he could have imagined. They were royally fucked. And no way could they just make Myles Fairfax disappear. The president himself would lead the hunt.

"So what do we do?" He looked at his friend. "This is a fucking mess."

He was grateful Neil chose not to point out that it was *his* mess and walk away from it.

"I need to think." Neil refilled his coffee mug and carried it to the window, where he stood looking out. "We obviously can't take down a bunch of SEALs."

"Obviously." Darius repeated the word, edged in sarcasm. "But we have a real crisis here. Myles Fairfax will dig into every nook and cranny and ferret out every tiny bit of information. If even the least little bit of this gets out, our worlds—yours and mine, as we know them—will collapse, and we'll be the ones in Raiford. We're smart. We should be able to figure a way out of this."

"And fast," Neil reminded him, "because with Fairfax in charge, things in Jeremy Hunt's case will move along at warp speed."

"The first thing is to get that tracker on Hernandez's car. Does Sprague know where he is now?"

"I do know that his offices are in downtown Tampa, although I heard he was one of the attorneys moving his office into one of the new waterfront buildings. I can have it checked out. I'll also have him sit people on the office and his condo. Wherever he is, he has to go to work or come home eventually."

Darius wanted to wring someone's neck. His entire life was falling apart before his eyes. And he couldn't seem to get a handle on it.

"Okay, but what if we don't find him until tomorrow?" he asked. "What if he's holed up someplace with Fairfax and the SEALs and Sierra Hunt?"

Neil set his mug down, took a deep breath and let it out slowly.

"Okay. Take a breath. Even if Fairfax goes to see Hunt tomorrow, it will still take time for him to go through the process of pulling his strings to file for an appeal. And he can't dig up dirt on all the other attorneys in one day."

Darius shook his head. "Don't be so sure. That man has a staff the size of a small army. He can find out anything about anybody. I'm telling you, this is heading for disaster."

"Fine. Then what we need to do now is cover our tracks. For one thing, there's no way for them to find where we disposed of that woman's body, so we can mark that off the list."

Darius nodded. "Yes. Good. I agree."

"But ask yourself this. Did you manage to choose someone who does not have friends who will look for her? Are looking for her now?"

Darius shrugged. "I thought so. I have my own version of Sprague, someone who does really dirty jobs for me. He's the one who found her for me, and he knew exactly what I needed."

"Let's hope so. All right. Look. Give me every bit of information you have about her, and I will have Sprague set someone to do a quiet search for info. He's expensive, but for this we need him to handle everything. There's no one better. The people he uses have cleaned up messes worse than this, and we're lucky we can afford it."

"I know you're right." Darius dropped into a chair and leaned forward, his head in his hands. He wasn't used to being in this position. He was always the one pulling the strings and pressuring others.

"Once we clean this up, my friend, we need to step very carefully until there's no longer a chance the spotlight will fall on us."

Darius swallowed the bitterness in his throat. "Agreed."

Neil pulled out his cell phone and spoke rapidly into it. When he hung up, he nodded. "He's waiting to hear back from me. Are we a go on this?"

"We have to be," Darius told him. "We have to figure out how to make sure there is no evidence of anything for them to find. No body. No witnesses. No nothing."

"Maybe," Neil pointed out, "the best thing is just to let him get a new trial date for Jeremy Hunt and let him be acquitted."

"And what if in the process Fairfax uncovers the whole thing? Or if Hunt is acquitted, and they decide to open up the investigation again?"

Neil just shook his head. "We're going to make sure that doesn't happen. If the body can't be found and no one else knows anything about that night, then we're good. You know the chances are Jeremy Hunt even knew you were in that car or who was with you are slim to none. If you hadn't panicked, we wouldn't be in this position."

"I just could not take that chance." Darius rubbed his temples where he felt the beginnings of a headache.

"Fine. Let me call Sprague back and get him started on this. We'll figure out how to clean it up as we go along."

"All right, but tell him to meet us here. We need to have a full-out planning session so we leave as little as possible to chance." He paused. "And I still want to figure out a way to get rid of the Hunt woman." He held up his hand. "I know, I know. You think it's a bad idea."

"I think it's a dangerous idea. Why can't you leave it alone? With Fairfax on the case, getting rid of her means nothing now."

Darius shook his head. "There's a better than even chance that Fairfax can clear Jeremy Hunt without anything pointing back to me. The cops won't want to dig it all up again unless they're pushed, and she's the one who can push hard. You know she won't rest until she finds out how this whole thing started."

"You get rid of her, and they'll be digging for clues forever."

"I'll make her disappear," Darius told him. "No body, no case and nothing leading back to me." He held up a hand. "I'll be careful, but I won't rest until she's erased."

Neil shook his head. "We'll discuss this after we see what happens next. We aren't really in the habit of eliminating people. Meanwhile, let me make that call to Sprague and get him out here for a meeting. While I do that, call your admin and tell her to cancel your appointments today. You'll be busy."

"Will do." Yes, he'd be busy but not the kind he wanted. He hoped to hell something worked because he had the unsettling feeling he'd lost control of the entire situation.

Chapter Eighteen

Sierra stood on Viper's large patio, looking out at the water, thinking how peaceful it was in comparison to the turmoil churning inside her. The day had been long, all of them sitting at the table, going over everything from the beginning, looking for inconsistencies. Checking things on their laptops. Several times Myles Fairfax had called someone in his office to give them cryptic messages and sent them documents to look at.

But there still seemed to be more questions than answers.

Now Viper was cooking steaks on the grill while Hannah and the other women were fixing the rest of the meal. Sierra had offered to help, but truth to tell, she was feeling completely drained.

Hannah had shooed her out to the patio and insisted she try to relax.

"*I know what a challenge that can be,*" the other woman had said. "*We've all been through it, so just know we're with you. Whatever you need, please just ask.*"

The door slid open behind her, and she turned to see Myles step outside. He held a rocks glass in one hand and a wineglass in the other, which he handed to Sierra.

"I think you can use this," he told her, his deep voice warm and kind.

She took it gratefully. "Thank you."

"You holding up okay?"

She shrugged. "I've been holding up all this time. I'm not about to fall apart yet. Not while my brother is still in prison."

"I'd say holding it together is a better description," he told her. "I think you need another sip of that wine."

As she took a second swallow of the smooth liquid, the sliding door opened again and Eagle joined them. He walked immediately over to Sierra, put his arm around her and gave her a gentle squeeze. If not for Jeremy, she would have given anything to just melt into him and forget all of this.

"Everything okay out here?"

He was asking the question more of Myles than Sierra.

Myles gave him a lopsided smile. "I think it will be okay once we get Jeremy back into civilization." He looked at Sierra. "There are some things that disturb me about the incident that supposedly set this all off. I'd rather we discuss it out here where it's quiet." He nodded at the patio table. "Can we sit?"

"Of course."

Once they were settled, he studied her for a long moment as if trying to read her expression or maybe what was in her eyes. She knew he had taken this case as a favor to Tom and she was aware that he'd been studying her all day as they worked through the monstrous pile of files.

"Let's talk for a moment about the accident. I'm surmising, after examining everything, that this is the only event that could have kicked off this tragic chain of events. Do you agree?"

He looked from Sierra to Eagle and back.

"It's the only thing that makes any sense," Sierra said at last, "even though it seems to have no connection."

"No more connection than your brother had to the woman he's accused of killing. And by the way, I've had an entire team working on that since Tom called and sent me the documents, and bizarre does not begin to describe it."

For the first time since this had started, Sierra felt her brother might actually be freed. His sentence overturned. This man believed her. This man who was one of the best attorneys in the country truly believed her about this.

"Thank god. I mean, if there was something funky about the accident, Jeremy would have insisted on calling the police right away, even with the pouring rain. It was just a little fender bender and whoever was in the car was just anxious to get going."

"Going over the possibilities of what might have needed to be concealed," Myles mused, "the most extreme thing that comes to mind is a dead body. If they were willing to kill a woman to frame your brother because of what he might have seen, it's got to be something more than just a husband cheating on his wife with another woman."

"That's what I thought," Sierra agreed. "But every attorney down the chain told me I was crazy. They said, among other things, that there hadn't been any unsolved murders that would fit the situation."

"Yeah, well." Myles' mouth twisted in disdain. "There wouldn't be. If whoever this is was that anxious to get away, and there was a body, you can bet it's somewhere now that we may never find."

"Then what can we do?" Sierra gripped her wineglass so tight she had to stop herself from cracking it. Instead, she took a sip to steady herself.

"We have to work backward. That means checking missing persons reports and seeing if there's a likely candidate."

"God." She leaned against Eagle. "It just seems so hopeless."

"Not at all," Fairfax assured her. "Difficult but not hopeless. Luckily, I have an excellent staff who can handle assignments like this. I'm interested in the identity of the person in the car. I find it interesting, Sierra, that you're the only one that mentions that it happened at The Library. Nobody else even brought it up or questioned that it might be a factor."

"Do you know about The Library, Myles?" Eagle asked.

"I do. I actually have some clients who are members."

Sierra stared at him. "You do? Does that mean that you can—"

He held up a hand.

"I know what you're going to say and anything I do has to be handled with care. Let's take this one step at a time. I'm going to meet with the prosecutor and see if he'll tell me why the accident was never brought up at trial."

"He might not be too anxious to stick his foot in this," Eagle warned.

"Doesn't matter. It's the rule of law, and I'll make sure he follows it. Also, today we discuss another key point in this mess, and that's the woman whose body was found in Jeremy's room."

Sierra wanted to scream but she didn't. This man who had an international client list was taking his time to help Jeremy. She'd tell him whatever he wanted to know. Do whatever he needed her to do.

"I swear he didn't know her," she assured him, hoping he'd finally believe her. "I never, ever heard him mention a Rose Aitken, and we talked about everything."

"Even strange women he took to hotel rooms?" He held up his hand as she opened her mouth. "Just triple-checking the waters. I did some investigating after I spoke to Tom, before I said yes, and apparently no one in the universe has a bad word to say about your brother. So there's a real bad smell here."

"I've been trying to tell people that very thing," she cried, then took a deep breath and leaned into Eagle.

"But it's still important for me to satisfy myself that the case meets our standards. What sticks out here is the fact someone has gone to a great deal of trouble to cover up something that could easily have been dismissed. The fender bender didn't seem to be of any consequence, but someone made it a major event. Now I have to find out who set Jeremy up in this elaborate frame and what there was about the accident that made them do it. Because that accident is the only thing out of place in the three months of your brother's life I checked out."

"If you have a relationship with The Library, is there a way you can see if anyone knows anything about the fender bender?" Eagle asked.

"I plan to." Myles nodded. "Very quietly, of course. And I have investigators doing a deep dive into Rose Aitken's life to see what we can find there, too. If indeed this was a setup, there has to be a reason she was chosen."

"If the key person who generated this disaster is a member of The Library, there's your answer to why no one wanted to take the case after the original verdict. Someone with enormous power is pulling the strings and they won't let go easily."

Sierra slumped in her chair. "Then—"

Fairfax held up a hand. "But they haven't come up against me. Whatever power they have I can match it, so I'd say their little game is about to blow up. I can tell you more after I meet with Jeremy."

Viper, who had been grilling in the outdoor kitchen on the other side of the patio, walked over to where they were sitting.

"I'm about to tell Hannah that dinner is ready. Come on in and get in line."

As they rose, Myles took Sierra's hand.

"We're going to fix this," he assured her again. "I feel it. But be prepared it's liable to get nasty."

"Can't be any worse than it is," she told him. "I'm ready."

Eagle gave her a hug. "*We're* ready. Let's go eat."

They had just served themselves from the buffet Hannah set up and seated themselves at the table when Myles Fairfax's phone rang.

"Excuse me," he told them. "It's one of my tech guys. I need to take this."

He stepped away from the table into the living room, phone to his ear. No one said a word, instead silently picking at their food while they waited. When Myles returned, he was smiling as he slid into his chair.

"A piece of good news," he told them.

"We could certainly use it," Sierra said.

"Did we find out something new?" Eagle asked.

"I hope we're going to. The head of my tech team has been working on some new programs and equipment. I sent those videos from your security camera, Sierra, as well as the shots from your camera, Hannah. He's running them through his programs and he thinks he can get more than a guess on it."

"Oh, god." Sierra set her fork down. Suddenly her stomach was tied in a huge knot. "You mean we might actually find out who these people are?"

"I'd say at this point it's at least fifty-fifty, which is better than we had before."

"One more thing." Fairfax took another sip of his drink and set his glass down. "I have a call in to the department that runs CCTV for the city. I want to take a look at the local traffic where you were driving the day of the accident, Sierra. Then I'll have my senior tech guy run the license plates. Nobody is completely invisible. I'd bet even money their cars are not registered to shell corporations the way the ones you all drive are." His smile was anything but humorous. "We'll find out who these people are that think they can literally get away with murder."

"You mean like whoever actually killed the woman Jeremy supposedly did?" Sierra asked.

"I do. I've learned over the years that every single thing has little threads dangling from it. I just have to find them." He looked across the table at Tom. "I'd like to get a real early start to the prison in the morning."

"No problem. Just tell me what time, and I'll be there. It's already set up with the warden."

Sierra suddenly couldn't swallow. It occurred to her that everything she'd been trying to make happen was actually going to occur, and better than she'd imagined. The fact that this nationally famous attorney had dropped everything to come here for Jeremy and was going to meet with him tomorrow made her suddenly freeze. What if when he got there he didn't like her brother? What if he changed his mind? What if — ?

Eagle put his arm around her and gave her a gentle hug.

"It's going to be fine, darlin'. I promise."

Myles smiled at her. "I haven't lost yet, and I don't plan to start now. Keep the faith, okay?"

She blew out a breath. "Okay. And I think I'll have some more wine."

Throughout dinner, she was torn between gobbling down her food or not eating at all. The anticipation and anxiety were a volatile cocktail bubbling through her system. Now that something was actually happening, she was turning into a nervous wreck. She appreciated the fact that no one made an issue of it and that everyone treated her as if this were just another meal.

Myles took several calls during the meal, always moving into the living room to talk, telling them very little each time.

"I don't like to give information out in dribs and drabs," he told her. "But it's coming together, and I promise you when it does, you'll be the first to know."

"Thank you."

"But tomorrow looks to be a busy day. I know I'll have a lot to discuss after my visit with Jeremy, so my suggestion to you is to go home and try to get some sleep."

As if, she thought.

"'Try' being the operative word, right?"

Eagle took her hand and looked at everyone.

"I think that's a great idea, so we'll take your advice and split."

He held her hand on the drive home, not saying a word for which she was grateful. Once inside, he led her down the hallway and into the bedroom.

"Come on. Let's get those clothes off so I can go to work on that luscious but tense body."

She stopped and tugged her hand from his.

"Eagle, I don't think I should let you make me feel good tonight. Not with everything going on and things coming to a head for Jeremy."

He cupped her face in his hands and looked directly into her eyes, the blue in his own darkening to navy. Tonight, instead of the hunger she usually saw there something else flickered—caring, concern, and even…possessiveness.

"Darlin', you won't be a lick of good to your brother if you're all wound up like a rubber band. Let me make you relax. That way you'll be able to think better if Myles has more questions for you. Or needs your input for something."

She let out a sigh. Maybe he was right. Lord knew, tonight she could really use his attention.

In the bedroom, he pulled the covers back on the bed then helped her out of her shoes and clothes. Then he lifted her onto the bed and carefully placed her facedown with her head cradled in the pillow. She turned her head so she could watch him and saw him shuck his shirt and shoes.

"Aren't you getting into bed with me?"

"Soon. First, I'm going to give you one of my highly rated massages, guaranteed to get rid of all that tension."

"Oh?" She squinted at him sideways. "And exactly how many women have given you a rating on your massage?"

"Not nearly as many as you think, darlin'. Believe me. Now just get comfortable and close your eyes. Leave it all to me."

She'd been sure she wouldn't be able to do that, but it turned out to be easier than she thought. Eagle was a magician with his hands, as if she didn't already know. First, he wrapped the silk scarf around her eyes, so she was drifting in a cocoon. It helped her shut out everything, just as it had the other times, and fall into a deep, soft, black cloud.

"I found this massage oil," he told her in his deep, sexy voice. "When I warm it in my hands, it increases its effect on the body a whole lot."

He climbed onto the bed and straddled her hips. She felt the effect of the warm oil at once. Whatever it contained, it woke up every one of her nerve endings even as its soothing effect slid through her body. In the next moment his hands, soft as angel's wings, were sliding up and down her spine. He gently kneaded the muscles on either side before lifting his hands to her shoulders.

"Damn, Sierra. Your muscles are tighter than an old lady's girdle. Maybe you needed more wine."

"No," she murmured. "I just need you."

"Well, you've sure as shit got me. Now take a deep breath and let it out slowly."

She did as he asked, and as she exhaled, he began to gently rub the muscles in her neck and shoulders. He didn't squeeze hard, just let his fingers play with her muscles, loosening them a little bit at a time. He spent a significant amount of time on each group of muscles, working his way slowly down her spine then back up again until she finally felt as loose and relaxed as jelly.

More oil, warm and seductive. Then he began to work on her arms, shoulders to wrists and back again. And when they were totally relaxed, he slid down to straddle her thighs and began to massage her buttocks.

What?

Behind the blindfold, she blinked. She'd never had her ass massaged before. Gripped tight in sex, maybe, or kneaded as she rode someone's cock. But this was totally different. This soothed her and eased her and yet…*damn!* Aroused her at the same time. Was she becoming a sex addict? With Eagle, probably. She'd never had sex this good in her life. And now that she was thinking about that, the pulse in her pussy began to throb gently, just enough to send little flares of heat through her body.

Relax, she told herself. *This is to relax you, not to have wild, crazy sex.*

On the other hand, wild, crazy sex with Eagle relaxed her in a way it never had with anyone else. There was something about him that she connected with that sent her hormones into overdrive.

What would happen when this was over? Would he still want to—?

Wait. He said something about that, right?

"Whatever you're thinking about," he told her in his deep voice, "get it out of your brain. You're starting to tense up again."

"Oh-kay."

She inhaled a deep breath, let it out slowly and shut all those questions out of her mind.

He went back to kneading the muscles of her ass, and, when she was relaxed again, shifted his position once more. Easing her legs apart, he knelt between them and began to massage her thighs, one at a time. Each time he reached the top of a leg, the knuckles of his hands would brush against the lips of her cunt, sending shivers through her.

"No spankings or anything tonight," he told her in a soft voice. "I just want you to relax and let the stress fade away, at least for the moment. I know you'll be uptight tomorrow waiting to hear Myles' report after he meets with Jeremy. Although I'm sure once that happens, he'll be more committed than ever. So tonight, let's just think about Sierra. Let me pleasure you and make you relax and feel good. Okay?"

"Mmm," was all she could manage as his fingers worked their magic on her.

He stroked up and down her legs, ankle to thigh, and down again, knuckles lightly touching her hot center. She did her best to lie still but, cocooned in the darkness as she was, his touch brought every sense to life, accentuated every sensation. The hot little shivers spread from her cunt to the rest of her body, increasing the thrum of her pulse and making her nipples harden and ache.

Just when she was ready to beg him to make her come, he turned her over with gentle hands, moved up her body and began the routine again. He used his fingers gently but firmly on her shoulders, her arms, and down to her waist, gently squeezing her flesh.

She had been tense as a wire when they'd arrived at his sprawling home on the water. But the house was so soothing and now, just as Eagle predicted, her muscles were so much looser and more relaxed. Except a different kind of tension now gripped her body, a hunger for this man's touch stronger than anything she'd ever experienced. Ever expected to experience. And after a very few short days it was obvious to her she didn't want to walk away from it. She just hoped Eagle meant everything he kept saying.

His hands moved down to the muscles of her stomach and rational thought left her brain.

He used his fingers in the same gentle, rhythmic way he had on other parts of her body. The thrumming in the heart of her pussy was getting stronger and she had to be wetter than a river by now. Easy for him to slide his fingers into her. No, his cock. Yes! His cock!

The blindfold increased the effect of his touch, shutting out everything else.

He eased his body back so he was straddling her legs and continued to work on her thighs, sliding his thumbs up the inner flesh and just teasing the lips of her pussy. By now she was moaning with a combination of need and pleasure, intensified by the darkness that wrapped itself around her. By the time he shifted again, she was vibrating with need and hunger.

Eagle maneuvered himself so he was between her lower legs, spreading them wide and now giving the lightest of massages to the outer lips of her cunt. Heat spread through her, like millions of little fingers plucking at her skin, inside and out. The oil was both soothing and stimulating. She heard soft moans in the air and realized it was her, so consumed with pleasure she couldn't help herself.

By the time he finished working on her, every muscle in her body was loose as a piece of silk, yet her body thrummed heavily with need. And she wanted him inside her more than she wanted her next breath.

At last, when she didn't think she could stand it for one more second, he moved off the mattress and gently turned her over.

"I could do this all night, you know," he teased.

"Oh, god, no." The words just blurted out of her month. "Oh, please. Please, please, please."

His laugh was low, rough and sexy.

"What's wrong, darlin'? I thought you liked the massage. Sure took the tension out of your muscles."

"I do. I did. But…"

"But what? It makes you horny?"

She blew out a breath. "Yes. Please, Eagle."

"Please what?"

"Please fuck me?" If she hadn't been so unwound, she would have shouted the words.

"Well, then. Since you asked so nicely, I think that can be arranged."

She felt the bed shift as he climbed off, heard the faint sounds of his jeans hitting the floor and the tear of the foil covering the condom. Then he was back. Turning her face down on the bed, he gently lifted her to her knees and placed a string of kisses along her spine.

"Mmmmm." She could stand him doing that forever.

He slid one hand between her thighs and stroked her pussy, brushing back and forth over her clit each time and sending streaks of desire through her body. When he eased a finger into her, she pushed back against him, but he slid it out and held her hips in place with both hands.

"Uh-uh, darlin'. I'm calling the shots here."

Well then, start calling them, damn it, she wanted to say. In all her life, she never remembered being this turned on by a man or craving him the way she did Eagle. And right now, she wanted all of him.

As if he could sense what she was thinking, he pressed the head of his cock into her opening and very slowly eased himself inside until he was fully seated. She squeezed him with her internal muscles, and his hands tightened on her hips in response.

"Slow and easy, darlin'," he told her. "There's no hurry."

Yes, there is. I want to come now!

But Eagle was in control and that made her even hotter. Slowly he rode her, sliding his cock in and out with unbearable deliberateness. Every drag of that thick shaft against her inner walls drove her need even higher. She was almost at the point of begging when his fingers tightened on her hips, and he increased the pace. Now he moved faster and faster, and she moved with him. With the blindfold shutting out everything else, every sensation was magnified a hundredfold.

She was almost there, almost there, the tightening in her muscles telling him, when he reached around her to find her clit, squeezed it and thrust hard into her, once, twice, three times.

And they exploded together, spinning into dark space as the orgasm shook them both again and again and again. When the last spasm finally subsided, he eased her down flat again, kissed her shoulders and took off the blindfold.

She hummed as lassitude overtook her.

"I have nothing left," she murmured.

"Good." He gave her lips a soft kiss. "That's the way it's supposed to be." He stared into her eyes. "I never want it to end. Ever. Tell me you feel the same."

"I do." She said the words without hesitation. They had so much to learn about each other, but the basics were all in place. "Count on it."

"Then let's get this problem taken care of and get on with our lives." He kissed her again then grinned at her. "But first, let's get that shower."

Chapter Nineteen

Darius disconnected the call and had to restrain himself from throwing the phone across the room. He had barely slept the night before, and his nerves were shot already, a very unfamiliar situation to him.

Fuck, fuck, fuck. Things were getting progressively worse.

"What now?" Neil asked.

He had arrived at Darius' house early this morning so they could finish putting a plan together to hopefully put this whole fucking mess behind them. So far, everything they'd come up with held a large element of danger, but they were beginning to think they didn't have much choice. This only underscored it.

"That was our contact at Raiford."

A series of unexpected circumstances had put one of the guards at Raiford in their debt. Neil was always fond of saying he could never tell when he might need someone, and right now they needed him. If only he had better news.

"What's the good word? Or bad word, I guess."

"Myles Fairfax was at the prison this morning very early, per special arrangement with the warden. He was there for three hours, after which Jeremy Hunt was moved out of general population to a secure, sequestered area. Damn it."

Darius punched the arm of the chair. He was losing control and he was a man given to being in control.

"That means Fairfax is taking his case for sure. Our guy will have no access to report on anything."

"I'm telling you." Darius took a deep breath, trying to settle himself. "We should have killed the sister in the beginning. Everyone would have focused on her and not worried about the brother. Plus there'd be no one to rattle the blinds the way she has."

"And exactly how do you think you'd get away with it?" Neil asked. "Jesus, Darius. You are totally losing it."

"The same way I got away with the others."

"Which, I might point out, would have been unnecessary if you hadn't lost your mind."

"Okay, I've got it." He wondered if he'd have a stroke trying to deal with this.

"We have to pull out all our contacts," Neil told him. "You know Fairfax will file for an appeal, and I don't think there's a judge that will turn him down. They wouldn't want to deal with the repercussions."

"We have to find out if whoever gets the appeal will decide whether to grant it without a hearing. My guess is not, since it received so much publicity. Reach out to your contacts at the courthouse. If they set the time for a hearing, we have to make plans for her not to reach the courthouse." Darius glared at his friend. "And don't lecture me on why we're in this spot, please."

"You have another wild hair up your ass?" Neil asked.

"Yes, and let me tell you what it is. It may be wild, but we don't have many choices. These SEALs have the Hunt woman squirreled away somewhere and that would be our only chance to get at her. If she's gone, there's no one left to push this, and Jeremy Hunt is in no position to put pressure on the cops for whatever happens."

Neil rubbed his jaw. "I know I'm about to hear what this nutty scheme is. I think your luck's run out. That's why we're in this position to begin with."

"I get it, okay? Can we get past it, please, so we can fix it once and for all?" Darius walked over to the built-in bar, dropped two ice cubes in a rocks glass and poured a fat inch of Pappy Van Winkle over them.

"Jesus, Darius. It's not even noon yet. Get a hold of yourself."

Darius knew his friend was right. He'd never been this rattled in his life, but he suddenly saw everything falling apart. All because he'd accidentally killed his play partner at The Library—a woman having sex for money and whose real name he didn't know. Probably no one would have cared and probably Jeremy Hunt hadn't seen or cared who was in the car he'd dinged. But Darius had worried overmuch about it and here they were.

Well, if he could handle this, they were almost home. He had no idea what Sierra Hunt would say in a courtroom, and he couldn't take a chance. He'd get with Sprague again, the only person he knew who could pull this off and be done with it once and for all. No evidence, no case, and people could scream the house down, Fairfax included. But to no avail.

"Did Sprague get the tracker placed on Hernandez's car?" Darius asked.

Neil nodded. "He did, and fortunately without too much trouble, but not until last night. I want to know where Hernandez is now and where he goes for the rest of the day."

"And you think that will lead us to where these SEALs are? And where the Hunt woman is?"

"That's the plan," Neil told him. "But we also need to know if and when Fairfax files for an appeal, which I'm sure will happen soon. I hope to have word on that this afternoon. He probably already had the appeal ready to file, and I assume we're unlucky enough that his meeting with Hunt went well. Then it's just a matter of taking the paperwork to the court and processing it. I'm going to contact that guard at the courthouse you helped out of a jam and ask him to keep an eye out for any action."

"Good. Very good." Darius found himself pacing and forced himself to stop. He had to keep his shit together.

"I'm trying to decide if we should contact all those attorneys you put the squeeze on and tell them to keep their mouths shut. Or are we better off figuring they want to stay as far away from this as possible, so we shouldn't do anything to bring more attention to it?"

"This time I'm going to leave the decision up to you." Darius blew out a breath. "Neil, you have to know how grateful I am to you for all of this."

"If that's so, then do me a big favor. Watch your behavior and activities for the next several months so you don't call any attention to yourself. And keep away from situations like the one that started this whole mess."

"That's certainly the least I can do. You have my word."

"Good. Then let's map out our strategy." He looked at his watch. "And I want to know if that tracker is working."

"Neil?"

He looked over at Darius. "Yes?"

"We still have to kill Sierra Hunt. If Fairfax is able to get an appeal and have a new trial date set, we have no idea what she can testify about, but I can't take the chance. You can see that, right?"

Neil sighed. "We'll discuss it. Okay? That will have to be good enough for right now."

* * * *

Sierra had a hard time getting through the morning. Eagle had made coffee and heated cinnamon rolls for breakfast, but she could hardly swallow the food. Viper had called very early to say Tom had picked up Fairfax at five-thirty a.m., and they were on their way to Raiford. The meeting with Jeremy was set for eight, and Tom would call when he had something to tell them.

"I'm torn between wanting the visit to be fast," she told Eagle, "and wanting him to take his time so he can be satisfied Jeremy is innocent. And ask him all the questions he needs to."

They were sitting in the living room with fresh coffee, looking out at the view of Hillsborough Bay. The setting soothed her, and she was glad Eagle had insisted she stay here with him. The last thing she had expected in the middle of this crisis was for a relationship to explode like this, one that was more intense and complex than any she'd ever had. She hoped it lasted beyond this situation. Eagle had hinted as much but then, as she knew very well, shit happened.

Worry about it when the time comes.

"What did you think of him?" Eagle asked. "Fairfax."

"I was very impressed. And stunned that he would actually take Jeremy's case."

"He told you why," Eagle reminded her. "He dedicates all these cases to his brother-in-law."

"Yes, and that success gives me hope."

He tried to keep her occupied while they waited by asking her about her life and her career and why she chose it. She was proud of the fact that she could focus enough to answer his questions when her brain was filled with thoughts of Jeremy and the meeting going on right then.

She nearly jumped off the couch when shortly after noon Eagle's cell rang.

Eagle looked at the readout.

"It's Tom. Let me put him on speaker." He pressed the buttons. "Hey, Tom. You've got both of us. Good news or bad?"

"I'd say good. In fact, very good. Myles was very thorough in his questioning of Jeremy. And after he finished, he called his office to get them started on some things, but he's convinced we have a very good case to file for an appeal."

"Oh, thank god." For a moment, Sierra felt so weak she was afraid she'd faint.

Eagle reached for her hand and gave it a reassuring squeeze.

"Can you give us an idea of some of the points?" he asked.

"After listening to everything Jeremy had to say, all the things his attorney never brought up or introduced into evidence, Myles has decided the most effective and speediest claim to use is ineffective assistance of counsel. It seems Jeremy gave his first attorney access to a great many things that at least would have called into question the situation and none of them were used."

"Damn."

Sierra was glad Eagle was doing the talking because she couldn't make her mouth work.

"So what happens now?" he asked.

Myles' voice came over the connection

"Tom's driving, so I'll answer the rest of the questions. I had my staff prepare the appeal, just leaving the pertinent parts of it to be filled in. We passed the original deadline to file an appeal, so I'm asking for an extension which, considering all the errors I am uncovering, the judge will grant. If he's an appropriate judge, he won't fight me on this. Then we have to set a date for a new trial."

"What if they won't give us the extension?" Her stomach was already cramping at the thought.

"I've dealt with these before," he assured her. "There were so many errors of procedure here no one's going to give me a hard time. I promise you that. Eagle? You there?"

"I am." He squeezed Sierra's hand again.

"Who's got the best printer? You or Viper?"

"We all have the same one. They're top of the line. Why?"

"When I called my office, I gave them the final information to fill in. Then they'll email them to me, but I'll need to print everything out to take to court."

"Either place is good," Eagle assured him.

"Okay. Let's do it at your place. I'm calling the courthouse as soon as I hang up here to get on a schedule today."

"We'll be waiting for you."

The moment Eagle hung up, Sierra burst into tears.

"Hey, hey, hey." He cupped her chin in his hands, using his thumbs to brush away the tears. "What's with this? I hope those are happy tears, because this is all good."

"They are. Really. I just didn't think we'd ever get here. Oh, Eagle. Thank you, you and your partners, for taking me on as a client. Thank you for doing what you do and for helping. I'll never be able to repay you."

He smiled and brushed a kiss over her lips. "Oh, I think I have a few suggestions on that front. I'm saving them for later."

She gave him another hug. "It'll be worth it. I promise."

"Let's figure what to do about lunch. Myles won't want anything heavy, I'm sure, but he'll need something. Maybe a sandwich? They should be here about one o'clock. Let's go see what we can pull together that they can eat quickly."

Her hands were still shaking as she helped Eagle put lunch together, but she managed not to make a mess of things. When the doorbell rang, she felt weak at the knees again but pulled herself together. She'd have plenty of time to fall apart after this was resolved.

When Myles strode into the kitchen, he walked directly to her.

"If I ever get married again," he told her, "I hope I get a wife just like you. Jeremy is so fortunate to have you for a sister."

"I can hardly believe this is going forward."

"It damn well is. When I file the papers today, I'm going to push for a fast hearing. None of this scheduling business. You were right, Sierra. There's a lot of odd stuff attached to this. Stuff that smells. I'm flying in the private investigator I use because someone's pulling the strings, and I'm going to find out who."

"You still think The Library's involved?"

He nodded. "Someone with power had to make sure you couldn't hire a lawyer, good or bad. As I said, I think it goes back to that fender bender and whoever was in the other car. You've got some filthy-rich asshole who thinks he can get away with anything. Well, not this time. And when I get it all together, I'm going to make it my business to see all those attorneys are disbarred."

Her jaw dropped. "You can do that?"

He winked. "Watch me."

Half an hour later, he and Tom were headed down to the courthouse, and she gratefully accepted a glass of wine from Eagle. It would calm her enough to wait for Myles to get back and let her know when the hearing date was.

"I can hardly believe it's happening," she told Eagle. "I'll be thanking you for the rest of my life."

He winked. "Sounds good to me."

Chapter Twenty

Darius disconnected the call and resumed his pacing. Neil had confirmed that Tom Hernandez had driven to an address on Davis Islands very early then headed north. They had ended up at Raiford, not unexpected, and their whereabouts would continue to be monitored.

"Okay, the meeting at the prison is finished. Let's see where they go from here," Neil had reported.

"Assuming they stick together," Darius said.

"I'm pretty damn sure they will. Fairfax doesn't have his own transportation. And hopefully it will lead us to the SEALs and the Hunt woman." Neil sounded certain.

"I hope to hell you're right. Listen. I'm not going into my office today and I told my admin I'd be out of touch for a few days. I'm not worth shit right now and won't be until this thing is resolved." Darius clenched his teeth in frustration.

"Darius." Neil's voice was flat. "You have to be prepared that this won't end the way you want it to."

"Well, one way or the other I'm getting rid of the Hunt woman. Without her, I wouldn't be in this mess."

"I'm not going to point out again that it's your own actions that put you in this situation. Anyway, let me take care of a few things, and I'll be over. Maybe we'll have a final location on where Fairfax goes after leaving Raiford. I have a feeling things will be happening quickly."

He paced and cursed until Neil finally arrived, by that time ready to explode. He hated not knowing what was happening. He was going to tell Neil to have Sprague text him with the regular updates on where Hernandez's car was. Operating in a vacuum was shit. Besides, it was his ass on the line, so he needed to be plugged directly into the information.

"Well?" he demanded when he let his friend into the house.

"We may finally have gotten a little lucky."

"Coffee's ready. Grab a cup and let's have it."

Darius paced in irritation while Neil took a long swallow of the hot liquid.

"I have news," he told Darius, "and it's worth the wait."

"And that is?" Darius was ready to explode.

"The tracker has given us the location of the spot where Hernandez picked up Fairfax and it's actually very good for us. It will give us some options. It's at someone's house on Davis Islands."

Darius stared at him. "Do we know whose?"

"We have to work on that. If you remember, everything to do with these SEALs is registered under shell corporations. But I thought we might do a little drive-by. We can do it very casually, and no one will think anything of it."

"Really?" Darius cocked an eyebrow. "And how exactly do we accomplish that?"

"You'll see. And we're going to do it in a couple of ways that will give us visual confirmation of all our questions." He checked his watch. "We should be hearing from Sprague again any time now. And I'll tell him to add you to the text list."

"Tell him since I'm paying for all this, that would be a good idea."

Before Neil could answer, his phone chimed, and he studied the text.

"Okay, my friend. We're going to take a little ride and you're going to see how unexpectedly easy this is going to be. Come on."

"Would you like to tell me where we're going?"

"You'll see." Neil headed for the front door and the circular drive in front of the house where his car was.

Darius ground his teeth, forcing himself to bite back his words at least until he knew where they were going. They drove through the South Tampa neighborhood where he lived and headed toward downtown. He was about to comment when they avoided most of the downtown area and took the bridge over to Davis Islands, an archipelago of gorgeous and expensive homes. Once over the bridge, Neil turned left and followed a street that wound around and along the waterfront.

"If any of the Galaxy men live here," he commented, "they must have a shitpot of money."

"I told you. Remember? They won more than a billion dollars in the Powerball lottery. Plus they charge two arms and legs for their fees."

"Sierra Hunt doesn't have that kind of money," Darius reminded him.

"They also take cases that interest them and don't charge. Okay, here we go. Check out the gray stone place on the right."

It didn't make Darius feel any better to see the sprawling one-story house with the stone wall fronting it. There was a car parked in the circular drive by the front door. Neil drove by slowly enough so he could also see between it and the house next door to the lawn that stretched to the water. Beyond it, Hillsborough Bay sparkled in the sunlight.

"I don't know what I was expecting," he said, "but certainly not this. That must be Hernandez's car in the driveway."

"Let's make sure." Neil pressed speed dial for Sprague and gave him a description of the car. When he hung up, he nodded. "That's it."

He turned the car around to make another pass at the house but stopped when the front door opened. Two men exited, both tall, lean and muscular, both with dark hair and granite faces. They climbed into the car as if they owned it and everything around it, a gate slid open in the stone fence, and they pulled out onto the street.

Neil was about to pull into a driveway and wait for the car to pass but it turned the other way.

"We don't have to follow them," Darius reminded him. "The tracker on Hernandez's car will tell us where they are."

"As long as they don't find it."

"They won't," he said with confidence.

"Okay, let's drive around the island and get a look from all angles," Darius said. "I have an idea."

* * * *

Sierra had barely been able to keep herself together, as wound up as she was. She'd been turned down so many times by so many lawyers it was hard for her to believe that one of them—and the cream of the crop at that—was actually doing this.

"Your brother got a raw deal," Myles told her. "Even a junior attorney could have seen it. But the pressure was on from the very beginning, and it came from someone with a hell of a lot of power. And it filtered from top to bottom. My guess is attorneys were blackmailed and pressured to turn you away."

"They rushed this through the courts as fast as they could," Tom pointed out. "Then did their best to sweep it under the rug. Sierra, if you hadn't been so determined, your brother would be serving life with no chance of anything."

"Again, I don't know how to thank you for this."

Myles smiled, his eyes crinkling. "Getting the appeal heard and the verdict set aside is all the thanks I need. Oh, and Tom and I will also be following the trail of breadcrumbs back to whoever started this train wreck."

Myles pulled his suit jacket back on and picked up his briefcase, which contained all the completed documents bearing the correct information. "I'm on my way to file this right now before the court closes for the day. I'm going to request an expedited hearing, with the reasons stated in my application."

"Do you think you'll get it?"

Sierra thought his smile was pure confidence.

"Oh, yeah. Been there, done that, got the wins to show for it. Come on, Tom. Then we can come back here, and maybe Viper will take us out on his boat. We can take a little ride to relax at the end of the day. Sound good?"

She nodded, still stunned at how fast this was all happening now.

"We'll get it done. I've got people all over those attorneys as we speak." He looked over at Tom. "Okay, my friend. Let's roll. We've got a lot more to do today."

The afternoon hours seemed to move like molasses. Sierra knew Eagle was doing his best to keep her busy until they heard from Myles and Tom. She didn't expect the actual filing to take long but as Myles had told her, it depended on how busy the court was that day.

She paced, drank iced tea, tried without success to sit still. When Eagle's phone rang, she nearly jumped out of her seat.

"Yeah? Uh-huh. Uh-huh. Good. That's good. Head on back, and we'll go from there."

"What?" she asked when he disconnected. "Tell me already."

"Application for appeal is already filed and somehow Fairfax worked his magic to get an expedited hearing. Day after tomorrow."

"Oh, my god!" She knew that was next to impossible, but again it showed the amount of influence Fairfax had and the strength of his reputation. "The man is definitely a miracle worker."

"Yes, he is. He said his people should have information on what connects all the other attorneys who turned you down, especially the one who started the chain. He and Tom are going to stop by The Library on the way back here. Apparently, he knows the manager and did him a favor once."

"Myles Fairfax's favors ought to be good for a big payoff." She looked up at Eagle. "Right?"

"After what I've seen so far, I'd say yes. Listen, it will be a while before they get back here. I know you're just a bundle of nerves. How about a swim to relax you?"

"I don't have a bathing suit."

He curved his lips in a sexy grin.

"Now, you know with solar screening you don't need one. No one can see you but me." He squeezed her hands. "No sex, although it will take an extreme effort on my part to hold back. Just a little something to take the edge off."

Why not? she thought. She was wound up so tight she was afraid she might snap apart if she didn't take it easy.

"Okay." She nodded. "I think you're right and I can use it."

"But let me text Tom to let us know when they head home. Just so they don't catch us literally with our pants down."

He fetched towels from a cupboard by the pool and stacked them by the hot tub. Then he took Sierra's hand and led her down into the water. He pushed the button, the surface of the water began to bubble and, as she stepped down into it, she thought, well, if anything could distract her, it was this.

* * * *

Darius leaned back in the passenger seat, closed his eyes and raked his fingers through his hair. He could feel himself falling apart and couldn't seem to do anything about it.

"We should have followed them."

"For what?" Neil's voice had developed a sharp edge. "The tracker on the car is working. You don't want to put yourself in a more precarious position than you already are."

Darius closed his eyes. "How the fuck did this happen?"

"You keep asking that, but you already know the answer. We're doing what we can to fix it." His phone sounded. "That's Sprague. He said Fairfax filed the notice of appeal and request for a hearing."

"Well, that will take some time. He's not about to hang around here for months and that will give us a chance to finish cleaning things up."

"Don't count on it," Neil snorted. "Sprague texted me that the hearing's in two days."

"Two days?" Darius sat upright in the seat so fast the seat belt dug into him. "What the fuck? Who did he pay off? It usually can take up to ten months."

"You know the man's got clout. Now we know just how much."

"Fuck. Neil, I don't care what you say. We have to get rid of Sierra Hunt. Without her, the case goes away. No one else is pushing this hard. No one else even cares. We can work our usual magic, be done with it and life goes back to normal."

"Darius, my friend, you're delusional. You think Fairfax is going to walk away from this case just because she's dead? Her brother is his client, and they'll both be out for blood."

"She'll never rest until she finds out who's pulling the strings," Darius insisted.

"And what about the SEALs? She's their client. You think they'd just walk away from this? Are you taking stupid pills all of a sudden?"

Darius kept his mouth shut, but he saw Sierra Hunt as the root of all his troubles. He had to get rid of her, even if only to satisfy himself. He'd contact Sprague directly. He was the one with the most power. He was sure Sprague would do whatever he asked.

"I think I need to go home," he said at last. "I don't think the SEALs and Fairfax will be doing anything more today. I can call Sprague and ask him to put some men on this house so we know what's happening."

"Listen to me," Neil said. "Did you see any place they could conceal themselves? Any place they wouldn't stick out like a sore thumb?"

"The water. Did you see all those boats out there? They can blend right in. And while they're doing that, they can look for other places."

"Please think carefully about what you're doing. We can find other ways to shortstop this."

"And stop them from digging into a path that might lead back to me?"

"Yes, if we're careful."

Darius sighed. "I'll think about it."

* * * *

Sierra was glad she and Eagle had gotten out of the hot tub and pool when they did, although she could have stayed there for another few hours. But as it was, they barely had time to dress before Tom and Myles returned. She was very grateful Tom had called to tell them they were on the way back so they had some warning.

Now, dressed in jeans and one of Eagle's Tampa Bay Lightning T-shirts—she was stretching her limited wardrobe and she was also a hockey fan—she sat with the three men in the living room, listening to the latest turn of events. She was glad Eagle had served them all drinks first.

"I always say doing favors for people doesn't take much effort but can pay off big-time," Tom said.

"Agreed." Eagle nodded.

"It was your favor." Myles looked at Tom. "You get to tell the story."

Tom took a slow sip of the bourbon in his rocks glass.

"Myles and I both have a couple of clients who are members of The Library. They come from old families and a ton of money." He looked around at everyone. "Discretion is what counts the most with these people and that's what we focus on."

Eagle grinned at him. "You really are the soul of discretion, aren't you? Even we didn't know that."

Tom just smiled and winked.

"So how much can you share with us?"

Myles took another slow swallow of his drink.

"There is a man who is a member of The Library. He comes from a very old Tampa family and has enough money to support the entire city and surrounding communities. He's been prominent in politics, as a kingmaker not a candidate. Has a foundation that provides college scholarships and grants to educational programs. Serves on community boards—"

Eagle held up his hand. "Okay, okay, he's the second coming of Jesus, but what does that have to do with anything?"

"He also has a rather dangerous little habit which I had to dig really hard to discover. I knew there was something. There aren't many people who could pull off framing Jeremy the way it was done and have that many people shut up about it."

Eagle stared at him. "I get it. How about telling us who it is and why he did it?"

Myles looked at each of them in turn. "His name is Darius Holland, and he —"

"Really does have more money than god," Sierra burst in. "Holy shit. The man practically owns the city."

"The man also has some nasty little habits," Tom told them. "He is very heavy into BDSM, although his is the extreme kind."

Sierra had a hard time not looking at Eagle, who casually reached over and took her hand. *Let them think he was just…whatever…*

"And by extreme kind," Myles went on, "we're talking about activities that no responsible dungeon would sanction. That some people who practice BDSM would not even consider part of the lifestyle. A lot of them involve nonconsensual torture, and I have no idea why people get off on that. But they've gotten Holland barred from every BDSM club in the state and maybe elsewhere."

"Not a lot do get off on it," Tom reminded him, "but there are people so desperate for money they will do anything. One of Holland's fetishes is erotic asphyxiation, but he always takes it to the extreme."

"If he's banned from the clubs, where does he indulge in this?" Sierra asked. "His home?"

Myles shook his head. "No, he has live-in staff, and his kids might be there. He's been using The Library."

Sierra stared at him, shocked, and she knew Eagle had to be, too. This was as far from what he was introducing her to as Alaska was from the South Pole.

"And they let him do this?" Eagle asked.

"He's paid for a lot of improvements at The Library, even covered the mortgage when they expanded. Plus he's brought them a lot of wealthy, important international clients that polish the place's reputation."

"But what does that have to do with Jeremy?" Sierra wanted to know.

"Apparently he got a little too enthusiastic with one of his subs and she died. Armand, the night manager, thought the woman was drunk and helped him get her out to his car without anyone knowing what was going on. His driver was waiting for him, and they pulled out of the side entrance. However, it was raining heavily, and they apparently didn't see other traffic and ended up in a fender bender."

"With my brother," Sierra guessed.

"Exactly." Myles nodded. "He had his driver thrust a bunch of money at Jeremy, tell him he accepted responsibility and Jeremy should just get his car fixed. It was raining so hard your brother was just damn glad to get out of there."

"But then…"

"But then he was afraid to leave anything to chance. He decided framing Jeremy for murder was the best way to distract him and keep him occupied. Then he used his…shall we say influence…to make sure no other lawyer would represent Jeremy after the conviction. Which, by the way, was a disgusting travesty of justice."

"So that's how it all played out," Tom said. "But Myles was very good at ferreting all this out and letting people know there are consequences for what they did, which he would make sure were applied."

"So what happens now?" Sierra asked.

"The appeal hearing is in two days. I'm calling in all my resources to gather every bit of information about this disaster before then so the judge won't have a choice but to set aside the verdict. There will not be a trial, at least for Jeremy."

Sierra blinked her eyes, hard, against the tears welling in them.

"I don't know how to thank you. Really."

"Keep yourself safe until we've got Darius Holland locked away," he told her. "And I mean that. The manager at The Library said he overheard a discussion between Darius and his close friend Neil Maguire that he thinks eliminating you will get rid of all his troubles. No one will pursue this without you pushing them and it will all go away."

"I plan on being her personal bodyguard," Eagle told him and squeezed her hand again.

"We just need a few days to get everything on Holland locked up and we can all breathe again."

"No sweat. She won't leave my side."

"Good. Okay, gather the troops. Let's have dinner and figure out who can do what in this situation. Then I need to start preparing for the appeal hearing."

Chapter Twenty-One

"There's something funny going on out there," Eagle said, "and despite him wearing a stupid ball cap, I know one of the men in that boat is Holland. I thought so yesterday and still think so."

"I can't believe how many hours you've been watching it." Sierra walked up beside him. "Can't you do something about it?"

"Not unless I want an all-out shooting war, which is what I'm trying to avoid."

Eagle stood just inside the pool screen with his binoculars and studied the boats in the water. There were usually a dozen or so of them taking after-dinner rides at the end of the day, watching for the sunset. After living in this house for more than a year and watching them on a daily basis, he knew which ones were regulars, and which ones were cruising out there just now and then. He was still searching for the right boat for himself, but he liked watching the ones in his area in the evening.

Which was how this one had caught his attention. He'd first noticed it the day the application for an appeal had been filed, mostly because it was a sleek, good-looking deck boat carrying two passengers. The boat didn't stay in one spot but moved all around the area in this part of the bay. It would crisscross around, head off somewhere then come back. He hadn't thought much about it. The bay was always filled with boats, especially in this stretch of nice weather.

It could have been one of his neighbors out for a little pleasure ride, but in the year he'd lived in this house and observed activity on the water, people didn't focus on one area.

"This is the second evening that boat's been out there dicking around."

"How can you even tell?"

He grinned down at her. "I'm a SEAL. We're experts on boats."

"And you really think it's Darius Holland? And who do you think is with him? And how could he even know where your house is? Or who you are? Or any of that?"

"Good question," he told her. "Very good question. My itchy spine tells me it's either him or someone who works for him. Maybe a couple of someones. If it is, I'd like to know how they found out where I live and that you're here with me, because you know that's why they're here. Tom plainly said that Holland probably thinks you're the cause of all this."

"Which I am," she told him. "And happy I did it. Is there a way to find out?"

"Once I get my hands on him. Here. Hold these a minute. I need to call Viper." He pulled out his cell and punched speed dial for his friend who lived about two miles from him and bordered the same stretch of water.

"Hey, man. Are you getting any boats in your area that seem to either hang out or keep coming back? Have you noticed?"

"Haven't paid much attention but let me take a look."

Eagle described the one he'd been watching. "See if there's one that looks like that."

In seconds Viper was back. "As a matter of fact, yes. It just circled past these houses and took off again, heading towards your area."

"I hope I'm wrong, but I think it's either Darius Holland or some assholes he's hired. But if it is, how the hell did he find out who I am and where I live? We know Sierra's their ultimate target, but how did they find out she's here?"

"Some very good questions."

"I don't know what they've planned, if it's them. I sure don't want to get involved in some kind of shootout."

"Tell me what I can do."

"You guys got anything going on right this minute? Can you just sort of drop in?"

"Sure. I'll have Hannah bring her drone."

"Okay. Thanks."

"Is he coming over?" Sierra asked.

Eagle nodded. "Hannah, too. And she's bringing her new drone with her."

She stared at him. "Are you attacking the boat?"

"Nope. Just making him think I am. Darlin', I want you to go into the house. Please."

"I'm in the house," she pointed out. "And besides, that special screening makes it impossible for him to see me. Please, Eagle. I promise not to get in the way, but if something's going to happen, I want to know. I've been in this fight from day one."

He blew out a breath. "Okay, you're right. But just be sure you get out of the way if I tell you to."

"Got it. Let me go unlock the front door."

After a while, the boat headed out toward the open water, but then it turned left and headed along the shoreline before turning out into the open water again.

"Maybe they're just cruising around, scoping things out then they'll disappear," Sierra suggested.

"Holland must be on edge because the appeal hearing is tomorrow," Eagle reminded her. "He wants you gone. I think whoever is driving the boat is trying to throw us off track by making us think we're not their target, but I'm a lot smarter than they are."

She was so tense she practically vibrated with it, but she kept herself under control. She hadn't come this far after all this time, and managed to find people who could help her, to screw it up because she had no personal discipline.

"He's pulling away again," she commented as the boat headed out toward open water.

"Yeah, let's see for how long."

This time it was almost ten minutes before the boat reappeared.

"Okay, it's getting dark, and he's one of only a few boats cruising the area now." Eagle adjusted his binoculars. "Whoever the person is with him is sitting down and leaning over, as if he's putting something together. Damn. I wish Viper and Hannah would get here."

And as he spoke, the front door opened, and the couple hurried inside. They came out to the pool area very quietly, Viper with his own set of binoculars.

"Sorry," Hannah said breathlessly. "It took me a little longer than I expected to get Superman ready."

"Superman?" Sierra lifted an eyebrow. "Is that your name for Viper? And do I want to know why?"

Hannah gave a short laugh. "He wishes. No, it's what I call the drone, because he flies through the air with ease."

"Here comes another boat that looks like it might be sightseeing," Viper said. "Hannah, you almost ready?"

"On it," she told him.

Sierra watched as Hannah removed a drone from the leather case it was in, set it on the table and took out the controls. She got everything ready as if she did it every day. Oh, right. She *did* do it every day.

"I thought this would be a better solution than getting everyone over here armed to the teeth," Eagle said in a quiet voice.

Sierra almost had to strain to hear him. She knew he was speaking in low tones because voices carried over the water.

"Good thinking," Viper agreed. "The other boat pulled away so now it doesn't look like he has any other boats with him. But remember, anyone could be helping him, so we have to stay alert."

"I'd give a lot to know who Holland is with, and what his plan is. Will he try to land and come ashore? He'd have to know I'd be waiting for him."

"From everything we've learned, he's the kind of man who goes for the outrageous and thinks he's untouchable. Maybe he has something weird in mind."

"I don't think he does," Eagle said, "but we'll let the drone take a look for us."

"Almost ready," Hannah assured him and picked up another small case. "Okay, Sierra, want to give me a hand here?"

"You bet. Just tell me what to do."

"Bring that flight control board with you and the video receiver and come out in front with me. We don't want them to see us launch it from here."

Sierra followed her out through the front door and into the driveway. Hannah made some additional adjustments to the drone then used the controller to launch it.

"Okay, bring the screen over here so I can see what the drone's doing and make adjustments as I need to."

Sierra was fascinated, watching the other woman as she manipulated the sophisticated piece of electronic equipment. It wasn't long before it was over the water, and she saw the image of the bay and the boats scattered on the surface.

"Okay, let's take this inside." Hannah walked in ahead of Sierra who juggled the rest of the equipment. "Good, good, good."

The two women went out to the pool, Hannah still working the controls on the drone.

"Can you get it close enough to the boat to verify identities?" Eagle asked.

"Doing it now, but—holy shit!"

"What?" Both men asked the same question at the same time.

"Guys, you'll have to tell me if one of these men is Darius, but one of them has just finished assembling what looks as close as I can tell like a long-range rifle."

Eagle adjusted his binocs. "Shit. She's right. What the fuck? Everyone down!"

They all dropped to the floor except for Hannah. Out of the corner of her eye, Sierra saw the woman doing something with the drone's controls. The next moment, there was an explosion at the rear of the boat and both men, plus the rifle, ended up in the water. The closest boats began speeding away, not wanting the fire to spread to them.

"Let's go," Eagle shouted to Viper.

The two men ran out of the pool area and down to the dock where they dove into the water.

"That one man still has his gun," Sierra said in a shaky voice.

"Don't worry. The explosive charge I dropped knocked it into the water, and the two idiots are trying the decide whether to head for the sinking boat, swim away from the shore or battle it out with our two guys."

Sierra was fascinated to watch Eagle and Viper as they cut cleanly and swiftly through the water, grabbed the two men, knocked them out and dragged them to shore.

"Rope," Hannah said. "Or something. They'll need to tie these guys up before they come to."

"I have no idea where to find any. Oh. Wait." She ran into the master bedroom and grabbed the silk scarves out of Eagle's dresser. "Come on," she said, motioning Hannah to follow her.

They were waiting at the dock when Eagle and Viper dragged the two men up onto it. Eagle took the scarves from Sierra, doing his best to conceal a smile, as he and Viper bound the men.

"It's all recorded," Hannah told them, "so we have video to give the cops."

"Call Tom," Viper told said.

"I'll do it," Sierra said, grabbing Eagle's phone from a nearby table.

Neighbors were beginning to gather on either side of them to see what was going on. Other boats were also slowing down and moving closer to shore to scope things out. Eagle left Viper in charge of the two men and hurried down to the dock. Sierra heard him talking to people, and whatever he said must have reassured them because everyone began to move away.

Tom and Myles arrived and Tom called his connections in the Tampa Police Department. Then he called the other two Galaxy partners who arrived shortly with their women. Darius Holland and the man with him regained consciousness, looked at the people standing around them and swore.

"I'll sue you for everything on the books," Holland spat out.

"Yeah, yeah," Eagle snickered. "I don't think you've got much of a chance with what we've got on you."

Holland's gaze landed on Sierra.

"It's your fault, you fucking bitch. If you'd just stayed out of it, none of this would have happened."

"And my brother would be in prison for life for a murder he didn't commit." She knew she shouldn't do it, but she crouched down next to Holland. "Instead, you'll be the one, asshole. You should never have messed with me."

She balled up her fist and cracked it against Holland's jaw.

The others burst out laughing.

"That's some woman you've got there, Eagle, my man," Viper told him.

He grinned. "No kidding."

It was two hours later before the police left dragging Holland and his accomplice with them. Tom spoke to the police and said he'd send them a copy of the report he filed and fill them in on what was happening. Tom assured them he'd babysit the process and keep them in the loop every step along the way.

"The hearing on the appeal is tomorrow," Myles reminded them. "I'll make sure you get all the details as well as the reports on Holland and his pal. Then I'm going to see what I can do about expediting Jeremy's release." He looked at Sierra. "I don't think it will be a problem. Try and get some sleep tonight, okay?"

"I'll do my best," she told him, "although I don't know how successful I'll be."

"We owe Hannah a big thank you, also," Eagle reminded her. "Without that drone, we wouldn't have the visual evidence we need against those guys."

At last, they made plans to all meet for breakfast, and the others left. Eagle locked up the house and led Serra into the bedroom.

"I'll never be able to thank you," she told him. "Not in a million years."

"Oh, I think I can find a way." He winked at her. "But it may take another forty or fifty years."

Epilogue

"The wedding was fantastic," Sierra said, "and Peyton was a gorgeous bride."

Eagle nodded as he hung up his clothes. "Blaze couldn't take his eyes off her." He cupped her face. "But she isn't half as gorgeous as you are." He pressed a soft kiss to her lips, then gave them a gentle lick with his tongue. "Mmm. You taste good." He looked at her with heat blazing in his eyes. "But there are other places I want to taste, too. Like that sweet, sweet pussy of yours."

"What's stopping you?" She trembled, eyes darkening with a hunger that matched his.

He drew in a breath and let it out slowly.

"I have something I want to say first."

"Oh?"

He didn't like the slight flare of uncertainty in her eyes. "Nothing bad, darlin'. I swear. At least I don't think it is."

"Well. Let's have it, then."

"I know we've only been together a few weeks." He chose not to say "known each other" because he wanted to emphasize the together part. "But it's been the best weeks of my life. And I think it's been good for you, too. Right?"

She nodded. "Where are you going with this?"

"A lot's happened. First, we owe a huge debt to Myles, who managed a miracle here. I wasn't sure Galaxy could pull it off without him."

"I had faith in him," she assured him. "And I'm honored beyond belief that he took this on."

"Me, too. He got the verdict set aside. Jeremy's out of prison and his friends, the ones who never thought he was guilty, are rallying around him. His boss, who believed in him all along, said his position was waiting for him. Darius Holland and Neil Maguire and all the others involved in this are going to prison. The woman they used to frame Jeremy has been given a decent burial."

"And they're at the center of a scandal that keeps spreading. I know all that. Is there a problem?"

"Only if you don't agree to move in with me." He kissed her again. "If I didn't think it was too soon, I'd get down on one knee and ask you to marry me." He took her hand in his. "Please say yes, Sierra. Yes to a future that we can build together."

For a long moment, so long he began to worry about her answer, she didn't say anything, then she threw herself at him and wound her arms and legs around him.

"Yes. Yes, yes, yes." She sprinkled kisses all over his face. "We've lived a lifetime in a few short weeks. We don't need more than that to know this is right. None of your partners knew their women more than a few weeks when they got together and look how well that turned out. And friends like them are very hard to come by. I feel good about it."

Relief surged through him.

"Thank god," he murmured. "I think we should seal the deal, don't you?"

"What did you have in mind?" Her lips quirked in a tiny smile. "Because I've been a very naughty girl and I think I need a spanking."

Heat rushed through him, and his cock got so hard he was afraid it might break off. They had discussed this. "And we enjoy the same things," he reminded her.

"Yes," she whispered. "We do."

They undressed each other slowly, caressing each other. He kneaded her breasts and pinched her nipples, and she stroked his balls and squeezed his cock.

He licked her lips and her nipples before tying a scarf—a new one—over her eyes. Then he pulled the covers back on the bed and helped her lie down with her face in the pillow. Finally, he bound her wrists with another scarf then took a moment to enjoy the sight of her.

He had to work to keep from rushing this, but he applied the special warming oil, even sliding some between the cleft of her ass and rubbing it into her puckered opening. She moaned at his touch, so he did it again.

The he lifted her to her knees, still facedown, took a moment to rub her sweet little pussy and tease her clit and, without warning, smacked one cheek of her ass.

"Ohhhh." The sound was one of pleasure, not pain.

He smacked the other one, with the same response.

He set up a rhythm, one cheek then the other until her cries of pleasure blended one into another. She was so aroused that he could hardly keep himself in check. He swiftly rolled on a condom, knelt between her thighs and slid his fingers back and forth against the lips of her cunt. Each time he stroked her clit, it drew another sound of pleasure.

"Please," she cried.

"Please what?" he demanded.

"Please make me come."

"I think you meant to say that differently," he admonished.

"Please fuck me," she yelled, and thrust herself back at him.

'That's what I wanted to hear."

He pressed the tip of his cock into her opening, gave each ass cheek one more smack then drove hard into her, filling her with one stroke.

"I can't go slow, darlin'," he rasped, barely keeping himself under control.

"Then don't. Fuck me, Eagle. Fuck me hard."

And he did, driving into her again and again and again, until they both exploded with an orgasm that shook and shattered them. His cock pulsed inside her over and over and her inner walls squeezed him. At last the intensity began to fade until finally they were spent.

Forcing himself to move, he withdrew and disposed of the condom. Then he removed her scarves and turned her so he could look at her.

"I'll say it first," he told her. "I love you."

"I — I love you, too." She sighed. "I do, Eagle."

"Then let's make it permanent."

He stared into her eyes. "Are you sure?"

"I am. Kiss me, and we'll make it official."

And he did.

Want to see more from this author?
Here's a taster for you to enjoy!

Strike Force:
Unconditional Surrender
Desiree Holt

Excerpt

Slade Donovan, code name Shadow, moved silently into the room where the men on his Delta Force team waited. Tall and muscular, he was the essence of a warrior, his dark brown hair slightly shaggy with a gray thread or two showing here and there, and the expression on his chiseled face said *Bring it on.*

Lowering his gear bag to the floor, he dropped himself into an oversized armchair and pulled out his laptop. *First things first,* he told himself. Mission completed. Men all accounted for. Time to reconnect with the outside world. He turned on the machine and waited for everything to load.

He was more than grateful for the satellite setup at their base camp that allowed them all to communicate with the rest of the world. It was a great way to maintain contact with his 'brothers' in the many Spec Ops groups, not just on newsy items but on ways to do things better. He also kept in touch with the foreman of his ranch back in Texas and with the few friends he'd been close with for years.

While he waited for the computer to boot up, he glanced around the room at his men, the members of Team Charlie, sprawled out on the battered furniture, weary and battle-hardened. They still looked rode hard and put away wet, as the saying went in Texas. This last mission had sucked a lot out of them.

Just yesterday they had come down out of the Hindu Kush, the mountain chain that stretched from Afghanistan to Pakistan, tired, dirty and spent, although eminently satisfied. Despite the intel fuckup, the mission had been a success. One more terrorist cell destroyed, one more maniac blown to hell. And the troops fighting for the people of Afghanistan had one less bad guy — and his followers — to worry about.

Delta Force, the Army's top covert combat unit, had counterterrorism as its main focus and they performed their missions with cold single-mindedness. Like the one they had just completed.

Once they'd landed, they'd gone through debriefing, badly needed showers, a hot meal and fourteen hours of sleep. Now they were just hanging out, guzzling water and making plans for their imminent leave. They were facing ten days to let it all hang out, battle their demons and refresh.

"Damn, Shadow." Trey McIntyre, code name Storm and the team's demolitions and firearms expert, flopped onto the beat-up couch and looked over at him. "That last mission was a stone bitch."

Slade nodded agreement at Trey's comment. It had definitely been a shitstorm of epic proportions. Angry at the poor intel, at the danger it had put them all in, at the possibility the mission would fail, Slade had kept it all together. They'd regrouped, adjusted their plans and completed the assignment. But hellfire. He wanted to throttle everyone who had put this together.

"Fucking A," he agreed. "I told the captain the intel on this one sucked. You all pulled off a miracle and I'm damn proud of you all."

"No shit." Beau Williams made a rude noise.

With his sun-streaked light brown hair and green eyes, he looked like a typical surfer, fitting his code name. Surfer. Nothing could be further from the truth, though. Beau was their sniper, a job that required incredible focus and discipline.

The *ding* of a bell let Slade know his computer was now up and running.

When he clicked on the email icon, a flood of messages rolled into his inbox. As he scrolled through them, the subject of one caught his eye. He'd been searching for something he and his team could do together on their current downtime, something to work off the residual tension. Maybe this was it. Last time he'd talked them into it, they'd blown away the competition. Maybe he could coax them out to the ranch and get them to do it again. They might have plans or not, but they were all so drained after the last few ops he wanted them to recharge as a team where he could watch over them.

"Okay, you guys." The others looked over at him. "I've got something here that might interest you."

"What's up?" Beau stretched and yawned.

"Remember that shooting competition we took part in two years ago?" Slade glanced at his screen again. "The one held just south of my ranch?"

"Yeah." Marc Blanchard—code name Eagle—grunted. "We cleaned their clocks."

Beau grinned. "No shit. What about it?"

"There's another one scheduled for next week, right at the end of our leave. Handguns and long guns. Just like the last one." He paused. "I don't know what plans y'all might have, but how about hanging out at my ranch again and we'll go win a few more prizes?"

His spread was south of San Antonio, where he ran a small herd of cattle and kept horses he could ride fast enough and far enough to clear his mind. It had become his refuge, a place to heal after each mission and reconnect with humanity. He'd taken his team there a couple of times when they'd really needed to switch off from everything to pull themselves together again.

Beau sat forward, interest sparking in his eyes. "I can always use a chance to dazzle people with my skills. But, uh, Shadow? Besides the competition, will there also be women while we're there? That's *my* top priority."

Of course. Beau didn't care where or what as long as there were women.

"Did you notice a lack of them the last couple of times?" Slade grinned. "Yes, there will be women."

"Then count me in."

"Me too," Trey echoed.

Marc was suspiciously silent. Still recovering from the disastrous end of an even more catastrophic marriage, bitterness had etched deep lines on his face and colored his entire personality.

Slade focused his gaze on him. "Marc? You in?"

The man was silent for so long Slade wasn't sure he planned to give him an answer. Then he gave a short, quick nod. "I'm in for the shooting. We'll see about the women."

Slade had discussed Marc's situation many times with Beau and Trey. They all worried that, when he had leave, the man just crawled into a hole for ten days and drank himself into oblivion. Still, he always showed up on time sober and sharp so Slade really had no cause to say anything to him. Yet. But he could still worry about him.

"And speaking of meeting women," Slade went on, "remember the JAG lawyer I introduced you to when you were at the ranch two years ago? Paul Hutton? Old friend of mine? We had dinner one night with him and his wife?"

"Is he providing the women?" Beau joked.

Slade chuckled. "Maybe. In a way, that is. He and his wife are having a party. If you all promise to clean up good and not pick your teeth in public, we're all invited."

"I'm guessing it will be a little different than the entertainment last time, right?" Trey winked.

Beau laughed. "I'd say that's a big Ten-Four."

Slade nodded. "No private sex club this time. We tried it at The Edge and you all passed on doing it again."

Beau nodded. "Not our cup of tea."

"I like my sex with no holds barred," Trey added, "but not with a lot of other people around. Call me simple, but I like my privacy."

"Is that so the rest of us can't see how inept a lover you are?" Beau teased. "Afraid your women will take a gander at us and leave you in the dust?"

"Ha ha ha. Very funny. As a matter of fact, I don't want your women to get jealous of my style."

"Whatever." Beau flapped a hand at him.

"But I think we're all agreed the club scene isn't for us, right?" Slade looked at each of them. "Speak up now and forever."

"Yes." Beau nodded. "Right."

Trey nodded his assent. Slade glanced at Marc Blanchard, who hadn't spoken a word. The man was in a very dark place and had been since the implosion of his marriage. Slade worried about him, a lot. He'd thought the visit to The Edge might have lit a spark in him, but Marc had disappeared into a private room with one of the subs and hadn't said a word about it afterward.

"Marc? You agree too?"

Marc just nodded.

"Okay, then. We'll head back to my ranch and make plans from there. Let me dig through my email and see if there's anything else on that might interest us."

Slade liked sex as much as the next man and had a healthy appetite for it. He lived by the motto — *We go abroad to vanquish and conquer for country. We come home and vanquish and conquer for us.* And why not? Tomorrow could be their last day on Earth.

Sometimes he wondered, though, if that would be the pattern forever. He was totally committed to Delta. It was his life. He had nothing left over to give to a relationship. Something he'd learned to live with. Sure, he'd seen others do it, but it required a mindset he didn't think he had. There were those who had retired from Delta Force, at least from active missions. They taught, trained others — any number of things. But could he do it? He was a warrior, after all. The leader of Delta Force Team Charlie. Up until now there hadn't been room for anything else. Could he ever adjust to a change?

But then, as he stared unseeing at the computer screen, *bam!* A memory popped into his mind. One that had been haunting him for five years. No matter how he tried, he couldn't get rid of it. He wasn't a man given to dreaming about women — except maybe for the occasional wet dream. But a trip to Chicago and a party with friends had ended in a night of the most spectacular sex with the most incredible woman he'd ever met. She had stunned him. Sucker-punched might be a better word. Blindsided him. Silky auburn hair, emerald green eyes and a body that had made his mouth water. Perfume that had tickled his senses, a low musical laugh and the satiny feel of her skin completed the package. She had been so put together on the outside, but wildness had sparkled in her eyes.

They'd come together as two strangers, looking for nothing more than the moment. A brief but explosively intense encounter. He'd wanted to wash away the devastation of his most recent mission and she had wanted — whatever she'd wanted. They hadn't spent a lot of time discussing it. In his hotel room they'd torn each other's clothes off in their haste to get naked. That first coming together had been hot and frantic and had blown his mind. He'd felt like a teenager on his first hot date.

Every moment of that night still haunted him, indelibly etched on his brain, on his senses. He couldn't forget her plump breasts tipped with rosy nipples, or the wet heat of her sex and the way it had clenched around him when she'd come. He swore he could still feel the satiny caress of her skin as she lay pressed against him, or the silken fall of her hair brushing his chest — and other parts of his body.

Underneath her proper exterior she'd been a hot, sensuous woman who'd liked her sex as rough as he did. It had been the best sex of his life, ever, hands down. He had definitely been up for more of it the next day. Worn out and replete, he'd vaguely remembered falling asleep with her in his arms, but when he'd awoken in the morning, she had been gone, leaving him with an unaccustomed emptiness. He'd asked his friends about her, but all they'd known was she'd come with some other people they'd invited. They hadn't recognized the name and apparently nobody else had known who Mandy Wheeler Baker was. Maybe she'd given him a fake name, just as he'd done to her. Women came and went in his life, and that was fine with him. The way he wanted it. He was married to Delta and had no plans to change that any time soon. But not even calling on all his personal discipline could get one time with that woman out of his mind. One night, for fuck's sake.

How was it possible that after five years he still remembered every erotic detail of those long hours? How many times had he replayed it over and over, like a video on constant rewind? She appeared in his dreams, as if taunting him, and his cock swelled and hardened every time. Other women hadn't been able to erase her from his mind. He was arrogant enough to wonder if she thought of him after all this time but pragmatic enough to know the chances they'd ever cross paths again were slim to none.

He wanted her with a hunger that ate at him. Worse than that, they'd made a connection. An emotional link. Whatever. He'd have thought with the passage of time that feeling would fade. Instead, it had just increased. Grown stronger. He couldn't get her out of his fucking mind. And if he did find her? What then? Where did they go from there?

"Hey, Slade." Trey's voice broke into his reverie. "You still with us? Where'd you wander off to?"

He shook himself back to the present, realizing with a start he'd zoned out right there in front of his men. Bad, bad, bad. "Yeah. I'm here."

"Good to know." Beau cocked an eyebrow. "You looked a million miles away."

"So we okay here? If nothing else, for ten days you'll get to eat terrific food, soak up some sun and not have to do a damn fucking thing."

Trey nodded. "I'm in."

The rest of them murmured their agreement, even Marc.

"Okay. Let's make some plane reservations. We'll fly into San Antonio. Then I'll have the ranch chopper pick us up."

"Sounds okay to me," Beau agreed. "Let's rock and roll."

In less than twelve hours they were on their way out of Helmand Province, making a stop in Madrid to pick up a commercial flight to the States. Long hours after that they finally landed at San Antonio International Airport where Slade hustled them out of the door and down a long walkway to the private plane terminal. A gleaming black helo awaited them, a familiar figure leaning against it, arms folded across his chest, white teeth gleaming in a smile contrasting with his sun-darkened skin.

"Glad you're home, bro," he said, slapping Slade on the shoulder.

"Me too. Look at the bunch of ugly mugs I brought with me again."

"Hey, Teo!" Trey shook hands with the man. "Think you can put up with us again?"

"As long as the boss pays me extra." He winked. Teobaldo Rivera was the ranch foreman, fiercely loyal to Slade and excellent at his job.

Whenever Slade brought his team to the ranch with him, Teo always went out of his way to make sure they enjoyed themselves.

"Okay," he told them. "Let's get loaded up. The beer's chilling in the fridge and the steaks are thawing."

It was a tight fit for five oversized males, but Slade figured they could handle it for the short hop to the ranch. As soon as the chopper landed, they were out of the cabin. Slade shoved his hands in his pockets and looked around. He loved coming home to the ranch. It replaced the family he didn't have and the home he'd lost a long time ago. The sprawling ranch house off to his right rose two stories from the lawn around it, shaded by ancient oaks and maples. To the left stood the enormous barn that held his horses, any cattle that might need to be separated in an individual pen, and Teo's offices. Behind that nestled the building that housed all the ranch equipment, including the portable pens for branding. And beyond that, as far as he could see, the endless rolling pastures meeting the horizon of the blue Texas sky. Pastures that contained the small herd of cattle he nourished and bred and sold.

He inhaled the familiar scent of horses and hay and Texas sunshine and almost at once the tension riding him began to ease. He loved coming home to this place. He could regenerate, rest, ride his horses.

And there were always women to hook up with whenever he wanted, women he'd met over the years. Too bad none of them replaced the one he really wanted. He could almost see her here on the ranch, in jeans and boots, walking to meet him, two small figures hopping along beside her, filled with excitement. But he didn't know her real name, didn't know where to find her and no one seemed able to tell him. So all he had was the memory of the most incredible night of his life, a memory that plagued him whenever he opened his mind to it.

Fucking damn. He needed to find that woman or get over her. He was driving himself nuts.

While Teo went through his shutdown routine, he and his men unloaded their duffels and headed toward the house.

"Let's get inside," Slade told them, "and I'll get you all situated." He grinned. "Then we can crack open some cold ones."

The large ranch house had four guest rooms plus the master suite, a situation that worked out well for them. The air was still sun-warmed, even though the sun itself had dipped below the horizon, but a soft breeze added a cooling element. The air carried the heady aromas of hay and horseflesh and cattle, a mixture Slade loved more than any perfume. The spread was his haven, the place where he could put all the blackness of his missions behind him and feel like a normal person. If he ever did settle down, the woman would have to love it as much as he did — if being the operative word. Did the woman he'd dreamed about so much — ?

Damn! He had to stop this. He was losing his grip here.

"I see Teo got the beer out?" he commented as he jogged down the stairs and out to the porch.

The men had dumped their gear in their respective rooms and were already out there waiting for him.

"Yeah," Trey joked. "We're trying to save you some, but you know how it goes."

Slade glanced around, realizing one of the team was absent. "Be right back," he told them.

Slade knocked on the door of the room Marc had dropped his things in. He'd wanted to give the man a moment to himself on the off chance he'd come on downstairs and join them, but it seemed he needed either prodding or dragging. Slade had hoped with such a peaceful setting, surrounded by the natural beauty of Texas ranchland, with a gorgeous sunset painting the sky, he'd feel relaxed. Maybe even looking forward to the ten days here. But nothing relaxed him anymore. While the rest of them kicked back and did whatever, Marc, the team's weapons and demolitions expert, often used his downtime in practice and refresher training. Considering the state of his personal life, Slade was glad the man was a disciplined soldier, committed to the job.

"Yeah?"

Slade pushed the door open. Marc stood at the window looking out at the scene below.

"Okay to come in?"

Marc shrugged. "It's your house."

"Hey, guy. That doesn't mean you can't have privacy."

If anyone asked Slade he'd say the man had too much privacy. Too much time to think about the dark place he couldn't seem to get out of. A place where the image of his naked wife, high on the drugs he hadn't known she was addicted to, was riding their equally naked neighbor and screaming with pleasure. He once told Slade, in a rare moment of confidence, he wished he could bleach his mind to erase that scene that played over and over like a video on a loop.

'That's what I got for letting my cock tell me what to do instead of listening to my brain.'

Slade knew some of the background. When Marc had met Ria, he'd been stunned by her beauty and swept away by her vivacious personality. Naturally quiet and introspective himself, he'd nevertheless been drawn to her at once. His total dedication to Delta Force had precluded any type of lasting relationship. Until then. She'd told him she loved him and had made him believe it. The sex had been unbelievable, so hot it had scorched the air around them. When he'd had leave time between missions, he hadn't been able to get home fast enough to immerse himself in his incredible wife. The fact that she had chosen him when, he was sure, she could have any man she'd wanted, was in itself an aphrodisiac.

Slade and the other team members had met her, at a dinner where he'd proudly showed her off. None of the team members, including Slade, had been too enthusiastic about her, but that hadn't bothered Marc.

"You're just jealous," he'd ground out.

Then the roof had fallen in and his life had come apart. The scene he'd walked in on had been bad enough. He'd managed to control his rage to not kill the guy when he'd tossed them out into the street. But when he'd realized she'd been high on drugs rather than alcohol, he'd done a thorough search of the house, including her personal belongings, and found baggies filled with multicolored pills.

He'd called Slade, because he'd been out of his mind. Insane. Especially when he'd learned she'd been doing that for a long time, both the drugs and screwing anything with a dick. He'd been torn between wanting to kill her and kill himself. Slade had talked him down off the ledge and waited while he'd packed his things — not too many, he traveled light — and had walked him out of the apartment and out of her life. He'd found him an attorney who had told Marc to do whatever was needed to get a divorce fast.

He'd asked Slade not to ever bring it up again and had spent the rest of his leave holed up in a motel room, trying not to drink himself to death.

Slade wasn't an emotional person, but his heart ached for Marc, so damaged by a selfish, insane woman. He often wondered if Marc would ever get back to the point where he wanted to rejoin the living.

Now Slade cleared his throat. "Heavy thoughts there, Eagle. Admiring the great view?"

Marc turned, his mouth stretched in an imitation of a smile. "Just giving my brain a rest. Give me five and I'll be right along."

"I'll hold you to it. Beer's cold, so come on down."

Swallowing a sigh, he left the room and headed downstairs. He could already hear the others on the back porch where he'd left them. Maybe, just maybe ten days at the ranch would be the first step toward Marc regaining his sanity and equilibrium.

* * * *

Slade watched Marc snag a beer from the cooler, pop the cap and move to the far side of the porch. As usual, close to the group but still separate. Man. The guy was going to implode if they didn't figure out how to get him some help pretty soon. Slade thought about telling him to move closer to the others but decided to keep his mouth shut. This was supposed to be a vacation. Downtime. If he wanted Marc to heal, he wouldn't accomplish it by giving him orders.

"You know" — Trey leaned back in the lounger he'd appropriated, staring off toward the horizon — "I can see why you like this place."

"Yeah?" Slade raised an eyebrow.

"I'm not sure I could take the peace and quiet in large doses," Trey added, "or too frequently. But right now? I have to say it's great."

"I actually think I might agree with him, shocking as that is." Beau took a long swallow of his beer and let his gaze travel lazily over the view that stretched from the house. "I can see why you love it here, Slade."

Some of the horses were in the corral, their coats glowing in the sunlight. Beside the first bar, two of the hands worked on the hay baler and from the far pasture, two hands who'd been riding fences trotted their horses back to the barn. It always reminded him of a painting he'd seen in a gallery in San Antonio that specialized in Western landscapes.

"Best tranquilizer in the world," he told the other men.

"So what's on the agenda now, Shadow? Riding horses or riding women?"

Slade considered each of them — lean, tan, hardened men, men he felt privileged to have on his team. They'd forged a bond that was unheard of in normal circumstances. He wouldn't trade it for anything.

"I'm thinking we should just hang out here tonight, try to get back to what passes for normal for us. Kick back. Drink some beer. Grill some steaks. Tomorrow night is the party I told you about."

"Is this the party your friend is giving?" Beau grinned. "And how clean do we have to get?"

"Clean enough to pass muster. Yes, this is the one. So pretty damn clean." He took his own swallow of beer.

"I know he's JAG now," Beau asked, "but was he ever Delta?"

Slade shook his head, irritated at the question. "No, we went in different directions. He loved the law and the fact he could be Army and still practice it. He had his law degree, applied for Judge Advocate Group and he's been with them ever since. Dumb luck for him he got assigned to Lackland here in San Antonio and he's been here ever since." Slade looked hard at each of them. "And he's done a damn fine job. He puts his ass on the line every day in a different way."

"Okay, okay." Beau held up his hands. "I didn't mean anything by it. Any friend of yours and all that."

Trey took a sip of his cold beer. "Is this party for something special?"

"No. They just like to entertain. When he found out I'd be home for it, he insisted I come."

Beau lifted an eyebrow. "And us too?"

"Hard as it is to believe anyone would want your company," Slade teased. "But yes, he said to bring all you assholes."

Marc, who hadn't said a word up until now, shook his head. "I think I'll pass."

Slade leaned forward. "That's not an option, Marc. Even if you sit in the corner all night and glower at everyone, I'm getting your ass there, so just accept it." He unwound his tall body from the lounge chair. "Meanwhile, I think we could all use a shower. Then I'll throw those steaks on the grill. I don't know about you guys, but I've been waiting a long time for a decent meal. See you in an hour."

About the Author

USA Today best-selling and award-winning author Desiree Holt writes everything from romantic suspense to contemporary romance on a variety of heat levels up to erotic, a genre in which she is the oldest living author. She loves to research her novels, writing everything from military to laws enforcement to cowboys.

She is a winner of the EPIC E-Book Award, the Holt Medallion, International Digital Award, Authors After Dark author of the year, Romantic Times Reviewers Choice nominee and many others. She has been featured on *CBS Sunday Morning* and in *The Village Voice, The Daily Beast, USA Today, The (London) Daily Mail, The New Delhi Times* and numerous other national and international publications.

Desiree loves to hear from readers. You can find her contact information, website details and author profile page at https://www.totallybound.com

Home of Erotic Romance

Sign up for our newsletter and find out about all our romance book releases, eBook sales and promotions, sneak peeks and FREE romance books!

www.ingramcontent.com/pod-product-compliance
Lightning Source LLC
Chambersburg PA
CBHW020559260626
47157CB00003B/770